Praise for Kim Catanzarite

Captivating science fiction.

— BlueInk Review (starred review)

Kim Catanzarite excels in depicting changing family interactions and relationships against the backdrop of sci-fi events.

— Midwest Book Review

Irresistible appeal to fans of science fiction — crisp writing, superior storytelling, and intriguing characters.

— Christian Fernandez, The Book Commentary

A foray into intrigue that's thoroughly steeped in psychological revelation.

— Diane Donovan, Senior Reviewer MWR

If you love visually stunning sci-fi, you'll enjoy this story. [Her] writing is so cinematic that you feel the majesty and the mayhem—the glorious, the gory, the good, the terrifying—as if you've been thrown into the middle of it yourself.

— Independent Book Review

Catanzarite laces the story's intensity with character-driven moments . . . making this imaginative plot distinctly unique.

— The BookLife Prize

Well-constructed science fiction . . . and a chilling premise.

— Kirkus Reviews

Depth and substance right down to the final, startling, and deeply heartfelt plot twist.

— The Prairies Book Review

It is exciting and fun when you stumble onto a rising star . . . as I predict this series to be.

— Amazon Reviewer

I can only think of one word to describe the journey this author took me on and that is "Wow."

— Goodreads Reviewer

A hybrid science-fiction/thriller/mystery that I won't forget. It was a breath of fresh air.

— Brian's Book Blog

Other Novels in the Jovian Universe

They Will Be Coming for Us

Jovian Son

Bright Blue Planet

From the Angel of Death Series

Staked: A Vampire's Tale

THE MOON CHILDREN

KIM CATANZARITE

forster
publishing

A LUCY M SOCIETY BOOK

ISBN: 979-8-9912761-0-8 (paperback)

ISBN: 978-1-7359522-9-1 (e-book)

Printed in the United States of America

1 3 5 7 9 10 8 6 4 2

Published by Lucy H Society Books, an imprint of Forster Publishing, United States of America. Distributed by Ingram Book Group, www.ingramcontent.com.

Cover design by Damonza

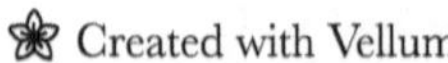 Created with Vellum

Disorder is not a mistake; it is our default. Order is always artificial and temporary.

— Farnum Street Media

Earth 2051

The Jovian Universe

Chapter 1

The Gulf of Alaska

Dana Peterman had spent the past four months worrying about the whales.

As she led her team of scientists across the hard-packed beach, with her husband, John, two steps behind her, she gazed over placid Glacier Bay, thinking, "Where are you? What's happened to you?"

The wind fluttered over her ears. It was a gentle June day, a warm fifty-five degrees with blue-gray afternoon skies that promised an uneventful evening as far as the weather was concerned. They'd lucked out on the sunshine, which was nice because it wasn't every day she and John organized a picnic-slash-party for their team of hardworking biologists, cetologists, earth scientists, social scientists, and others.

It was the least she could do for the dozen who came to work each day dressed in navy-blue cargo pants and matching sweaters only to spend hours listening to a glugging hydrophone or mete out multiple hypotheses to explain where thousands of whales could be hiding—and why.

There were other things to do, of course. So far they'd spent a lot of time climbing into wet suits and checking various parts of the bay for the whales' food sources—which were still there—and any new or overpopulated predators—which were not.

And now that it was June, peak whale-feeding season, the team had been uttering the words "nothing to see here" for so long that their growing boredom had turned into frustration.

As their leader, or "Chief," as they'd taken to calling her, it was Dana's responsibility to look out for the team's mental health and happiness. And this group of four humans, three Jovian hybrids, three clones, and two Jovian royals (herself and John) showed signs of losing heart.

"Where are we headed, again?"

The words floated up and over Dana's head, failing to break through her internal musings. She'd only realized Mandi had directed the question to her when John responded with, "Almost there. No worries."

"This way," Dana said as she continued to stare over the deep-blue enormity of the bay, walking at a slow pace upon the sand as the others followed behind.

The whales should have been there. They should have been feeding and breaching and peck-slapping their fins. The waters were ripe with krill and schooling fish, everything the fifty-ton mammals needed to bulk up for the three thousand–mile migration they'd take in the fall, and yet not one whale feasted in these waters. Not one sang a sad humpback song, spy-hopped its huge gray whale-head out of the water, or breathed out giant plumes of vapor.

The whales had been doing all these things each spring for as long as records had been kept. For all Dana knew, they'd been coming to Glacier Bay for millennia. So, why not now? What had changed?

She made a mental note to reach out to Caroline and ask if indeed the whales had been feeding in the Alaskan Gulf for millennia. Maybe long ago they'd fed somewhere else. If anyone would know, Queen Jovian—as the rest of the world had taken to calling Caroline—would.

Caroline's self-inflicted moniker emerged soon after she'd shown her true enormous-alien self in public—something Jovian royalty vowed *never* to do—and the fact that she'd done it only gave Dana a daily reason to shake her head. She and John weren't always proud to be Jovian. But the family generally did good work for the planet and, to a lesser extent, its inhabitants. Most important, Caroline allowed Dana and John to partake in their many humanitarian efforts, though Dana often disagreed with her when it came to beliefs, morals, and how to treat the population at large.

Dana cared about the human race—she cared for all creatures large and small. Empathy came naturally to her. If not in a human way, then in an alien way. That's why years ago Dana and John had been chosen to parent their adopted human daughter, Svetlana. None of the other Jovian royalty could have raised a human, let alone a teenager, and none of them wanted to. Dana had embraced the role and came to love Svetlana the same way any human mother loved her own child.

It made sense that she and John traveled to the Alaskan archipelago—this raw windy seaside environment that she adored—with plans to grow a village of five to ten thousand self-regulating individuals. She and John had been there for the humans throughout the global warming catastrophe, and now that the Earth functioned healthfully again—the air clean, the weather calm, the fresh water running and plentiful, the ocean (mostly) restored to its natural condition—she wanted to lead by example in a different way. She wanted all of Earth's inhabitants to see that life in its countless forms—human, Jovian, plant, and animal—could live compatibly in a natural balance.

The settlement prototype for living mindfully and peacefully on Earth with minimal disturbance to the community's natural surroundings would be an example the rest of the world and the soon-to-be-established colonies on Mars could follow. Life would no longer be the pursuit of riches and popularity, but health and wellness, and dare she say, happiness?

That is, if it worked out the way Dana and John hoped it would. Now they might never know. They had been about to take the first step on this journey when the mystery of the whales put the project on pause.

Dana stared over the water once again and worried about the lack of activity. Aside from a couple of gliding seabirds, no animals could be found whatsoever. It just wasn't right.

A year before they were supposed to break ground on the settlement, the three Federal Glacier Bay marine biologists who monitored the area reported an extremely odd occurrence: the whales had failed to arrive at Glacier Bay. Spring came and went, and the whales did not. Satellite imagery sighted them migrating in the Pacific Ocean, as was the norm, and then suddenly the pods had disappeared.

One theory for why they hadn't shown up involved an underwater earthquake that possibly scattered the whales or damaged their echolocation. The seismographs around the world had picked up on an event occurring within the same time frame the whales had disappeared but categorized it as "minor" in magnitude. Scientists hypothesized the event may have been more severe than the record showed.

Another theory claimed the whales followed larger-than-usual schools of fish in various directions due to healthier ocean temperatures. Perhaps they'd found new locations in which to feed.

Whatever had happened, the marine biologists in Alaska speculated the whales would be back on track the following year. The occurrence was an outlier, they'd hoped, a strange unexplained event.

Only here it was, the middle of June the following year, without even one whale to observe. The sea lion population, in addition, had stayed away as well as most of the other large sea mammals.

Because Dana, John, and their group had already planned to be in the locale, the job of examining what had happened to the whales dropped into their laps. Caroline's orders. Instead of building homes, a school, a medical clinic, along with the gathering places, gardens, and meditative parks that would surround them, the team would tend to the bay: observing, listening, and waiting. They would form hypotheses and puzzle out the mystery.

"You okay?" John asked. "Dana?"

Dana hadn't realized she'd stopped in the middle of the empty beach. With a look around, she greeted the silent concern of her team. The group had spread out, each member hovering in a bubble of personal space while waiting for her to lead them to . . . wherever it was she was leading them. A few of them gazed soundlessly at the bay, searching for whatever she might have been searching for.

Finally Vander, the only Evander clone in the group, said: "Beautiful day. So, what's on the agenda, Chief, and why all the secrecy?"

Dana had been stuck in her thoughts again. Perhaps she needed this day off even more than her young team did.

"I'm sorry," she said through a soft chuckle. "You've all been working so hard since we arrived, and I wanted to do something special for you. A surprise . . . because surprises are fun, right?" She laughed before shaking her head to clear out the cobwebs. "I guess I've already done a good job of piquing your curiosity."

"Yes, you have." Vander smiled at her, his air of casual confidence good for smoothing over the team's stress of not knowing what to expect.

Lena, one of the more stringent humans on the team, turned and said, "I hope you don't expect us to go in the water today because we didn't bring our wet suits."

"Oh, no worries about that, Lena," John was quick to answer. "There will be no seafaring expeditions today."

That was true, though Dana wished she'd brought her own wet suit. She'd spend entire days in the water, if she thought it would solve the mystery of the whales. But no, this was a day of restoration for the team. Her busy, hard-working team, whom she cared for as if they were her own family. They needed to have some fun, as simple as that was. An evening to let go of the hypotheses and dead-end theories.

"Well?" Anton, one of two Andrew clones, crossed his arms over his chest and stepped side to side. He and his "brother," Dru, never strayed far from one another. At the moment they stood ten feet apart, looking like impatient mirrored images. "What would you like us to do?"

"I want you all to relax," Dana said. "And I mean that in the most literal way possible."

The three humans in the group made screwed-up faces; humans hated confusion. The others waited without expression for her to explain.

"Look north," Dana said, pointing in the direction of the horizon. "Around that bend, just beyond those tall grasses. Can you see? We're heading to that army-green tent beyond the scrub brush."

"I see it," Mandi shouted. "Right there. Wait, is that a ping-pong table?"

Movement and muttering reverberated through the group.

"It's a party," Dana said. "Try not to look so serious."

"A party?" Vander's face lit up. "If I'd known we were having a party, I would have worn my best . . ." He gazed down at his sweater, before muttering, "uniform."

Dana smiled at this bit of humor. She and Vander "clicked," as humans liked to say, and uniforms were all the clothing any of the team had to wear. Vander was a clone of her grandson, and Dana did little to hide the fact that she favored him over the other members on her team. He shared the DNA of Svetlana's only child, the marvelous President Evander Peterman. The world's first human-Jovian hybrid who'd grown up to become the only twenty-first-century three-term commander in chief the United States had ever seen. A beloved leader, at least for a time.

Vander was a chip off the original block: charming, easy to get along with, handsome, a good person through and through. Dana hated that the human population assumed former President Peterman had abandoned Earth during its hour of need. Thanks to Caroline's public reveal of her alien form, the whole world expected a forthcoming alien attack and then former President Evander Peterman had disappeared.

The human race preferred to hate him and all of the clones that looked like him rather than to trust in the sensible explanation for his desertion: Evander had gone away to search for his eldest child, Natasha, who had been abducted and most likely taken to another planet. Hating their once-beloved president somehow gave humanity a right to scowl at every Evander clone in existence. Prejudice. That's all it was.

The hybrid named Sylvie twisted her long brown braid into a knot on top of her head. "It's been so long, remind me, what's a party?"

Dorian, a human, and at twenty-one the youngest individual in the crew took on a baffled expression. "Really? We're getting an afternoon off. Are you serious?"

"Yes," John said. "Come on, guys, let's have some fun."

Dorian's brow remained furrowed. "With, like, drinks and food and music and stuff?"

"I can see that we should have done this sooner," John mumbled to himself. And then in a louder voice, he rallied the group: "Follow me, everyone, and I'll show you around the site."

The scent of smoked vegetables greeted them, and if Dana wasn't mistaken, Jackson's shiitake and portobello mushroom burgers wafted deliciousness from the grill. His mother's recipe could not be beat, not by Dana or anyone else on this team of twelve, and that's why Jackson had volunteered to man the grill in addition to taking care of the entertainment. He came from a large family that he reminisced about often, and in the past, he'd claimed to know how to "put on a barbecue." Bryce had volunteered to be his helper and assisted him now.

The group rushed ahead. Anton found a huge inflatable ball and threw it to Dru. Vander chased after them while Mandi, Sylvie, and Dorian fell into a freestanding hammock set up for the occasion.

Jackson himself, a thirty-five-year-old human as large as one of Caroline's Leonard clones (and much warmer hearted) came from the Southern region of the country. He emerged from the tent holding a spatula and wearing an apron and a baseball cap with "CHEF" in big white letters.

Where did he get that hat? Dana wondered.

"Welcome to the party tent," he said with a wave. "Let the fun begin."

THE TEAM HAD EATEN their veggie burgers and coleslaw and sublime potato salad of the sort Dana had never before tasted. Afterward, they indulged in cake that was red in the middle and white on top, and too good to be true. And now Vander and Margot lingered in the tent, mixing drinks, while Anton and Dru, headed for the water with the intention of skipping stones. Mandi and Jackson —who may or may not have been falling in love—followed them. And Dorian, with his huge crush on Mandi, followed close behind. If the new couple had hoped for privacy, they wouldn't get it from Dorian. Dana smiled to herself as she thought, *He's too young to know when to butt out.* Bryce, Sylvie, and Lena grabbed the beach ball and tossed it back and forth, well behind the others.

Like the parents of the group, Dana and John remained at the picnic table. Dana sat with her back to the bay while John faced it full on. They both sipped a beer more for appearances than for any other reason. Alcohol did nothing to Jovians, and Dana never liked the taste. But she wanted the others to feel comfortable having a drink, so she made sure to be the first to take one.

"Remember years ago, when we were all about fresh water in the dessert and farming in regions ravaged by the throes of war?" Dana mused.

John smiled. "Those were *not* the good old days. Another reason to be happy Evander came along and set the planet straight."

Dana raised her eyes toward the darkening sky. "How quickly humanity forgets."

"That's the truth," he said.

The flames of a few tiki torches fluttered yards away. Bryce and Jackson had planted them here and there in preparation for the darkness to come. Where they'd found the torches, she had no idea, but she was glad that they had. It added a festive touch to the party, and in an hour or so, the sun would be down.

"I should be glad all we have to deal with are some missing mammals," she said in a pathetic way because that's how she felt in spite of how nicely the party was going.

"Hey," John said, "I'm as concerned as you are. But the whales are out there somewhere. Feeding somewhere. We just don't know where that is." His gaze hovered over the bay. "We'll figure it out. We always do."

He was right. Years ago, when the Earth choked on an abundance of carbon dioxide, they'd found ways to rejuvenate rainforests in Brazil and ecosystems in the jungle in Ecuador. They had built homes with nothing but reclaimed materials and settled grievances that stopped gangs from warring. They would figure this out too.

Dana lifted a crumb from the tablecloth and tossed it onto one of the dirty plates. "I just can't shake the feeling that something is off. I mean, *really* off this time."

"I can see that," he said. "You've been pretty quiet the past few days."

She bit her bottom lip. "Mm. Do you think there's some deviousness behind the whales' disappearance?"

"Do you mean human interference of some kind, or—"

"I don't know. It could be human. Or maybe not." She held his gaze, as steadfast as ever.

"I really don't think the Jovians would—"

"No, you're right. It's not Jovian."

"Maybe it's a new disease," he offered. "The ocean still isn't 100 percent. We know that much."

"But if it was a disease, dead whales would be washing up on beaches. We'd find their bodies, their skeletons. And the less-affected ones would still be here. Some would make it through."

John nodded in that way he did when deep in thought. "Maybe something turned them off about this bay," he said, staring into the distance. "Maybe something frightened them."

"I thought of that too. But the team has been diving daily. No one has seen anything suspicious under the water."

"Yeah, I know, but that doesn't mean it isn't there." He brought his hands up in a "Who knows?" way. "The truth will come out in the end."

"I guess so." Frustration pulled her mouth into a frown. "In the meantime, I'm upset that our plans for the settlement continue to be stalled. I suppose we could work on it on the side?" She raised her brow in question. "I don't want to put it off too long. Every day the world tends toward disorder."

She reminded herself that as long as she was helping, doing good work, and moving projects forward, she would be making a difference. Because that's what she did. She helped. Still, the settlement project was different, imperative. Every species on Earth, whether human or animal, needed to learn how to coexist. Without a goal of harmony, humanity could easily revert to its old, destructive ways.

"We can do that," John said with a nod.

"Okay. That makes me feel a little better." She

turned around to observe the team members dallying at the edge of the gentle surf. Lena hurled the beach ball in Dorian's direction, but instead of him catching it, it skidded across the water with a sizable splash. He shouted at the shock of it and kicked a wide spray into the air. Lena took the brunt of it, and howled, "That's cold, you little shit!"

The others paused from skipping stones to watch them, smiles brightening their faces.

John placed a hand upon Dana's shoulder, and she turned around to find him pushing his glasses up the bridge of his nose. "You still seem down."

He knew her well, as he should, playing the role of her husband for most of the last century. They were the only two Jovians who truly loved each other like husband and wife. Why the others never learned to love, she didn't know. Perhaps she and John had absorbed some of Svetlana's humanity over the years. Or maybe it was in their genetics. DNA was a twisty riddle; all one had to do was take a close look at Uncle Jimmy, the family outlier and most unusual of Jovians, to know that.

"I can't put my finger on it, but every instinct I have prevents me from letting my guard down," she told him. "It's like a woodpecker tapping on my skull, reminding me something is wrong."

"Ouch," he said, "sounds painful."

One of the team was coughing, and Dana hoped whoever it was wasn't coming down with a cold the rest of them would catch. Dorian came to mind, but when she turned around it was Anton who covered his mouth and hacked. Then Dru did too.

Maybe something really was going around.

She turned back to John, her shoulders slumped. "You know me. I can't relax until the puzzle is solved."

He took her hand. "Try not to overthink. Sometimes it's more about fear than—"

One of the team barked another cough in such a forceful manner that Dana turned around again.

The alarm in Mandi's voice carried across the beach. "Anton, what's wrong? Are you okay?"

Anton had doubled over and now raised his hand. "Just something . . . in my throat," he said. His complexion flushed as if a fever burned inside him.

Then Sylvie, a few feet away from the others, shouted, "What's going on with the water? Are you guys seeing this? It looks so steamy."

Dana refocused on the bay. Sylvie was right. A swath of fog stretched across as far as she could see. When had it formed? Fog didn't just show up without a drastic change in temperature.

"Back away from the water a few steps, guys," Jackson said, gesturing with a wave of his hand. "Till we know what this is."

"Maybe it's the Orcas," Dru said before he coughed again.

Jackson said, "What's with you two? Anton, your face is red. How much did you drink?"

"I had a soda," he said before doubling over into another coughing fit.

"Do you need water, or something?"

Anton hacked so brutally he gagged. When he stopped a few seconds later, he wheezed the word *yes*.

"Bryce, run to the tent and get a couple bottles of water," Jackson said.

Bryce, who'd continued to toss the ball with Sylvie, looked up and scowled. "Why me?"

"Just do it," Jackson snapped.

Bryce took off.

Small, crested waves formed on the surface of the bay. The last bits of evening light danced lightly on top—yet there was no noticeable breeze or gust of wind to speak of. A sound like water droplets hitting a stove ring fizzled through the air, and the fog continued to thicken.

The bay seemed to be simmering.

Dana fought a horrible cold swell of fear. She gave John a steely look. "This can't be what it looks like, can it?"

Down the beach, Jackson turned to face Dana and John, and shouted, "Are you seeing this?"

Then Dru said, "Anton just got sick. Something's seriously wrong."

John stared into Dana's eyes and said, "You think it's—but it can't be them. Can it?" He leaped from the bench and ran down the beach toward the team. "Get away from the water," he shouted. "Dru, grab Anton, and come away." He waved his arms overhead and continued to shout orders as he traversed the lengthy beach.

In her hurry to get up and go, Dana's toe caught the top of the seat of the picnic bench, and she slammed hands-and-chest into the packed sand, knocking the wind from her lungs. She scrambled up, coughing as her diaphragm returned to working order. Then she ran as fast as she could. "Sylvie, come away. Lena, to me. Hurry! Jackson, help the twins."

Dorian grabbed Mandi's hand and tugged her along at a jog before they both broke into a sprint. Sylvie and Lena followed, shouting, "Where should we go?" as they crossed paths with Dana running toward the danger.

"Get back to the tent, or farther even. Just keep going!"

John had entered the simmering bay, the haze wrapping itself around him. He bent over, touched the surface with the palms of his hands, and began to mutter something indecipherable.

Anton had fainted to the ground, and his body tremored upon the sand. Dru hovered over his clone brother, his own complexion sickly and red, and his cough coming in harsh grating hacks. Blood spattered like fat raindrops upon the ground. Jackson stood beside Dru, one hand on his back, at a loss for what to do.

As Dana reached them, Dru's eyes rolled back in his head, and he passed out upon his unconscious brother.

"What the hell is happening?" Jackson said. "Why does it smell like ammonia out here?"

What Dana believed to be the answer didn't make sense. There was no possible way and yet everything pointed to it. She held Anton's wrist in search of a pulse and eyed Jackson pointedly. "Roll Dru onto his side and try not to take deep breaths. Small sips of air. You're human. You'll be all right."

Jackson nodded, then maneuvered Dru onto his side. "His lips are blue. Fingernails, too."

Dru's cheeks darkened from flushed to deep red, brilliant blotches of cerise spread over his raw complexion. The same was happening to Anton. Their chests rose and fell erratically, the air through their lungs rattling like dried grasses subject to harsh wind.

Jackson pulled back and shook his head in muted horror.

"Can you carry Anton?" Dana asked. "We need to get them as far from here as possible."

"Is it safe to move them?"

Before Dana could answer, the skin across Anton's cheek began to bubble, blisters forming like cheese under a broiler. "It's ammonia poisoning, and it's only going to get worse. Take him as far away as you can. Hurry!"

Jackson bent to one knee and lifted Anton's long, lean body over his shoulder, rising with some difficulty before he took off, wobbly at first, then straighter and stronger as he achieved a quick clip.

"John, come out of there," Dana shouted. "We have to get Dru away, and I can't do it alone."

John stood knee-deep in the roiling water, still bent at the waist and touching the surface with the palms of his hands. The bay bubbled for as far as Dana could see. Plumes of steam unfurled like subtle slow-motion fountains, the scent of ammonia strengthening with every second that passed. Dana withstood a coughing fit so fierce she worried about breaking capillaries in her eyes. John continued to speak the strange language she had never learned, had never needed to learn considering the Moon Children had been banned to Europa and she would be an Earth dweller for life. But his whisperings didn't do any good. Whatever was happening had already begun. There was nothing he could do to stop it.

"John, please," she shouted. "We're losing him."

John closed his mouth and stood straight, waking himself from his trance-like state. Finally he started out of the water.

The cloud blanket that had unfurled over the stewing bay began to creep onto the land.

Dana held Dru's upper body, her arms wedged under his armpits, and when John joined her, he reached for Dru's legs, ready to carry him away. But the fog was upon them.

"We're too late," Dana shouted. "Get down! Hold your breath for as long as you can."

Dana lay Dru down, then fell onto her stomach and watched John do the same a few feet away. She pressed her cheek into the packed sand as she squeezed her eyes closed. Holding her breath, she clenched her fists, and used her arms to cover her head. John grasped her right ankle; it gave her some comfort to know he was there.

The thick vapor crept over them, like sunburn over Dana's exposed parts—her hands, the back of her neck, her semi-exposed cheek. She continued to hold her breath while the wheezes from Dru grew fewer and further between. Even without breathing, she somehow experienced the awful smell, the taste of ammonia settling upon her tongue. It must have penetrated the walls of her skin. Or maybe she only imagined the taste.

Her eyes squeezed tight, and tears emerged from their corners. While she waited for the cloud to pass, counting every long second—two, maybe three, minutes total—her body ached for oxygen. Finally the last of it had passed over them, and she let out her breath and heaved the subsequent inhale, the horrible odor leaving her dizzy. She fought for air, retching in between breaths, and listened to John do the same while Dru lay still and silent beside them. The last bit of the fog traveled through the party tent as it spread into the scrub brush beyond, heading for the forest after that. *A destination they can retreat to,* she thought. She continued to watch. To see if she was correct. To see if it really was the Moon Children.

The fog reached the forest's edge and stalled. The cloud thickened, deepening in hue, condensing to a darker gray color with silver glints. No longer spread out, it piled up, became a tower three or four stories high, much closer to opaque now, much less like mist and more like a solid wall.

The column began to quiver, as if its insides were reproducing, its exterior vibrating. She could make out a jumble of legs and feet, arms and elbows. Torsos and backsides, shoulders, knees. An occasional full-body silhouette.

Small bodies with circular heads.

The different parts organized. It wasn't long before a sudden clap of thunder broke, and all the creatures within dropped to the ground like pieces of a shattered puzzle. Bodies gave way to gravity, their feet connected with a drum procession of earthy thuds. They stood for a moment, getting their bearings. Their forms nondescript, a silvery-gray blur like the cloud they had floated in on. Reams of small individuals in their solidified state. Mobile and swift. They ran for cover like a herd of gazelles fleeing an enemy, seeking shelter in the shadows of the forest beyond.

DANA CRAWLED TO JOHN, who lay prone. She touched his cheek and jaw, and he opened his eyes and gasped a whiny breath before raising his head and scanning the surroundings. "Are they gone?" The whole of his body clenched for a moment. He coughed and then turned his head and spat.

"For now," she said.

John rolled onto his side, his eyelids twitching at the destruction that was Dru's physical form. It was as if the young man had drunk poison and showered in acid. What was left of his skin was burned and peeled. His hair was all but missing, a few tufts here and there, the skull exposed. Dana looked away, unshed tears hindering her sight. It had been a long time since she'd witnessed such horror.

Feeling like she'd forgotten to do something, she stood, regretting that choice as she wavered, off balance and dizzy. A ripple of nausea rose from her middle, and she waited for it to pass.

A scream in the distance reminded her of the rest of the team. Dru was dead, and she needed to help the others, needed to see if any of them could be helped.

Though she ran, it took forever to cross the beach.

She reached Bryce first, pale but standing, grabbing his forehead as he moved about nervously in hunched-over shock. Clearly alive. Then she came upon Dorian, sitting with his back against a tent pole, shaking and crying just a few feet from Jackson, who kneeled upon the ground. The body beside him was Anton's—even more deteriorated than Dru's had been. Clearly the Andrew clones had not stood a chance against the Moon Children's ammonia cloud. She wondered how the Evanders would fare, considering Evander was the son of Andrew.

"Vander," she whispered, gripped with sudden panic. "Where's Vander? Has anyone seen him?"

No one answered at first. Jackson gazed up at her with dull, watery eyes. "I don't know where he went."

Dana called to Vander as she moved out of the tent and toward the ping-pong table. He had not been near the water's edge. He had opted to stay behind with Margot. The memory of his voice flashed through her mind: "I'm too full to skip stones," he'd said.

Dana moved faster, the horrid air burning her throat. She came across Sylvie and Lena, both on all fours, gagging and spitting. "Are you okay?" she said when she reached them.

Lena looked like she wanted to kill someone. "What is that horrible fucking smell? It's disgusting and I can barely breathe."

"You're a scientist," Sylvie said. "What does it smell like to you?"

"I know it's ammonia. But why would the beach smell like ammonia?"

"I'll explain later," Dana said. "Have you seen Vander?"

"No," they both answered at the same time.

"Over here," Mandi shouted from the dunes in the near distance. "Vander fell face-first in the scrub brush."

Dana followed the sound of Mandi's voice but didn't see her. The tall grass and scrub brush were two-to-four feet high, and Mandi likely crouched on the ground beside Vander.

Suddenly she popped up and waved Dana over.

Dana raced in her direction. She would never forgive herself if something happened to Vander. "Is he all right?" Her chest vibrated with thudding beats.

"I'm not sure," Mandi said. "He's breathing, and his pulse is good."

Dana would do everything in her power to save him. Mandi had rolled him onto his back. He was unconscious, a thin line of blood oozing from a narrow triangular cut at the top of his head. Probably from when he'd fainted. His lips appeared pasty and dry, but he wasn't coughing, and his chest moved up and down without a hitch. Skin still covered his handsome face. No blisters, just a bit of rose in his cheeks.

"He's not waking up," Mandi said.

Dana lifted his hand and patted it. "Vander, come on, now, wake up."

He lay as if in the midst of a dream. His expression unperturbed. At peace.

Dana met Mandi's questioning eyes, then began jiggling his shoulder. "Vander, please wake up."

He twitched and uttered a small cry before his eyelashes fluttered open. He stared at the sky. "Is he gone?" he said.

"Is who gone?" Dana asked.

Vander sat up quickly and scanned the area around them. "The old guy with the messy hair. Uncle Jimmy, I'm pretty sure it was."

Dana laughed with relief as the urge to hug him came over her. He appeared healthy. Normal.

"He was here, at the party with us," Vander said. "He ate a huge plate of potato salad."

"That sounds like something he'd do," Dana said. "But he's not here. How do you feel? Is your throat burned? Are you breathing all right?"

"Nothing hurts." Vander gazed at her with clear, blue-green eyes just like the original Evander's. "Uncle Jimmy said it's begun. He said they're here, and we have to get ready." Vander scratched the tender scruff of his chin, then rubbed his forehead.

Dana already knew the Moon Children were here. Perhaps the real message was *how* to prepare.

Vander said, "I don't know what he means by that."

Dana pressed her lips together before she spoke: "It's the Moon Children. Did he say what we should do?"

"All he said was the Jovians can't do it alone. It has to be all of us—humans, clones, hybrids, *everyone*. He spoke very seriously for a funny old guy."

"Okay," Dana said. "We will prepare as best we can."

"I don't get it," Mandi said. "I didn't see any old man. I didn't see anyone at all. All I saw was fog. A chemical cloud. I don't know how you prepare for something like that."

"You're right. It was a chemical cloud. Of sorts," Dana said. "And it's the reason the whales don't come here anymore. But I'll explain more later."

"But we entered the water about a hundred times," Mandi said. "There was nothing unusual there."

"I think they probably were there. I think they've been here for quite some time. We just couldn't see them," Dana said, then paused to study Vander again. "You're sure you're all right?" she asked, drawing him in for a hug.

"I'm great," he said.

"Okay." She let him go and got back on her feet. "You two stay here. I'll return in a minute. I have to inform the others."

She moved deeper into the dunes and gazed into the forest beyond. The sun had all but set and an eerie dusk darkened the sky. What was left of the Moon Children's haze prevented her from seeing the stars. She came to a cleared area and sat, then attempted to enter a place of calm in her mind.

Vander had weathered the poison much better than the others. She and John had survived, the humans and hybrids fared well. Dru and Anton had died horrible deaths. She worried for the Andrew clones of the world.

She opened her mind to the oneness, in all its patchy imperfection.

"Caroline," she said. "We need to talk."

She hated to report to Caroline as if she were a soldier in the field, but today that's exactly what she was.

The attack on Earth had begun.

Chapter 2

Kirksberg, Pennsylvania

The room in which Caroline Jovian waited was white. The design and decor, minimalist in nature. Rectangular windows, a light-gray low-pile carpet, white painted shelves. The faint scent of ammonia mixed with citrus cleanser. Dim rays of the rising sun came through in a bland way, as if tired, slow to wake.

The quiet that comes with solitude surrounded Caroline. It held her like a pair of hands, reminded her that every moment was one to be lived through, one to be withstood. She crossed her arms and rested them on the conference table that extended before her.

Perhaps what the room lacked most was that thing humans called "spark." The energy one felt when inspired. But that should not be on a day like this one, a special day on which Starbright International would launch its second passenger ship on a trajectory to Mars. Miranda's construction-and-settlement project would enter Phase II early that morning, moving forward as it should. And yet, where was the satisfaction in it? The sense of accomplishing one thing in order to move on to the next?

Caroline felt nothing.

Inspiring the humans to move to Mars hadn't been difficult. Plenty of them volunteered to go, deeming it an extraordinary opportunity compared to the prospect of living on Earth governed by aliens, governed by Caroline, more specifically. As a race, the humans were frightened. The first thousand to leave the planet did so willfully— eagerly. Scientists, scholars, construction workers, ordinary civilians and their children. And all Caroline could think was *the more, the better*. Let someone give Mars another try. Maybe this time those who occupied it wouldn't fail so miserably. Once, a long time ago, Mars had lived. Let them try to resuscitate it.

She took a deep breath and sighed out of boredom, staring across the room at its dull, white walls.

Was she tired? Such a human affliction, to be tired. Jovians didn't tire. She never had. For years she had embraced the role of the determined leader, having to protect the planet, to make sure destiny did not take a turn for the worse and render it fruitless, dead. No, she wasn't tired or bored with the job. To her, there was nothing else. She would continue to do whatever she needed to do for as long as she needed to do it. For as long as the ocean tides swelled and the winds blew, and the sun rose and set on this, her beautiful bright blue planet.

She would never let what happened to Mars happen to Earth.

When the attack on Earth came—David predicted it would happen any day now—she would be there to defend with her special force of Leonards and her army of clones and hybrids and whoever else desired to continue to live there. The humans would have little choice. There would be many willing to do whatever needed to be done.

She sat in her high-backed chair, in the barely-there

morning light, and awaited the arrival of the others. She and her fellow Jovians met in this room twice weekly, sometimes more often: Miranda, Leo, David, when he was up to it. Over the years, attendance at these meetings had dwindled. Just the four of them and Head Leonard (the leader of the security squad earned his name when nearly half his head required replacement three years ago after the Battle of Philadelphia). Head Leonard played the role of her personal protector, and for each meeting, he stood sentinel in the hall.

Where was he now? Why was no one ever early for these meetings?

Not long ago every seat at this conference table had been filled. Only three years prior, her grandson, Evander, occupied the chair across from hers as her second in command. Before that, Edmund had filled the role. He'd played the part of her husband as well. Humans loved a power couple, so the Jovians had coupled themselves, though coupling did not come naturally to them. Constance had a seat at the table as well, and so did James, though James had been asked to leave soon after Evander was born. He visited Earth on occasion, and when he did, Caroline always knew he was there. Something about his presence jangled her brainstem. The famous Uncle Jimmy, known throughout the galaxy and, some said, in other galaxies as well, remained a mystery to her—to all Jovians. She had not seen the last of James, she was certain.

James's partner, Constance, was an altogether different story. Contrary to her name, Constance's loyalties most certainly lay elsewhere. Caroline knew that now. The question was where, and to whom? Unlike James, Constance had taken a subordinate role on Earthly matters. Quiet and grandmotherly, she drew little attention to herself, never made demands, rarely even made suggestions. She'd headed the clone program after James was asked to leave, and she'd taken orders in stride.

A groan came unconjured from Caroline's throat. She tapped her fingernails in an acrimonious rhythm over the rigid top of the conference table. She wasn't too proud to admit Constance had fooled her.

Even before the oneness had weakened, Caroline had not been able to read Jimmy and Constance as well as she'd read the others. Even when David still possessed his supreme powers, and the Jovian oneness had not yet waned, she often found herself in the dark when it came to their activity, their thoughts. Now that the oneness had withered, Caroline received hazy messages that overlapped and blurred and twisted like a never-ending ball of twine. Half the time she couldn't reach the Jovians she intended to reach, and when she did, she couldn't decipher their messages. And that only led to questions.

Caroline had never liked questions.

She sat back in her chair, tipped back her head, and rubbed her neck. Change was the way of the world. The oneness had changed. She accepted that. But she didn't like it, just like she didn't like this new *lack* she suffered from. The bland white walls, the meager light that gave the conference room a shadowy, regretful aura. The memories that reminded her of individuals who once lit this room from the inside out. The excitement had dwindled, if Caroline could call it excitement. No, Jovians didn't feel emotions like excitement. It was energy. Yes, it was the energy that eluded her.

Was it only she who was afflicted? Maybe she'd been living in the tubes for too long. Three years was a long time to remain indoors.

She gazed at her hands and the rings that adorned them, then touched the blue sapphire, which had always been her favorite. Perhaps the lack began when Evander first slipped through her fingers. It was the right thing to do, encouraging him to leave, letting him search for his daughter. But she couldn't pretend doing so had not . . . *How would a human put it?* . . . "bothered" her. His leaving was perhaps the first time she'd been bothered by anything for as long as she could remember. And she hadn't expected to feel that way.

Certainly Evander's mother, Svetlana, and her insolent ways, had bothered her. But Svetlana's presence was more a ripple than a wave. Other Jovians had left before Evander. Edmund had been her partner since the very start of the original Earth Project millennia ago, and he had left. That was his choice. She didn't debate it, and she wasn't bothered by it. Edmund was Jovian through and through, just like she was Jovian through and through, and Jovians did not waste time debating. They did not waste time indulging in or showing emotion. Human emotion had never made sense to her. Things were or they were not. The world was one big bundle of facts and nothing more.

And that may have been the problem. Where she saw black and white, Edmund and Evander saw shades of gray. The human side of Evander, especially, had bewildered her —the way the humans worshipped him because he was one of them, because he spoke to them as if they were on the same playing field when clearly they were not. Evander possessed some intangible force that brought people together. Foremost was his charm, which in itself was baffling because Caroline knew full well Jovians were *not* charming, not appealing to the human race in general.

And yet the humans loved Evander, and their love for him brought them together as a people. He was something they could all agree upon. He had unified them, a fact that gratified Caroline now and always would, she assumed.

Evander was a rare gem indeed. The thought came with an unsettled feeling in her middle. The physical manifestation of being bothered, she supposed. An emptiness in her stomach, which she ignored.

Her son, Andrew (Evander's father), had bewildered her as well but not in the same way. Conceived in the Starbright lab, Andrew never knew he was a lot more Jovian than human. Which made Caroline wonder if Jovians were more like humans than she dared to admit. How was it that Andrew, a product of herself and Edmund, could be so scientifically Jovian and yet undetectably so? Andrew had never made sense. But when you live in a world that's black and white, a fact doesn't have to make sense for one to accept it. You accepted it and moved on.

The problem at this point was that Caroline found herself looking back. Wondering. Being bothered.

She took a deep breath and sighed as she released it. She never used to sigh.

And now this general feeling of lack had descended upon her like a thickening fog, and it led to questions. Questions kindling in her mind, the small flames demanding she tend to them lest they rise up and set her boring blonde bob aflame. Where she once understood the world as black and white, she now suffered doubt.

Doubt was altogether new to her, and she didn't like it.

With an air of dread, she also suspected why it was happening.

Constance had done it to her. The Jovian who seemed so grandmotherly and compliant, so easy to deal with, had changed everything.

It happened during the Battle of Philadelphia. The day the human-clone protest at Independence Lawn turned into a conflict that captured the attention of the entire planet. Caroline made an appearance on the field when only a few original humans remained there. The clones, on the other hand, had come out in droves.

In order to bring the oneness back to full force and regain control of the rebellious clone and hybrid population, Caroline had broken a sacred Jovian rule by showing her true self to humanity. It was an infraction of Jovian law of the highest decree, but that was not where she had planned for her transgressions to end.

The universe had given her an opportunity, and she meant to take it. A chance to snap the clones back into line, and for her to ascend the Earth's throne once and for all. How dare the clones rebel in this manner? How dare they go against her word? Did they believe they could fight her and win? They were no match for her. She was their god. It was she who had made them, she who had put James, and later Constance, on the cloning project to begin with. Caroline's plan was the reason they existed. And if they wanted to remain on her planet, they would have to do as she said—obey her—from that day forward.

In Jovian form, Caroline stood nearly six stories high. Black and sleek and flawless, with long, strong limbs and a mostly featureless face. *Perfection*, was how she thought of herself. The moment she transformed that day on Independence Lawn, the oneness had returned, clear as a ringing bell. She controlled every one of her clones' minds and bodies—and rendered them motionless.

At that moment, the chaos had ceased. Each one of the small bodies on the lawn stopped moving. Through the newfound channel, Caroline used the oneness to impart everything she wanted them to know. Then she approached Drew, the leader of the clone rebellion, a duplicate of her son, Andrew. It was he who had dared challenge her authority. Didn't he know how easy it would be for her to show his loyal followers just how helpless he was, how helpless all of them were? If she wanted to, she could end Drew with a mere clench of her fist.

Plucking him from where he stood on his tiny manmade perch was the equivalent of lifting a child's action figure in her palm. With his unmoving body in tow, she turned toward the stage, amused by the bird-like thrum of his heart, the daintiness of his limbs, so fragile, so easily drawn and quartered should she choose to do so. She carried him back to the stage, where everyone on the planet could see just how powerless he was.

That was when she sensed someone standing behind her. She turned to see who it was. An older woman stood in the middle of the lawn.

It was Constance. A nimbus surrounded her like a cloud of steam rising from her skin. She appeared silvery and pure; something about her was as strong as metal. Something not quite Jovian. Whatever it was, Caroline couldn't look away. Constance's kind eyes gleamed in her direction. She seemed to shed light from the inside.

This was not the norm.

As Constance maintained eye contact with Caroline, she lowered her chin, perhaps indicating that she did not agree with whatever Caroline planned to do next. Without sounding a word, she planted a statement in Caroline's mind: "You will not harm him. Jovians are a nonviolent people, and that is how it shall remain."

The strength of the statement filled Caroline's insides, rattling her bones and making her doubt herself for the first time in her very long life. *What am I doing?* She looked at Drew, motionless, in her too-tight fist. Did she really mean to harm him? To end his life? Was she no better than the humans who so often resorted to violence?

Quickly Caroline turned and set Drew on the stage

behind her. She stepped away from him and considered what to do next.

"Release them," Constance demanded.

It was then that a strange tingling sensation in Caroline's hands drew her attention. A prickling of her skin like fine sandpaper grazed over her fingers and wrists and forearms, all the way up to her shoulders, spreading over the whole of her. It was the feeling of cells being sloughed.

Constance continued to stare back with a knowing look in her eyes. Calm. Demanding. Caroline sensed an aura of satisfaction, then gazed upon her own body once again. Her arms and her trunk had begun to fade. Her hands, no longer opaque and black became a shimmering translucence. The prickling continued, and Caroline's true form slowly, consistently dissolved.

Alarmed, she said, "Yes, Constance, I will do as you say. There. They are released."

And yet, layer by layer, she continued to thin until she'd been peeled down to invisibility, until she stood alone within her consciousness. Merely a thought hovering. Constance's words in her mind said, "That's right, Caroline, go now," before the world around her vanished.

Caroline stepped out of the memory as she shivered with repugnance. *Why had Constance done it?*

Immediately after she'd disappeared, she found herself back at Starbright, safe in her pod in the Jovians' residential tubes. Back to her meager human form. Dressed and ready for the remainder of the day. Evander was leaving the planet. Everything on Earth had changed because of what she'd done. Humankind now knew that the Jovians—Caroline and her people—possessed supernatural powers of the sort humans could only imagine and fear.

And she'd introduced herself as Evander's grandmother, so they knew the former president they'd loved and admired wasn't human, either.

But they didn't know the whole truth. They didn't know Constance had been standing on that lawn and that she'd stopped Caroline from carrying out her plan to kill Drew. They didn't know Constance was the reason Caroline had disappeared before their eyes.

And now, three years later, Caroline could no longer ignore the awful change she'd experienced, both in her body and her mind. She no longer had the ability to transform, to become her true self. Whatever Constance had done had stripped her of that faculty. The very thing that made her Jovian was gone. And while Caroline could function in human form very well, the power that once resided within her, the capability that backed every one of her self-assured thoughts, every one of her bold moves, was gone.

She felt the lack in every uninspired breath she took, wondering if this punishment would last forever, whether Constance would one day return to Earth. If she did, would she restore Caroline's natural ability? Did she even have the means to do so?

If Caroline was no longer her true self, who was she?

All she'd ever wanted was to remain in control of her bright blue gem of a planet. And so she continued to lead, to act in a strong and unquestioning manner, and to promote the appearance of power she no longer possessed.

No one knew how powerless she was, and she intended to keep it that way.

Miranda entered the conference room, sat in the chair across from Caroline, and said, "Gotta love this weather. Perfect for shipping a thousand more humans off this gorgeous planet. I only wish it were a million more."

Caroline greeted Miranda with a wordless glance. Her current second-in-power proved a sorry replacement for Evander's kindness and charm. Miranda did what she did mostly for her own good—she enjoyed the stature that came with being Jovian royalty—and she pledged her devotion to Caroline.

Miranda's loyalty had never been a question. The same couldn't be said for Evander.

Leo was the next to enter the conference room, wearing the casual business attire he was known for: a golf shirt and dull beige pants. There had been a time when Leo wore a suit to the office, but Starbright formality had dwindled over the decades. Just more evidence of change, Caroline supposed. David did not enter the room after Leo, though she had hoped he would. The weakness that plagued him had come on strong of late. She would pay him a visit as soon as the meeting ended.

Like a black smear across the room's white walls, Head Leonard marched in next, in security squad attire. His threatening presence never failed to stop conversation. A clone of Leo, Leonard had been modified to such a degree over the years that sometimes Caroline forgot Leo had supplied the DNA that made him. At this point Leo was nothing like Leonard, who had muscled up to a Goliath degree. His mind, like his head, was half AI, half human. Half black zirconium, half pale human flesh. Since the shooting incident three years ago on Independence Lawn, he'd become more humorless and menacing than ever. Caroline appreciated that. Because prior to having lost her power to transform, that's what she'd thought the planet needed: a team of unforgiving protectors to help keep the humans and clones in line.

As leader of the security squad, Head Leonard also captained the Starbright special forces detail made up of a dozen Leonard clones, all of them similarly formidable. They'd been rumored to use force when necessary, though if that were true, Caroline had never seen evidence of it. Admittedly, neither had she looked very hard.

Head Leonard approached the conference table and unrolled a paper screen upon it. "All systems go," he said, pushing the ends flat. Then he returned to his post outside the conference room door.

Miranda and Leo leaned in to better view the image of President Annalise Abela and her designer-suited entourage of government officials as they appeared in an enclosed booth at the Cape Canaveral Space Launch Complex located between Jacksonville and Miami, Florida. Abela held a microphone. "Today, we double down on what's already the beginning of the successful settlement on Mars," she began. "With our second launch, we are literally creating a new community that's safe and healthy for all mankind. For anyone who has dreamed of space travel, the future looks bright!" Abela paused as the attending public clapped. "To the thousand pioneers on this ship, we wish you Godspeed."

The screen showed the rocket powering up against a backdrop of a watery-blue dawn. "Ten, nine, eight, seven . . ." Abela's voiceover counted backward with confidence.

The engines roared and within seconds the rocket hovered, then lifted, boosters firing. The ship climbed into the sky, gaining speed, a billowing column of exhaust in its wake.

A band began to play. A parade was set to march as soon as the rocket ventured out of sight. It would be a celebration led by President Abela, as if the human population still respected her authority and believed she was in charge. Maybe some of them did, Caroline supposed, though plenty of others accurately assumed their commander in chief took orders from the Jovians—and had done so for the past three years. Abela both ran the country (Caroline had no desire to become submerged in such mundane tasks) *and* she bowed to Caroline's every request, no matter what it might be, thus guaranteeing herself a second term.

The camera returned to the group of government officials, who smiled and clapped and bobbed their heads in an enthralled manner.

"There they are," Miranda said with a chuckle, "our fear*ful* leaders."

Miranda often tried to make a joke, but Caroline rarely saw the humor in it. She didn't understand humor. She knew what it was but saw no reason for it. Miranda was the best actress in the Jovian family, the most convincing human—or that's what Svetlana had once claimed—but Caroline didn't consider it a compliment. Who wanted to be good at being human?

The rocket produced its hot exhaust and penned an arc across the sky. The one thousand beings tucked into their pods surely prayed they would make a safe landing on Mars. The method of travel may have been antiquated, but it was the best they could do without disrupting humanity and its delicate technological evolution. Humans believed new technology came in drips and drabs, so that's how the Jovians fed it to them. Still, Caroline was losing patience.

"Not bad for 2051," Leo said.

"I'd hoped we'd be farther along by now," Caroline told him. "Why are they still using fuel?"

"It's only for the initial boost. The humans love their Atlas VII Rocket."

"It's unacceptable," she said sternly.

"When are the next thousand scheduled to go?" Leo asked.

"Six months," Miranda, who headed up the program, said, "if not sooner."

He nodded in a curt manner. "I'll make sure they're off the fuel in time for the next one."

"Wonderful." Caroline clasped her hands. "That will be all."

"Actually, I have something else—" Miranda turned to her but then held back the words.

Caroline met her gaze. "Yes, Miranda?"

"It's not to do with the Mars program. An incident has occurred in Alaska."

"Tell me," Caroline said.

"Dana attempted to reach out via the oneness but had some trouble getting through, apparently. Possibly because she uses it so seldom."

As much as Caroline wished it weren't true, David's failure to fix the oneness had become obvious to everyone in the family despite attempts to blame the problem on other things. At this point, the Jovian system of communication was stretched and ripped and pocked with holes. It irked her that David couldn't fix it, nor so much as figure out why it neared complete shutdown.

Edmund had sabotaged it so Caroline couldn't communicate with the clones; that much she knew.

"And what has happened in Alaska?" Caroline asked.

"A couple of days ago, Anton and Dru of the eco-environmentalist group perished."

"Two Andrew clones. What was the cause?"

"Ammonia poisoning," Miranda said with a raised brow. "They were on the beach when it happened."

Caroline sifted through possible reasons why ammonia would be found in quantities of strength on Earth, let alone in a body of water such as Glacier Bay.

Miranda gave her a pointed look. "Dana believes it was

the Moon Children. The hybrids and humans became ill, some worse than others, but they have recovered. She and John became sick but not for—"

"The Moon Children were banished to Europa two millennia ago," Caroline said.

"Yes. That is true."

"They have no means of transport. They're ill equipped for travel of any significant length."

"We have no idea how they traveled or why, but Dana says she witnessed the attack from start to finish, and it was in fact the Moon Children. She watched them transform and saw them take shelter in a nearby forest. She says it would explain why the whales have not returned to Glacier Bay."

Caroline's eyes bore into the tabletop in front of her. *Could this be Edmund's work? Would he be so reckless as to transport an invasive species to Earth to rid her of her army of clones?* She decided he absolutely would.

"The Moon Children are the attack on Earth," Caroline said plainly.

Something like relief washed over her. Not because the Moon Children were not a formidable opponent but because she finally knew what was out there, what was coming for them.

Miranda put on her game face. "What would you like me to—"

Leonard barged through the conference door. "The doctor is here, Ma'am. It's urgent."

Caroline recognized Andy, an Andrew clone, as he entered the conference room. He wore the usual white lab coat, buttoned-up to the top and as pristine as ever except for what appeared to be a rust-colored smudge across the wrist of one arm. "I'm sorry for the intrusion, but David has requested an audience at once."

He seemed agitated. More like a nervous human than a Jovian clone.

Miranda and Leo rose from their seats.

"Only Caroline," Andy added in an apologetic tone.

Caroline studied his face. If the oneness worked as it should, she would already know whether this was dire news or something else. Whatever it was, it must have been important. Andy—and David, for that matter—wouldn't interrupt a meeting, especially on a morning like this one, during which a rocket launch took place. She hoped this wasn't evidence of David's weakened condition. The oneness barely worked as it was, and now with the Moon Children on the attack, she needed him to recuperate. She needed him at 100 percent.

But maybe she was getting ahead of herself. He had requested her presence, that was all.

"We should hurry," Andy said, his voice carrying a quiver Caroline didn't like.

She stood and said, "Yes, I'm coming."

CAROLINE EXPECTED Andy to lead her to the laboratory, but he rushed past its entrance and made for the elevator that whisked them to the astronomical observatory.

David wants to see the sky, she thought. *The sky gives him strength. It will help him heal.*

She understood why he loved the observatory. Being in its cool, earthy atmosphere was almost as good as being at one with the stars. Every Jovian agreed. The way the light entered through the central oculus like a thick, swirling, almost-tangible luminescence proved heavenly and resuscitative. Spending a few moments in the observatory was like ingesting liquid well-being.

Andy opened the door for her, and she entered the

circular space filled half with watery light, half with midnight-gray shadow. A mechanical element sat at its center—a pod set upon the floor where the wide, squat telescope normally resided. The pod caught her by surprise, clicking a gentle cacophony of rattles and taps. Caroline had remained just one step inside the door, and Andy strode past her as he hurried to the pod and observed the screen propped by its side.

Up until that moment, she'd imagined David would be perched cross-legged on the stool by the far wall. He often meditated there, absorbing messages and insights. Interplanetary knowledge.

"I don't understand," she said. "Why have you placed a pod—"

"Please come closer," Andy said and waved her forward as if she were some clone he was going to treat. "He wants to see you."

Caroline stood deliberately taller as she moved with cautious steps toward the center of the room.

A scent she didn't recognize bothered her. The bitter char of burned wires. Something heated to the point of destruction.

The clicking sounds that emanated from the pod mixed with the tap of her high-heeled shoes. *Tap-tap-whir-click-tap-tap-click-whir*. Once she was able to see inside, the shock fluttered her eyelids. *David, no*, she thought as she forced herself to observe him.

His body lay in the tranquil reflection of light funneling in from the oculus above, the glow of morning brightening his pale-gray complexion. Thankfully, his lids were down, and he didn't see her reaction to his appearance. The orbs of his eyes underneath remained active, as they always had, still working tirelessly—or attempting to —to keep the oneness intact, she assumed.

She could not help but feel the thinness of his body as if it were her own brittle skeleton and parchment-like skin. She cringed at the tubes and monitors hooked and inserted, as if he were just another weak human, a non-alien passenger prepped for deep space travel.

"Why have you put him in a pod?" she asked.

She sensed Andy's hesitation to answer.

"The pod is keeping him alive," he said, softly.

How dare he utter such words in front of David! David wasn't dying. He couldn't be. What did Andy know? Andy was just a clone. A clone of her son, who hadn't lived past the age of thirty-one. He was weak. All the Andrews were weak.

"He can't die," she said. "He won't."

"His life force is tragically low," he responded in a gentle manner. "It has been all morning. He asked me to bring you here because—"

"Leave us," she said, cutting him off from the words she did not want to hear.

In her periphery, Andy became rigid, then took a step back and nodded. He tended to the equipment, touching the attached screen here and there, before making brisk work of retreating from the room and closing the door without so much as a tick.

Caroline gazed at David, horrified by his scarce breaths and sunken cheeks. His face, once so boyish and youthful, looked bony and old, the skin deteriorated. A white infirmary garment covered most of him, but the limbs, uncovered, appeared brittle, delicate. His body, like hers, had not aged much over the years—until the past few months. Admittedly, he'd grown thin over the years, pale, heavy-lidded, but that was only his physical form, his human self. Underneath he possessed powers greater than any other Jovian. Or so he once had.

Could he be dying?

She crossed her arms over her chest. Is this what they were all destined to become? Stripped of their true selves, of their Jovian powers? Dying the way humans do? Caroline knew that Jovians did not live forever, but she had never watched another of her kind die. True Jovians lived for millennia. When they made plans, old age and death didn't work into the equation. It wasn't something they thought about the way humans did.

Today David resembled a cut flower, dehydrated and faded. Was the supreme one ready to let go? She couldn't imagine it.

"David," she whispered, "wake up."

The pod clicked and whirred in place of a verbal answer.

Caroline stood tall in her usual way, putting on a determined gaze meant to camouflage her internal consternation. She didn't need this right now. Not with the Moon Children invading, and Edmund—and possibly Evander—conspiring against her from Io. Not with her own inability to take her true form, and with the oneness collapsing—wholly collapsing should David perish. If he died, he'd leave her vulnerable. Weak. As weak as he was lying in that pod.

And then Miranda might attempt to step in. As loyal as she was, she would want Earth for herself.

That can't happen, Caroline told herself.

She touched David's small, dry hand. A layer of residue rested on top, something like dust.

He opened his eyes. His chest inflating as if he'd been underwater for a time and desperate for a full breath.

"David, oh thank goodness." She heard her own voice and wished she'd reacted in her usual unemotional way, without worry or sadness, but something had changed. *Everything had changed,* she remembered with sudden dread.

"Caroline," his voice lacked timbre, the vitality drained from it.

As she looked upon him, she sensed avalanches sliding down mountains, cliffs wavering and toppling into the sea, streams of lava decimating forests.

The possibility that she would soon be without him hijacked her ability to breathe.

"I have come to my end," he said, through pale-gray lips. "I have done all that I can do."

"You are the supreme one," she said as if he needed reminding.

"I have pushed too far and am unable to come back."

His breath smelled of burned forests. Caroline sensed the life rushing out of him, the end coming fast. Her instinct urged her to protect herself, to prepare to take her true form, though she knew that was no longer something she could do. Instinct told her to guard against his passing as if it were the start of a battle she'd be up against until the end.

"Don't say that, David. I need you here now more than ever. Pl—" She stopped just short of begging.

"You must fare well," he said, and she wondered if he had heard her. "You must carry on. My forces will transfer in manner and form."

His lids dropped closed, then shakily rose, his eyes portraying the numb appearance of blindness. The pod and its tubes clicked and whirred at greater frequency, though not in an alarmed way, unfazed by David's dire announcement.

Caroline's desire to refuse him became tangled in the back of her throat. Couldn't he find the strength to hang on?

"Pull back," she said, her voice straining. "You're tired and overtaxed, I understand, but it's not the end. You can come back from this."

His blue-green eyes, a mere echo of their original vibrant hue, reached for her from deep hollows. In that moment, she felt him fall like a handkerchief wafting to the ground. She squeezed his hand in an attempt to catch him, to sturdy him.

His lids fell closed.

"Tell the boy," he whispered. "You must tell the boy."

The clicks and whirs came to an abrupt halt.

Tubes deflated, pressure released.

David emitted an exhale, his body flattening like a book that had been closed.

The clouds must have scattered because rays of morning sun spilled from the oculus above and drenched them in a sudden burst of warmth. David's body seemed to compress even further under its brilliance. He was wasting away right in front of her.

Is this what the end looks like for Jovians?

She fought a terrible urge to pull him up, to snatch him from the hands of death.

But the pod erupted into flames, and Caroline jumped back.

"David, no. I demand you stay!"

As his body became lost within a deep-blue blaze, the last traces of the oneness in Caroline's mind flickered and went out.

She backed all the way to the wall, and the pod collapsed to the floor. The blue flames fed upon his body for a few slow-moving seconds before a brilliant flash filled the space and rendered Caroline blind.

When the glare faded from her vision, a mound of ash smoldered at the center of the room. The absence of

David plunged into her like a knife and pulled her toward the floor. Her knees buckled, and she fought the swell of doom that dragged her down.

She didn't recognize her own voice when she murmured, "Don't go."

A disturbing silence grew where the oneness had once babbled.

She came to sit with her arms draped over her knees, her upper body slumped in defeat.

David's command to "tell the boy" echoed through her memory.

"Dmitri," she said, hardly able to form words. "Dmitri, I need you."

Chapter 3

Metka, Russian Federation

The dancers moved to the music they made with their drums and their voices—and their costumes—which Dmitri supposed could not be called costumes because what they wore onstage may have been how the Koryak dressed every day. The Koryak's clothing looked to be made with animal skins, which may have been genuine, and had fringes in various places and tassels along the edges that jingled with small bells.

Both the men and the women wore their dark hair long and came from the far eastern side of Russia, a place Dmitri had never visited in person. On the internet, he'd learned they were an indigenous people who lived in harmony with their environment, in a place called Kamchatka. He doubted he would ever visit that part of the country considering its rough terrain was the sort that proved difficult for wheelchair users. Besides, he and his mother rarely left Metka.

The mixture of the thuds of the dancers' feet upon the community center stage and the chants coming from their mouths and the many bells tinkling from tassels on their costumes came together to make the music the group danced to.

The dance made the music, and the music made the dance, he thought. There was something satisfying about that.

At eleven years old, Dmitri had never danced before. He could clap and sort of bob from side to side, though not to the beat of the music, and that was the extent of it.

Because he'd been born with a disease that caused a lack of control of major muscle groups (not exactly muscular dystrophy or cerebral palsy, but a combination of the two, his parents used to say), Mother treated him like he was fragile. Ever since Father went away, and Dmitri and Mother left America to live in this village three hours by car from Moscow, she had become more protective of him than she used to be.

Dmitri assumed she wouldn't let him dance even if he had been born without disabilities.

He understood why Mother was so protective. Uncle Jimmy had taken Natasha away three years ago, and Father was still on a mission to retrieve her. Mother had refused to go with him. She didn't want her family to live anywhere but on Earth. When Father became president, he'd promised the space travel would end. Which was good because doctors said Dmitri would not likely survive a space trip, especially not one to Mintaka, though the travel pods had successfully transported other disabled people to Mars and Jupiter. Still, there was no way Nadia Peterman (Mother's married name) would chance it, he knew. The former first lady of the United States had temporarily lost her daughter and her husband to space travel, and there was no way she was going to let Dmitri's feet, or his wheels, leave the safety of Earth's terrain.

That's how they ended up in Metka, the place Mother

had grown up. It was easier to hide out here, she'd told him. Easier to stay under the radar.

They also ended up there because Metka was far from the Jovians, who still lived in Pennsylvania as far as they knew. Mother didn't trust that Great-grandmother wouldn't try to lure Dmitri away—and she intended to keep her son to herself. She'd told him many times.

When the dance performance ended, each of the Koryak pressed the palms of their hands together in a thankful manner and bowed their heads, receiving applause from the audience. It was at this time that Dmitri detected a sudden change in the oneness. The oneness was the part of his mind filled with Jovian chatter. It was there, as it usually was, while the dance of the Koryak took place, and then suddenly it was not there—like he had toggled a switch that had turned it off.

How strange, he thought, and he rapped the side of his head a couple of times the same way Mother occasionally kicked the side of the dishwasher to get it started.

But it didn't work for him.

He slid his hand into a pocket on the side of his chair and grasped his cluster of keys. In a jagged, uncontrolled trip to the space beside his ear, his hand held the keys so he could listen to them jangle. Jangling was his favorite sound. The doctor told Mother he did this as a way of self-soothing. He supposed that was true. More than that, however, it was a way to bring the Jovian oneness into focus, to better hear Great-grandmother's voice, or to do other things like speak directly into people's minds, a skill that depended a great deal on whose mind he tried to enter.

Mother disliked the Jovian side of him, so he never talked about the oneness. She knew he was part of it, knew he'd been born to it—and yet she also forbade him to use it. But he had no way to switch it off, so he let it ramble like a radio in the background, like a song he couldn't hear well enough to decipher the words.

Even now, with the keys jangling, the oneness eluded him. The fact that it had gone mute was wrong, very wrong. Maybe even bad. Most likely it was bad.

After the dancers skipped off stage, the audience came to life, filling the space with the loud hum of words. Mother helped Dmitri get his jacket on, one roving arm at a time, then placed a blanket across his lap and began to wheel him up the aisle of the auditorium. It was then that he thought of David. Actually, he didn't just think of him. An image of David *appeared* in his mind. David in a dark space dissected by a cylinder of light. The bottom of a well maybe. The light came from above. A sparkling sort of illumination like tiny diamonds in a sunbeam that spread over David's unmoving body.

The light surrounded David for a moment, and then it went out with a sound like a slammed door.

Dmitri dropped his keys into his lap and gasped. Great-grandmother's voice came through the darkness. It was much louder than the murmur of Jovian oneness. "Dmitri," she said.

Was she crying? He'd never heard her cry before.

"I need you."

His hair stood on end. "We-ah have to get back," he blurted, straining as he usually did to pronounce the words in an understandable way.

Mother bent over the handlebars at the back of his wheelchair, and said, "What happened, did you drop your keys again?"

"No," he said, his mouth twisting. "To America, we must go—"

"America?" She made a face and then resumed moving up the slope of the aisle, trailing the rest of the crowd to the exits that led out of the building. Someone opened the door for them, and the night air rushed over Dmitri like a shock of cold ocean water.

"Mother!" he shouted.

They moved a little farther to get out of the way of the people behind them and then she squatted beside him, a cloud of vapor escaping her nose. He looked into her eyes, which brimmed with suspicion. "Are you okay?" she asked.

In the parking lot in front of them, people opened car doors and climbed inside. Engines roared to life. Others started the walk home.

"You must listen to me-ah," he said with strenuous sincerity. "I—"

She didn't wait for the rest of what he wanted to say. "We were having such a nice time. Why do you have to ruin it by bringing up America?" She paused. "Have you been talking to Caroline again?"

He didn't want to lie, so he kept his mouth closed. He hadn't been talking to her; *she* had been talking to *him*.

"Caroline cannot be trusted. She is the reason your father left. Why do you disobey me?"

It was too bad Mother wasn't part of the oneness. Then he wouldn't have to use his mouth to speak to her. Once, when he'd attempted to communicate with her using only his mind, she mistook what she heard as an indication that she was "losing it." He had to convince her it must have been the TV in the next room, and never tried it again.

He grabbed the pen from his shirt pocket and located the small pad from the pouch on the side of his chair. Sometimes his fingers worked better than his mouth. He did his best to write, *No. Father went to retrieve Natasha.*

He handed her the pad, and she gazed at it. Even in

the darkness he could tell her face grew red. She may have been boiling on the inside.

She returned the pad to him and said, "This is true. I suppose retrieving Natasha turned out to be a lot more difficult than your father imagined, considering he left three years ago. But that doesn't change anything. I don't want you talking to Great-grandmother or any other Jovian—unless it's your father. Or Uncle Jimmy. Those two only," she said.

Dmitri stared at her. The only voice that ever came through the oneness clearly was Great-grandmother's. And he'd never successfully replied to her. So far, it had been a one-way street.

"Do you hear me?" Mother spoke loudly whenever she wanted him to say yes.

"My ears work very well," he said, his neck tweaking in such a way that his chin jutted toward the sky.

She deflated and mussed his hair. "I know they do. Let's go home. It's cold out here. Do you want your hat?"

"No-ah," he said.

They traveled several blocks in silence before arriving at their single-story house wedged in between two larger ones—unlike the White House in Washington, DC, it was inconspicuous, Mother said—with its tiny front porch, crooked gutters, and ramp on the side, which led straight into the little kitchen with old, yellowed appliances. They moved up the subtle incline, and she opened the door, bolting it locked behind them.

In America they had a team of eight secret service agents to protect them. In Russia, they had one metal lock that didn't come together perfectly, not that it wasn't enough to keep them safe. Few people knew who they really were. Mother made sure of that by shopping for "everyday clothing" for herself and using a made-up last name. She was a single mother with a disabled child as far as most people knew, and no one bothered them.

"It's late," she said with a sigh. "I'm sorry I yelled at you. I'm just tired. Let's get you to bed."

She was always tired. He hated that sometimes she had to lift him. But he was getting stronger. His upper body strength had grown to the point where he could climb into bed by himself. Lift up, slide over, butt on mattress, grasp one leg, pull and place, then reach for the other, pull and place. Then adjust, adjust, adjust, inching to the center of the mattress so as not to roll out in the middle of the night.

He wrote "I can do it" on the pad and raised it up so Mother could see.

It wasn't falling out of bed that woke Dmitri that night.

The pungent scent of forest fire came to him in a dream. . . .

His eyes startled open. Was the fire in his bedroom? A neon-green cloud surrounded him from head to foot as if he'd stepped into a glowing bubble. What he saw through it indicated no fire was near. A fire would produce light and heat, and except for the green luminescence that hovered around him, the room remained dark and the usual nighttime cool.

As he observed the strange glow, aware of the possibility that he was dreaming, a curious electric vibration began to course through his veins to the thrum of his heartbeat. It tingled and zapped like charged blood flowing through his limbs, tickling the tips of his fingers and toes. He knew the peculiar bite of electricity because when he and Mother first moved into the house in Metka, he'd plugged the old-fashioned lamp into the wall and accidentally grasped the metal prong as he did so.

Whatever thrummed inside him felt oddly similar, uncomfortable and at the same time good, like energy spreading through his limbs. He thought back to the prior day and considered what he'd eaten. Some foods gave him more energy. For instance, sour cherry juice. But he hadn't drank sour cherry juice since leaving America, and whatever this strange sensation was, it probably wasn't about food.

He assumed the tingle would strengthen, which it did. The electric vibration became an all-over bee sting that flashed through his arms and legs, and pulled them taut. His limbs stretched to such a drastic degree that his body rose from the mattress. The whole of him vibrated the way his teeth had when the dental technician cleaned them.

A picture of David sitting cross-legged on a stool showed up in Dmitri's mind. David within a cloudy green glow just like the one that surrounded him. Dmitri wondered if David would speak. But then the thrumming electricity in his veins staggered and dropped off. The vibration disappeared from his right-hand side. Half his body went limp and hung, his elbow grazing the top of the mattress, while the other half remained stretched and floating. It was as if he'd been partially freed from a net that had caught him.

He continued to hang. The green cloud that surrounded him dispersed. As he wondered what to do, whatever power that had held him cut off altogether, and he rolled onto the mattress and careened over the edge of the bed like a waterfall over a rock wall. His elbow knocked the wooden floor with a loud thump, softening the collision for his head.

He lay there for a second on his stomach, trying to determine whether he'd dreamed the whole thing and maybe the dream had ended with him falling out of bed.

But the burning scent lingered in the air, and he didn't feel like he'd been sleeping. His eyes were open—he carefully touched them to be sure—and then he realized that he'd touched his eyes with a hand that normally would not be so careful but would have poked his eyeball or hit his face.

He rolled onto his back without too much trouble, his arms listening when he commanded them to push up from the ground. Not only did they listen but they supported him. In no time, he sat upright, resting on his rear end.

He pulled in one leg and then the other so that his knees bent before him. His limbs remained still. Obedient. Unhindered by involuntary twitches and spasms. He used his hands and arms to maneuver the bulk of his weight onto his feet the way Natasha always did. Sit on butt, legs in, arms back, push with hands . . . and stand.

He was standing!

His muscles weren't used to this, so they wavered a bit.

He bent his knees and pressed into his feet a few times. His balance was pretty good.

Is this how most people feel? he wondered.

He felt so tall.

"I'm standing," he said out loud. "This is very strange."

His words had arrived fluidly. He sounded like other people. What was happening to him?

He *must* be dreaming, asleep in his bed.

But when he looked at his bed, his body wasn't there. He wasn't lying down. He was awake and upright. In the mirror Mother had hung on his bedroom wall, his image stood at least four feet tall.

He and his reflection exchanged baffled glances.

And then he lifted a leg and thumped his foot on the floor. And he did it again with the other one. And he pumped his arms and pretended there were bells attached to the sleeves of his pajamas. Leg thump, leg thump, arm pump, arm pump, just like the Koryak at the community center earlier that evening.

"I'm dancing," he whispered. And then he shouted, "Mother, look at me, I'm dancing!"

Across the hall, he bounded through the door to her room and stood at the end of her bed. "Mother, wake up!"

She squinted at him from her pillow, her hair veiling her face. "What time is it?" She sniffed loudly and cleared her throat. "Dmitri Peterman, what are you up to?"

He stepped back toward the door and swiped the light switch, then raised both arms out to his sides. His body formed a T, and he turned in a circle. "I'm standing!"

Her expression wrinkled her forehead. "I don't understand. How are you doing this?"

"It's David. He gave me his power."

She groaned and rubbed her eyes. "David gave you power?"

A smile took over his face. "Look, I can dance like the Koryak." He thumped his feet a couple of times, though they didn't make much sound because Mother had an area rug on her floor.

"That doesn't make sense," she said. "A person can't just *give* you their power. Do you mean Caroline's David?"

He stopped dancing and approached her bedside, hands clasped behind his back. She wasn't as happy about this as he was. "Yes. David, the supreme being. He died today."

She closed her eyes, and they seemed to vibrate in their sockets. "How do you know this?"

"I didn't talk to Great-grandmother, I promise. I saw David. Not in person. In my mind."

"In your mind?"

"He came to me. He was there while it was happening."

Mother pinched the bridge of her nose. Whenever she did that, it meant she was confused—and confusion made her angry. "Tell me what happened," she said. "Tell me everything."

"Okay," he said with a nod. "First a green light surrounded me, and then I felt a zap, like I did when I touched metal to the electrical outlet, and I saw David in my mind. He gave me his energy the same way electricity flows through wires."

Mother's mouth opened, and she seemed to want to say something, but no words came out.

He felt like his explanation was taking too long, so he started talking faster: "Energy cannot be created or destroyed. But it can be transferred. Great-grandmother said one day it would be my turn. And now I am walking and talking like other people as though this is my normal even though it is not." He did a couple of squats to demonstrate, still a bit wobbly as he dipped down and then straightened his knees on the way back up. "I've never been able to do this," he said, like she didn't already know.

The grimace he encountered in response told him she was worried.

"What can Caroline mean by this?" Mother glared at the ceiling as if she were angry with it. "Oh no," she said loudly. "No, no, no. That cannot be right. You tell her no for me, Dmitri. I told you never to speak to—"

"I didn't speak to her!" he shouted.

Suddenly his legs crumbled below him. He collapsed as if someone had swiped his feet out from underneath him. The muscles in his arms and legs tensed and then cramped to a painful degree, and he groaned.

Mother jumped down from the bed. "Dmitri, stop it! Oh my God."

He couldn't stop his muscles from contracting, and he writhed from side to side. Mother held him in her arms until the spasms lost steam, and he lay still.

Both he and Mother heaved breaths in and out.

It appeared that the worst was over. But after the spasms ceased, Dmitri suffered a terrible drain of energy, as if all the power David had given him poured onto the floor and took everything he had originally possessed as well. He didn't have the strength to keep his eyes open let alone to respond to Mother's question of whether he was okay.

He woke in his bed as he would any morning, only the light didn't shine like morning light. A dull ooze of dimness spread across the floor he'd danced upon the night before. Afternoon light. Which meant he'd slept for a long time. Which was weird because he was still tired, his limbs heavy, hard to move. He remembered the strength that had propelled him to stand and how Great-grandmother had called for him. Surely she knew where he was. Would she come for him? She'd sounded frightened, and that was strange. What did she need him for?

He raised his arms and attempted to rub his eyes but ended up only grazing his forehead. Without the oneness, he had no way to hear Great-grandmother. She'd called out to him; surely she expected him to come. And David had attempted to give him his power. Maybe it would return. Maybe if he stayed in bed long enough, the green glow would reappear. Having all that power was weird, so different from what he was used to, not that his usual was terrible. But if he had David's power, it would be a lot easier to return to Kirksberg.

He lifted his keys from the night table and held them above his head. The gentle tinkling centered him, but the oneness failed to come through.

His wheelchair waited for him in the usual place beside his bed. He grasped one of the handles and tried to pull it toward him but accidentally pushed it into the wall instead.

Mother appeared in the doorway. She must have been listening for him, waiting for him to wake.

"*Privyet*, Mitya. How are you feeling?"

The Russian side of the family often called him "Mitya."

"I am fine-ah," he said, the disappointment in his tone hijacking his words—and from the frown Mother gave him, he could tell she heard it.

She sat on the bed by his feet and put her hands on her lap. "Whatever happened last night was strange and maybe even wonderful for a little while—"

"Yes, it was. For a little while." *I danced. I spoke like other people. I felt surprisingly strong.*

"I'm sure it was. But it couldn't last. It was just one of those things that happened, and no one can explain why. A momentary . . . thing." She shook her head the way people do when unable to come up with a better word. "Plus, the way you live normally is nothing to feel bad or ashamed about. It's not always easy, but nothing in life is."

"That-ah is true," Dmitri said. "But I *can* explain it. David did it. I told you last night."

"Yes, you did. But it's gone now. And that's okay." She leaned toward him and mussed his hair. "You are wonderful as you are."

"Maybe it will come back."

"Uh-huh," she said, offhandedly. "Maybe. You never know. But it didn't last very long."

He could tell she hoped it *wouldn't* come back. Not because she didn't want him to walk or to speak more clearly or to feel unusually strong, but because she didn't trust anything that came from Father's side of the family. She hadn't trusted them even before the Jovians took Natasha without asking. And then Father went away, so in a way they'd taken him too.

She stood and opened a dresser drawer, making a shirt-pants-and-socks pile and handing it to him. "You must get dressed because we're going to Aunt Helena's. It's Alexandria's birthday. Can you believe she's going to be twenty-eight?"

"No-ah."

"She's getting to be an old lady like me."

"Ha," he said. He concentrated on pulling off his shirt, trying to focus on his arms' movements so they would do what he needed them to do—and then he felt something unusual. A tingle of energy in the place where his neck connected to his head. Very quiet and gentle. Like the tiny fire from a matchstick warming the base of his skull.

David's energy? he wondered. Or had he only imagined it?

"No way!" Alexandria shouted at Dmitri with delight.

They sat in her bedroom with the door closed, the only two "kids" in the family hanging out while the adults discussed the boring details of ordinary life. Dmitri, parked at the foot of her bed, had just told Alexandria, seated in the middle of the mattress, what happened the night before. How he'd stood, walked, and even danced. She often babysat for him because having a disabled child was a challenge for a single mother, and Alexandria was a kind person who liked to help. She also didn't leave the house too often, so she didn't have a job. She lived with something called "agoraphobia," and only visited Dmitri at his house when she was feeling "well."

"People leave the house," Alexandria had once said, "and sometimes they don't ever come back."

She meant Father, who she knew as Evander.

Evander and his mother, Svetlana, had lived in Alexandria's parents' house for ten years. That's because Alexandria's mother, Aunt Helena, was Svetlana's adopted sister. When the Jovians tried to take Evander away, Svetlana left America with the help of the FBI and came to live in Tula with Helena. Tula was the town next to Metka.

One night Evander, who'd grown up very quickly, went on a date with Nadia—Dmitri's mother—and never came back because the Jovians had come for him. Svetlana had left to find him and then she never came back, either.

So, in a way, Alexandria wasn't wrong. People did sometimes leave the house never to return.

"I can't believe you could do all of that. Stand and run and dance?" Alexandria said with big, amused eyes. "Or wait, this is *you* we're talking about, so maybe I *can* believe it." She pulled a silver flask from some crumpled tissue paper in a box on her night table and took a drink.

Maybe it was a birthday gift?

"I guess that's Jovian magic for you," she said. "I wish so much I was part of your family. You have no idea."

"But you-ah are afraid of Jovians."

She finger-combed a tangle of her long hair, then took a closer look at its ends before tossing it to the side. "That's true. But I still wish I had your sometimes-very-surprising genes."

Alexandria had learned to speak English back when

Svetlana and Evander lived with her family. Those first ten years of her life, she told Dmitri, were the most fun she'd ever had. She was born the same year Father was, though at present time she resembled a young lady and Father already had gray in his hair and wrinkles across his forehead. Mother said it was because Jovians aged differently than humans. Jovians did *most* things differently.

Alexandria had loved Evander like a brother and still missed having him in the house, though Aunt Helena always said it was for the best that he no longer lived there.

Dmitri said, "You are part of my fam—"

"Yes, I know. I'm the boring human part. Which means no one's sending me superpowers in the middle of the night." She raised the flask in his direction and took another drink.

"Who gave you that?" he shouted with glee.

"I was waiting for you to ask." She laughed loudly and gave him a mischievous sideways glance. "A boyfriend of mine."

"*Boy*friend!" Alexandria never spoke of friends, let alone boyfriends.

"Okay, okay, *boyfriend* may not be the right word." Her cheeks formed smiley mounds on her face. "He's an admirer." She broke into laughter and turned red for a minute before going back to her normal pale color. "He's just this new neighbor who wandered over to my house a couple of times. I accidentally let it slip that my birthday was coming up, and I guess he wanted to show me how much he appreciated the cups of coffee I made for him."

"Ugh, a boyfriend," Dmitri said. "Gross."

She slouched for a second. "That's the most kid-like thing I ever heard you say."

"I'm eleven. Remember?"

"Yes, but you're Jovian eleven. Your dad was twenty

when he was ten, so—" She shrugged, her sweatshirt gathering around her double chin. "Back to my admirer and his gift. It's not gross because I'm practically thirty years old, and my parents won't let me drink in the house. It's kind of nice to have a secret bottle, you know?" She paused. "Plus, it's the only present I got so far."

One reason Dmitri liked Alexandria so much was because she treated him like an equal although he was just a kid. And even though everyone judged her larger body and eating habits, and worried about how she hardly left the house, she seemed pretty happy to him. He knew she enjoyed his company. He often told her things he couldn't tell Mother. Jovian things delighted Alexandria while they gave Mother headaches.

"I have a present for you too," he said, thinking she'd like one of his tricks.

He lifted his keys from the plastic pocket that hung from the side of his chair.

"Oh, cool," she said as she scooted to the edge of the bed. "One second. I'll get some paper."

"No. No-ah paper this time."

Sometimes Alexandria wadded pieces of paper into balls, and he concentrated on them so hard that they flew up and hit the ceiling or simply fell from the table to the floor. It was one of the more interesting Jovian things he could share with her and no one else. Once when he practiced at home, he shot a cough drop off his desk and it landed in his shoe.

She sat in silence as he raised the keys unsteadily overhead and focused on the sound of their stems clinking together. He stared at the way the keys swayed according to his body's unpredictable movements. And then he brought to mind the silver flask at Alexandria's side and grasped it with his internal fingers. He raised the flask from the bed, pulling it over Alex's head, and made it slowly spin as it lingered there, in the air.

It wasn't hard for him to do. Which was strange.

Alexandria yelped when she saw the flask floating right in front of her. "When did you graduate from paper balls!" Then she gasped. "Is this because of what David did?"

Throughout the day, the buzz that warmed the base of Dmitri's head had grown in strength and now radiated up the sides. He closed his eyes, feeling how the energy spread like massaging hands.

"Mitya, this is amazing," Alexandria whisper-shouted. "When did you learn to do this?"

He opened his eyes and the flask darted across the room, crashed into the opposite wall, and hit the floor with a clunk. It left behind a glaring, egg-sized depression. He hadn't meant to fling it like that and hoped he hadn't damaged her gift. Never had such easy power surged through his mind.

The keys slipped from his fingers into his lap as his head hummed in a comforting, energizing way. Instinct told him to stand, so he removed his feet from the chair's footrest and placed them on the floor. Then he pressed his weight into his legs as he stood. He bumped the wheelchair with the back of his thighs, and it rolled away from him. The muscles in all four of his limbs buzzed.

"It's happening again," he told her.

Alexandria sat straight up, bracing herself. "Oh, my goodness. Are you going to walk?"

He started with his right foot, then left, then right, continuing in a circle around the room. Then he jumped a couple of times, a bit unsteadily, just to see if he could. He lifted the right knee, then the left, and danced like the Koryak again. Alexandria clapped. He stomped his feet and waved his hands in the air. When he attempted a spin, his legs collapsed and he crashed into the wall near the depression he'd made with the flask, ending up in a heap on the floor.

Alexandria ran to his side. "Are you all right? What happened?" She helped him sit up.

He waited for a seizure to follow, for the drainage of power to overtake him. But it didn't.

"I have to go to America," he said. "Great-grandmother needs me."

Alexandria's jaw hung open in awe. "How are you doing this? You sound like a different person. Is this David's power too?"

That didn't matter to him at the moment. What mattered was going to America. He grasped her shoulders and stared into her eyes. "Please say you'll take me to America."

"You mean to see Caroline, Queen Jovian?"

"Yes. In Kirksberg."

"Me? Really?" She drew back, fear tensing her usually soft, jovial face. "But how? I mean, I don't have that kind of money. I don't know if I can. I wouldn't know how to go about any of it."

"I have money," he said, his words flowing, "but Mother won't take me. I *must* go but I can't do it alone. I'm too young. I still need assistance."

"These changes won't last?" she asked.

He shrugged just like she had a few moments before.

Alexandria's faraway stare let him know she was seriously considering his request.

"It's very important, Alex. Great-grandmother is powerful. She wouldn't call for me if it wasn't serious. David is dead. I don't know what will happen if I don't get back there, but I know it won't be good. It won't be good for anyone."

She glanced at him with fear in her eyes. "What does she need you for?"

He breathed in and shook his head. "I only know that bad things will happen to Earth if I don't go."

At that, Alexandria stood and retrieved the flask from the floor. She opened it and tipped back her head, pouring the liquid down her throat. When she came up for air, her blue eyes watered, and she coughed a little. "I'm not sure I can go to America, let alone leave the house—"

"You can. Of course you can," he said. "I'll be there. I'll help you." He raised his eyebrows, nodding, hoping she would nod along with him. "It will be an adventure."

She raked back her long hair, her hands pausing at the crown. "I always wanted to have an adventure."

"I know!" Dmitri said, smiling broadly. "And this will be fun! Your mother will never take you to America. This could be your only chance."

She drank from the flask again, possibly finishing off what was left.

"You're right," she said. "I need to do this for you and for me. Of course I will take you. Of course. When do you need to go?"

Chapter 4

Kirksberg, Pennsylvania

When the bunker's heavy metal door slammed closed the way it did whenever someone hurried inside, Fran Vasquez startled and gazed upward to make sure the "someone" was his wife, Lisa.

"I saw one of the Leonards in town, standing at the edge of the park," she said as she hustled down the steep staircase that led to the wide-open room Fran and the other resisters called "the pubspace." Short for *public space,* it fulfilled all the Coalition's needs for community living.

"He'd come out of the pharmacy a few minutes before," she said, pausing to remove her jacket, "so I guess that gives him a reason to be there, but I don't know. No one followed me, as far as I can tell. But still. Anyone else think it's too close for comfort?"

Not bothering to look up from his comm, Drew reclined as much as one can upon a bar stool without toppling over backward. "As long as it wasn't the one with the robotic head, I'm not worried," he said. "Did you get the supplies?"

"It wasn't Head Leonard. And, yes, the medical kit is now complete, no worries." She raised a small shopping bag in her hand.

"Did he see you?" Fran said. "Your face, I mean."

"I don't think so. He was at least a block away, and I had my hood up and sunglasses on."

Lisa's ability to thwart danger rivaled that of a trained ninja. She possessed a natural, paranoid ability to sniff out a bad situation. Fran took comfort in knowing he could move any plan forward with complete confidence based on his wife's stellar instincts.

"What does your gut tell you?"

"Just that he was probably picking up cough drops . . . or aspirin."

Fran nodded. "Cool."

Ironically, the leaders of the Coalition (a group made up of clones, hybrids, and anyone who fought for freedom for all) had settled into the abandoned Jovian bunker only days after Caroline showed her true alien self at Philadelphia's Independence Lawn. It had been Drew's idea to move into the place the Jovians occupied when Edmund and his team arrived on Earth in the 1960s, and at first Fran considered it an outrageous one.

Dug deep under farmland not more than two miles from Kirksberg's Starbright International facility, the bunker's secret multiple-room structure housed a vast array of reference materials, strangely advanced weather predicters, star finders, and energy sources. The circular design and its content pointed to ancient, otherworldly creators and architecture. The general consensus among Coalition members put forth the idea that Edmund had not built the bunker in the sixties but that beings who came decades (or possibly even centuries) before him had readied it for some future travelers' arrival.

Jovians, they surmised, had been coming to Earth for a very long time.

"Can I get you a coffee? There are donuts over here." Fran gestured to the center of the table where he sat, and Lisa made her way over, passing Drew as she did.

Built much like a spaceship, the bunker's circular pubspace created a core that encouraged social interaction. At its center was a seating area resembling a bar with stools set around it: this was where members of the Coalition ate, met, scrolled, chatted, and researched, with plenty of screens for viewing and sharing views. Outside of the bar, wooden tables and chairs to accommodate gatherings of six or more filled much of the space, with shelves of serious-looking tomes lining walls like a library. In between shelving, cubicles with computers and other technology nestled. Beyond these spaces, corridors led to a ring of residential rooms, modest-sized community kitchens, bathrooms, and exercise and wellness areas. Facilities for about one hundred occupants. At present count, eighty or so lived there full-time, including Jovian clones, hybrids, some humans (mostly those who worked in Starbright offices before joining the cause).

Edmund and whichever Jovians had landed on Earth with him in the 1960s had abandoned the bunker in 1970, when the Starbright International office facilities officially opened, complete with its covert residential tubes, where Caroline, aka Queen Jovian, currently lived.

Fran and Lisa had moved into the bunker soon after Ida Moore called to warn him of the impending attack on Earth, urging him to reach out to Drew, co-leader of the Coalition. Fran had never liked Drew much, but he trusted him because Evander did. And who would know more than Drew did about Jovian plans and whereabouts? If he said the Jovians hadn't given the bunker a second thought since they moved out in 1970, Fran believed him.

So Fran and Lisa joined the resisters who'd moved into the bunker with the objective of keeping an eye on all things Jovian while staying out of public view themselves.

Fran observed his wife as she stirred some sugar into her coffee. He reached out and squeezed her forearm. "You okay?"

"It's never a fun trip when you run into a Leonard," she said.

Rumor had it, Caroline ordered her Leonards to hunt former employees, afraid they would turn family secrets over to the media. Fran wore a target on his back considering he'd headed up Starbright's security squad and his son, Max, was the one who had accidentally shot Head Leonard. Drew was in a similar boat, in that he was once Caroline's favorite clone, always willing to do her bidding until Svetlana woke him to the idea of personal autonomy and free thinking. That eventually led him to organizing the protest at Independence Lawn, which had turned into The Battle of Philadelphia.

Since then, the Leonards had tracked down and beaten several of the clones who'd been active in the protest, a huge turn of events considering Jovians had long been a nonviolent race.

"Whenever I see one of those brutes, it makes me glad Max left the planet," Lisa told Fran.

"Me too," he said, but the truth was he missed his kid and most days kicked himself for letting Max board that spaceship with Evander. It was three years later, and they'd had no word whatsoever. Evander had promised to find a way to reach out, and he wasn't the kind to break promises, which only made it hard for Fran to resist worrisome thoughts.

"You good?" Lisa asked.

Fran had been zoning out, staring at the ground. "Yeah, yeah," he grumbled. "It just bugs me that Max will be thirty this year. That's a big milestone we're missing."

A few feet away, something Drew read on his comm made him sit up straight on his stool. "This is interesting. I'm getting intel on two clones who died of ammonia poisoning in Alaska a couple of weeks ago. There's a rumor it happened in Michigan, recently, too. On the beach of Lake Superior. All the deceased were Andrew clones."

"Why would that be?" Fran said.

"Is it normal for ammonia to naturally occur near water?" Lisa asked.

"Freak accident, most likely," Fran said. "Or, maybe an industrial cloud from a nearby chemical plant."

"In both places?" Drew said as he continued to read.

"Yeah, that would be a strange coincidence to say the least," Fran said.

"Didn't Evander get rid of all the chemical-spouting industrial plants when he was in office?" Lisa asked.

Fran bit into a doughnut. "I'd be surprised if he didn't."

"Unless some of them continued to work covertly somehow," Lisa said, shrugging.

"The hybrids and humans involved in the Alaska incident fared pretty well for the most part," Drew said. "And two of the Jovian royalty were there when it happened too."

"Which ones?" Fran asked.

Drew swiped up on his comm. "Dana and John Peterman."

"Svetlana's adoptive parents," Fran said. "Were they hurt?"

"No. As far as this intel goes, they walked away."

"We need to talk to them," Fran said. "This could be the attack on Earth."

In Drew's usual nonflexible form, he said, "More likely two accidents caused by human error."

"Maybe," Fran said. "Do you know a way we can reach Dana and John?" He braced himself for Drew's angry or sarcastic reply. What he got instead was a deprecating tone: "They're Jovian," Drew said, "do we really want to do that?"

"I'm not saying we have to invite them to the bunker, but they're not your usual Jovians. They're humanitarians. I doubt they've sided with Caroline, if that's what you're worried about." Fran knew how naïve he sounded. "We should see if we can work with them."

Drew rolled his eyes and smiled in a mocking way. "I'm aware that you know them. Are you aware that whatever you know about them is only their cover? You realize that they're just like Caroline—only not as large in their natural forms. Either way, they don't care about humans. Or clones," he said, adopting a cold stare.

How this guy could be a clone of the original Andrew Jovian, the one Fran long ago called his best buddy, was beyond him. How different could two people be when they shared the same DNA?

Drew's voice sunk to an angrier level. "The Jovians only care about possessing this planet and using it to satisfy their own—"

"I'm pretty sure you're wrong about that," Fran interrupted in a loud, stern voice. Because that's how Drew needed to be handled. He may have been an all-right guy most of the time, but no one would describe him as *easy* or *nice*.

"Dana and John took Svetlana in and made her family.

I never would have guessed they weren't human if Svetlana hadn't seen Dana in her true form."

"Good actors," Drew said.

"What does that mean?" Lisa asked.

"It means they were chosen to play the roles of Svetlana's parents simply because they are good actors. Not all Jovians can pull off being human. Caroline can't, for instance."

"Whatever," Fran said with a grimace. "I still want to talk to them."

"Well, the oneness is out of service right now, so I'm afraid I can't help you with that. We'd need a phone number to reach them, and I don't have it. Do you?"

Fran didn't dignify the question with an answer.

Drew turned the comm screen in Fran's direction. "They were stationed in Alaska, Glacier Bay, where the incident occurred, according to this article."

"Plan B for the Jovians is to use the telephone?" Fran asked, frowning doubtfully.

"If there's another way, I don't know about it," Drew said with a shrug. "I'm not exactly on good terms with royalty since the queen declared me Lead Resister and held me in her clenched fist."

The door to the bunker slammed closed.

Lisa gasped. Fran reached for the gun in his shoulder holster.

Drew tipped back his head and shouted toward the ceiling. "You just scared the crap out of the humans. Can you maybe un-invisible yourself next time? Where were you all morning?"

The Jovian clone named Connie, wearing a white one-piece jumper, black military-style jacket, and boots to match, materialized halfway down the stairs. As the only clone with the ability to blend with her surroundings, she was special. And dangerous. *And useful as well*, Fran reminded himself.

"I'm so sorry," said the much-sassier knock-off of old Aunt Constance, Uncle Jimmy's better half (or pretend one, at least) who had replicated herself in much younger form. "I had a meeting at Starbright this morning. You do know I attend these things from time to time?"

"I knew," Drew scoffed. "*They* did not. Were you able to find out what's happening with the oneness?"

"I sure did. And it's not just broken," Connie said. The forthcoming news brimmed in her eyes. "David's gone."

Drew's mouth twisted with impatience. "What do you mean? Where did he go?"

"He passed away," Connie said curtly as she pulled her shoulder-length braids from the place she'd neatly pinned them upon her head. "He's dead."

Drew turned to her with his mouth agape. He couldn't seem to find the words.

"I thought Jovians lived for millennia," Fran said.

Lisa nodded. "And he was so young. I mean, I guess he really wasn't, but—"

"No, he wasn't," Connie said, "but he didn't have to die, either. Caroline might as well have killed him herself."

"Were you in the room when it happened?" Drew asked.

"I was in the conference room, eavesdropping on the meeting, when Dr. Andy called for Caroline to join him. It was too much of a risk for me to follow. Miranda and Leo stayed behind. Miranda said she wouldn't be surprised if David lay on his deathbed, the way Caroline had manipulated him into using his energy the past decade. She said no one could have withstood it."

"Miranda blames Caroline for David's death?" Drew said.

Connie's shoulders lifted. "Certainly seemed that way."

"What will this mean for the oneness?" Fran said. "Will Caroline still have control of the clones?"

"I wish it meant she didn't," Drew said, "but if the clones assume they're free, and they fall out of line, she can still take her true form the way she did in Philadelphia and snap them back in place. So, I'd say not much has changed as far as her reign of power is concerned."

"Damn." Fran eased back in his chair. "I thought we might finally catch a break."

"Then again . . . " Drew said with a tilt of his head.

Connie's smile widened in delighted anticipation. "What?"

"Now might be a good time to break her."

Chapter 5

Mintaka, Orion's Belt

Max liked the way space travel lent itself to musing.

Even while one manned the helm, which thanks to Jovian technology didn't require a whole lot from the pilot—far less than driving a car down I-95 in Philadelphia, for instance—a person could navigate and sleep, eat, or carry on a conversation with himself or his favorite AI without too much effort. For this reason, space and its vast stretches of nothingness in between rare instances of somethingness inspired contemplation. Meditation. All sorts of mental meandering.

That day, as Max headed back to Mintaka, also called "Delta Orionis," he entertained himself with thoughts of, well, spaceships, captaining, speeding through the galaxy, and how his new life overflowed with those things, a fact that still blew his mind. Not only had he learned to fly a spaceship, but he also possessed his very own called the *Orion Sparrow*. Its name was as cool as its sleek, flashy build.

The first time Max laid eyes on the *Sparrow*, something

deep in his gut, possibly his pancreas or liver, told him that one day the C-class flier would be his.

When he left Earth, he'd traveled with former President of the United States Evander Peterman for the equivalent of one year. Space time was not the same as Earth time, he knew, though calculating how many Earth days had passed since he'd been free of its gravitational pull was tricky. He'd always hated math in school and had no desire to waste precious bandwidth attempting to calculate in space. That's what AIs like Elsa were for.

Anyway, he'd taken a ride in (and later co-piloted) the *Mens Ex Spatio* from Earth to Mintaka with Evander and his loyal AI bodyguard, Elsa. The *Mens* was Evander's personal ship and what Max referred to as "Jovian Air" but translated into *headspace* from Latin. After the equivalent of about ten months (according to Elsa's calculations), the three woke from their pod-induced comas and rose from hibernation. Evander then spent about eight weeks teaching Max how to fly.

It was a dream come true. Every second of it, and Max couldn't have been happier.

He clearly remembered how waking from the ten-month sleep had been interesting, and not in an all-good way. He was pretty sure he'd never get the sour taste of coming back to life out of his mouth—and the feeling that he'd been dead for a time (not even dreaming, his life held in suspension with the pod's assistance).

While he had lingered in unconsciousness, tubes found their way into places he'd never thought they'd be programmed to go—but it made sense, considering the human anatomy and its basic needs. Anyway, he tried not to think about that stuff. It was like peeing and pooping on Earth; it had to be done, but the only ones who wanted to talk about it were the parents of toilet-training children.

Once he woke and became free of the pod's tubes and monitors, his first meal of space food didn't want to stay down. For three days he barfed up semisolid beige and yellow mush before finally some pudding form of kale (a leafy green vegetable of all things) settled in and became the thing that basically kept him alive.

He'd forever be grateful for Evander's role in teaching him to pilot. The former president was literally the coolest, most awesome person he'd ever met, and taking this trip into outer space to help Evander find his daughter, Natasha, became the best thing that had ever happened to Max in the thirty-ish years he'd lived and breathed.

Pinpointing birthdays was tricky considering there were no days and nights in outer space, and he'd never understood the method Evander taught him for keeping track of it. All Max knew was that he'd been away from home for about three years. Or four. Sometimes it felt like five. He really wasn't sure at this point, and he liked it that way. Otherwise, he might feel an obligation to hurry up and get back home to see his parents, who no doubt wondered if or when they'd ever see their son again.

At the end of Max's pilot training, Jovian Air arrived at a massive docking station with Max at the helm. He'd never forget what a beautiful sight Mintaka was, like an enormous and intricate lace collar of a blouse floating gracefully in space. Sleek black metal surrounded swatches of deep-blue and reddish-purple clouds. Mintaka, Evander had explained, was a loosely formed planet at the heart of a nebula. It was said to be one of the centers of creation, and at its strange and mystical core, there was nothing but dust and gas. In other words, its core, like the place itself, eluded definition. Evander described Mintaka as a site of pure creativity. A figment of every single being's collective imagination.

These ideas went over Max's head, of course, but as baffling as they were, he could get on board with them. Uncle Jimmy came from Mintaka, after all, and no one could figure him out, either. Yet there he was, a fat, balding, elderly man who seemed wise beyond his human-alien-whatever-he-was years.

That first day on Mintaka, Max had pulled Jovian Air into the docking station, shut it down, and accepted Evander's and Elsa's congratulations. He stepped out of the aircraft a new man from the one who had stepped in the year or so before. A confident, much more mature man. His parents would have been elated to see how far he'd come, how much he'd grown. They could have joined him on this soiree into the universe, and he still wished they had, but Dad had nixed the space travel without even thinking about it, and Mom wanted Max to have his own adventure so he could finally grow up.

The day Max arrived in Mintaka was also the day he saw the *Orion Sparrow* and succumbed to the tremor of knowing that he would one day pilot it. The way he saw it, the *Sparrow*, like his new life as a pilot, had been waiting for him.

And he was right. Evander soon gifted it to him.

First, though, they would locate Evander's daughter, which Evander did easily. Natasha, who traveled with Uncle Jimmy, ironically was an eight-year-old who at that place and time looked like a fourteen-year-old and acted as sedate and level-headed as an adult. She displayed none of the silliness Max remembered exhibiting at that age. Like father, like daughter, he supposed.

Space travel had notoriously aged Evander, and Max was seeing it happen firsthand. When they took off from Earth, Evander seemed about fifty years old, and when they arrived at Mintaka, he sported the wiry gray hair and scruff of someone of sixty to sixty-five. Frankly, it was scary to see, and Max often checked the little mirror he'd hung inside the cockpit to make sure the same wasn't happening to him.

Like now, for instance, when he looked into that mirror, he saw his usual unlined light brown skin, just like his mom's, the same brown eyes he'd always had, and buzzed hair, just like his dad's. No change in his good looks yet (he chuckled to himself), but he assumed that was no guarantee of what might happen in the future.

Max's first mission had been to transport Evander, Natasha, and Elsa to Io, Jupiter's Jovian-inhabited moon. They'd leave Jovian Air with Uncle Jimmy for reasons unknown to Max, but who cared? The *Sparrow* was his!

If he did well, it would be his first mission of many, so screwing up wasn't an option. And he hadn't. He had taken his precious cargo to Io, no problems whatsoever, outside of the fact that when they arrived, six months later, Evander appeared to have aged even more, and his daughter had grown into a gorgeous eighteen-year-old, a far cry from the middle schooler she'd been when they'd left Mintaka.

Evander and his daughter had business to tend to on Io, and the plan, as Max understood it, was for him to complete some missions of his own, then return to Io to pick them up for the journey back to Earth. When would this happen? He had no idea. He was simply to wait for Evander's call to appear on his wristcomm.

And here he was, still waiting for that call weeks—or was it over a month?—later. In the meantime, Max had successfully completed twenty back-to-back missions, dashing all over the Jupiter System and beyond, trans-porting Jovians, messages, and items here, there, and every-where. When the massive gas planet's orbit came nearest to

Mintaka, he was called back for an appointment with a superior he'd never met before. A person named Ida Moore who claimed to know his father, of all people. The reason for meeting remained unspecified. That could be good news, or bad. He wondered (hoped) she would inform him that the twenty-mission milepost he'd met warranted him a promotion—maybe even a medal of honor of some kind for piloting Evander and Natasha to Io. That would be nice. He often dreamed of medals and honors, not that he had anything to prove, but you know, who didn't like to be awarded?

As he laughed out loud, the oaky-brown mini pinecone he kept on the pilot's console stared back at him without eyes. Just before Max left Earth, his father had given it to him and said, "Don't forget where you come from." Over time, that conical little thing had become his most prized possession. If it could speak, he bet it would say, "A medal of honor would be all well and good, Max, but you promised your parents you'd come back home as quickly as possible. You've been gone for you-don't-know-how-many years now, and you're still not homeward bound."

"I know, I know," Max told the pinecone with resignation. "I'll get there soon. Evander should be reaching out any day, and then we'll go back together, I promise."

Max's parents no doubt missed him as much as he missed them. But they would also be happy for him. He'd never been so excited about life. Even if his being gone for so long upset them, they'd understand when he told them how much he had accomplished. How well he was doing at his job. The fact that he'd been given his own spacecraft would blow their minds!

God, he loved the *Sparrow*. He patted the console and said, "I adore you, you know that?"

Sometimes it occurred to him that flying was better

than sex, not that he'd had any sex in . . . he didn't want to remember how long it had been. Or with whom. Some hot-shot pilot he'd met during a layover on Ganymede.

"Can I be of assistance, captain?"

He'd never get used to Syndi chiming in when he spoke out loud to himself. He'd named his AI Syndi after its technical name, the Syndicate 1330. When prompted to label the AI, he'd started typing and accidentally pressed the Enter button before he was through. Typing had never been his strong suit. So, Syndi it was.

"Nope, I'm good," he told her.

"I'm available to talk anytime," she said.

"Yes, I know. Thank you."

One of an AI's duties was to make their pilot feel less alone. To keep them from losing their mental health marbles way out in nowheresville for long lengths of time. The thing was, Max never felt lonely out there. Or looney. The solar system was his happy place.

He grinned to himself as the *Sparrow* sailed into the metallic docking station that surrounded Mintaka. After visiting many space stations, planets, and moons during his missions, it was still the most amazing orbiting object he'd ever seen, and that made more sense than ever due to what he'd learned from the people and extraterrestrials he'd met along the way. Apparently the greatest creators in the universe originated on Mintaka. Architects, philosophers, futurists, freethinkers, builders, teachers. Mintaka was literally the innovation epicenter of the galaxy, possibly even the universe itself. An organic sort of space station, it began as a few sizable rocks circling a distant star of the same name. Those rocks had settled into the palm of a hazy, gorgeous nebula of reddish space dust that protected them from the star system that would have otherwise burned them—and all the life they sustained—to cinders.

It made for an abstract outer-space splash of a red-beige-maroon-colored sky that Max couldn't get enough of.

Space was much more beautiful than he had expected it to be. When he was a kid, he'd thought it was black with a few diamonds sprinkled in, but, man, was he wrong. Who needed attractive women to look at when the universe displayed so many colorful abstracts? Then again, if he ever met a beautiful female who took an interest in him, he was pretty sure he'd never say that again. For now, the wonders of space kept him from dreaming of eighteen-year-old daughters of former presidents—and that was a good thing—though he did wonder how old Natasha might be the next time she traveled. Maybe she'd speed right into her thirties. He hoped to be her pilot if she did.

Once the *Sparrow* powered down, and Max disembarked, he left the docking area and stepped up to the waiting station. He pressed the button for the elevator and listened to the hydraulic whir of a compartment traveling at a speed he'd never wrap his head around. It made a distinct whistling sound, like nothing he'd ever heard on Earth. When the doors opened, he stepped in—glad to be alone—and pressed the button for MAIN.

Two years ago, his stomach would have lurched as the lift whisked him miles upward, but he'd been in space long enough to become accustomed to sudden shifts in velocity. His e-skin helped his body to withstand the g-force. The elevator doors opened twenty seconds later (a counter in the lift let him know), and he exited into a wide-open space. A decidedly green one.

One of the Earth floors.

It was a park based on the famous one that thrived then died then thrived again (thanks to Evander) in New York City. *Central Park,* he thought but wasn't sure. Gravel paths traversed a grassy floor. A variety of tall, ancient-looking elms lent shade from the fabricated sunshine. The NOxygen clip he wore in his nose made sure the air he breathed provided enough O_2. Space air usually came with the stench of this chemical or that. Ammonia sometimes, sometimes sulfur. In Mintaka, however, it smelled like the real deal. Maybe thanks to the trees?

Bar 503, that's where he needed to go according to a Jovian Headquarters text he received with the name, location, date, and time. As if he were some CIA operative with a deadly mission. Usually assignments consisted of shuttling individuals from one moon to another. The number of moons in their galaxy neared three hundred, and Jupiter claimed ninety-five of them in its massive orbit.

The wide path of the park led to an old-fashioned New York neighborhood where brownstone residential buildings connected to a corner market, pizza place, and bakery wafting the mouthwatering aroma of fresh bread. Men and women walked by wearing dresses, blue jeans, flannel shirts. Angular haircuts in every color imaginable were the norm here. Of course, not all of them took human form. He came across many Jovians in their shiny, black, minimalist bodies. How they could tell each other apart remained a mystery to him. Slight deviations in head shape and stature seemed to be the only variations. He'd seen Jovians of all sizes, even seven or eight feet tall—none near as towering as the giant Caroline had revealed herself to be—none of them wider than an average-size human. And then there were other cosmic species that resembled Elsa, Evander's AI bodyguard. They wore uniform colors and moved with grace and precision, like humans minus the imperfections. He'd also met beings with reddish skin that came from Martian lineage. Their ancestors had left Mars when it dried up.

He looked down upon himself, at his black pilot uniform, and wondered how strange he might seem to these passersby. A real human space pilot. He was only one of a few hundred human pilots in the galaxy, and yet no one batted an eyelash in his direction. He wasn't surprised. Everyone he'd met on Mintaka had been as open-minded as they come. Friendly in their own way. But Mintaka was the exception, not the rule. Not everyone in the galaxy exhibited nonjudgmental behavior. The universe hosted its share of skepticism and discontent, prejudice and poison. Usually lurking in the shadows, where you'd expect to find it, but sometimes hidden in plain sight as well. Power struggles took place every day, everywhere. Just like on Earth. The entire universe ran on survival of the fittest, Max didn't know why.

He'd seen his share of sketchy dealings and unfairness.

At the end of the block, he came to a building of old, white stucco suffering chips, cracks, and dirt smudges. A window paired with an unassuming entrance directly beside it and small letters reading "Bar 503." This was it. He pulled open the door, squeaky on its corroded hinges, and stepped into complete darkness. He couldn't see his hand in front of his face and considered reaching back and reopening the door to let some light in, but then his eyes began to adjust.

Humans sure liked their watering holes dark.

Before him a U-shaped bar bumped out a half-circle from the wall, without a server to man it. Shelves of bottles cluttered beside metal advertising signs, mirrors, dimly lit neon, and dusty paraphernalia of the sort he might have found at a garage sale or antique shop back home: framed photos of people he didn't recognize and dusty, dented license plates.

No one was here. He checked his comm. He was exactly on time, and usually his appointments were as well.

This is definitely sketchy, he thought.

Then he heard an exhale and turned in the direction from which it came. The far side of the bar. Someone was there, in the corner. On a stool, hunched over, wearing a hooded cloak like a ninja. The head within the hood had to be small, not much bigger than a cantaloupe or grapefruit. The person themself, so dark and colorless in the dim lighting that they blended into the shadow.

Now that Max could see better, a tuft of hair below the oversize hood came into view. It was the silvery shade of moonlight. A jolt of worry rode his spine. Whoever this was looked more like an assassin than a Jovian communicator. Had he done something wrong? He couldn't think of what that might be.

Then they raised one bony hand and said, "Max, sit beside me."

The voice was old and scratched, most likely from Earth. It may have been a man or may have been a woman. Was Ida a name for a woman or a man? Now that he thought about it, he realized he didn't know.

"Your promptness is impressive, especially for a human."

He was close enough to see the face now. Its sharp angles and sunken cheeks, two straight lines for lips. Shriveled with age. "You're Ida Moore?" Max asked.

"Yes, yes, please sit. I have important news."

Seemed civil enough. Max climbed onto the adjacent stool.

"I don't want to alarm you," the old lady, or man, said, "but the attack on Earth has begun."

At that, Max suffered a mental gut punch. For a long time now the Jovians had been saying Earth would be attacked. He'd worried about it less and less as time had passed with no word of trouble. "My parents—"

"They're fine. So far only Jovian clones have perished. It's the Moon Children. Do you know the Moon Children, Max?"

"I don't even know who *you* are."

"I'm Ida Moore."

"Yes, I know your name, but I don't know who you are." Max squinted with suspicion.

"Your father and I work together from time to time. Like you, I'm from Earth."

"You *work* with my father, as in present tense?"

"The present," Ida and her oversize hood nodded, "the past, the future."

Max knew about time travel and how it was physically possible, but frankly that sort of thing spun circles in his mind the same way mathematical equations did, so he preferred to live in an Earthly way—without messing around with time. Leave it to Dad to keep a few galactic secrets under his belt.

"Look, Max, I'm an old woman," she said and Max thought, *Well, that's one mystery solved, at least.* " . . . and I don't have time to explain everything to you," she continued. "I work with the Jovians and have done so for a long, long time. That's all you need to know."

"Which ones?" he said.

"You want me to name—" Some light glanced over her large round eyes, too big for such a small head.

"Yeah. I do. Because if you say Caroline, I might have to—"

"Edmund, Evander, James."

That was good.

She paused to sip from the shot glass her face had been hovering over. He could tell by its opaque color that it was one of those dense superfood mixtures. Instead of leaving you drunk and lethargic like shots of alcohol do, they left you feeling as if you were walking on air. He'd never had one but old people were rumored to love them, maybe even needed them to stay alive out there.

His stomach growled. "You think I can get one of those? Or maybe they serve food here?"

"I sent the server away. We have important business to discuss. *Confidential* business," she said. "Do you understand?"

"Yes, okay." He mentally shifted into business mode.

"So, you don't know who the Moon Children are?"

"No, never heard of them."

"They're a species from the Jupiter System that originated on the moon of Io millennia ago. They loved Io and had no reason to leave, but the Jovians lived there as well and as the Jovian population grew, they claimed the land for their own people, designating the bodies of water the Moon Children's only allowable places of habitation. The Moon Children didn't like that option and rebelled by spreading their chemical clouds, which at first killed many Jovians. Only the family lines born with a natural resistance survived.

"As the relationship between the two species went from bad to worse, Edmund, a Jovian royal back then as he is now, promised the Moon Children's monarch a new home. That home was Europa. The Moon Children cannot travel on their own—they have neither the means nor the engineering intelligence—and Edmund convinced the monarch to travel with him to see it. She and her hive willingly boarded a spaceship with him.

"When they reached Europa, however, Edmund found a way to leave them all behind. Without him and his ship, they had no choice but to stay. No means of leaving. The

Moon Children don't like Europa's drastic cold, nor the fact that most of the planet is an ice-water crust. Living there requires them to remain in liquid form much of the time, and they prefer a solid existence."

"Ohh," Max said, "I *have* heard of them. They're the ones who can change from one form to another. Always thought that was so cool."

"They're interesting, that's for sure," Ida said, without enthusiasm. "Like I said, they're not travelers, so invading other planets has never been their thing—until Edmund offered their monarch transport for a group of Moon Children to Earth aboard a Jovian vessel. The queen would stay on Europa, where she remained safe and out of the way, and a small group of her hive would travel to Earth."

"Why would Edmund do that? And why would they agree?"

"The monarch agreed because she is desperate to leave Europa, I suspect," Ida said. "As for why Edmund did it, it's because he wants to drastically reduce the number of clones on Earth. When the Moon Children transform from liquid into a solid state, they first become a vapor, and this vapor, a concentration of ammonia, is enough to kill. It harms humans and hybrids, too, though not usually fatally."

"So, okay," Max said, wanting to make sure he had it all straight. "You're saying that Caroline's husband sent the Moon Children to kill Jovian clones? The clones the Jovian family took great pains to create on Earth?"

"No, I'm saying Edmund did it. He's *not* Caroline's husband the way your father is a husband to your mother. Marriage is an Earthly construct. Jovians couple up on Earth only for show, only because marriage is so ingrained in the human psyche that Jovians feel they must appear married in order to avoid suspicion among the human population."

She paused there and pressed her lips together contemplatively before continuing. "Edmund and Caroline, Jovian leaders, had a falling out. The clones were her idea, and she made them in a way that assured their devotion to her. In other words, she has basically built an army that answers only to her. But it backfired because her army of clones eventually wanted the freedom to choose: to pursue other ways of life. You're familiar with the protests, I assume."

"I'll never forget them," he said, as the memory of his gun going off—and striking Leonard—rattled his brain. "I wish I could."

"Many of us do." She sipped her drink in a careful way, as if every milliliter contained a blast of energy. "Caroline has grown overly attached to Earth, and because of that, she's also become power hungry. Edmund must be fearful of what she'll do with her power, or he wouldn't have sent the Moon Children, wouldn't have taken such drastic measures."

"Okay, so, you don't know what Caroline wants to do with Earth, and you don't know exactly why Edmund has sent the Moon Children to kill the clones?"

"I only know that he wants to diminish Caroline's power. The problem is he thinks he has the Moon Children under control, but he's wrong. They're a hive mind. They answer only to their monarch, and their monarch is deceptively strong and protective of her people. The Moon Children are under her command even more steadfastly than the clones are under Caroline's. The Moon Children do not think for themselves. They move as one massive, multiple-individual whole. All the monarch has to do is think, and her people react. It's like your body and how it moves in response to your brain."

"Cool," Max said, staring across the room as he took a second to imagine how that would work.

"And if some of the Moon Children disappear along the way, plenty more reappear in their place." Ida produced an exasperated exhale. "Which is why it's so hard to deal with them."

Max squinted at her as he scratched his chin. "Well, my head just exploded," he said.

"Don't worry about it. My head has exploded many times over the years. The details aren't important right now. What's important is that I need you back out there as soon as possible."

"Back out where?"

"Io." She turned to face him, her big, round eyes smoldering with intention. "I need you to take Evander home, back to Earth."

"Okay," he said, thinking there had to be more. "And . . ."

"Edmund is on his way there as well with another school of Moon Children and their monarch. I'm sure he intends for the monarch to negotiate with Caroline. But I don't know what Caroline will do in response. David has passed. With the threat to her clones, she'll be more vulnerable than ever."

"*Passed* as in he's dead?" Max said with surprise.

"Yes. Can you handle this assignment? It's of the utmost importance, and I can't ask just anyone to do it."

"Of course I can handle it," he said quickly. "But you may not need me. Evander's plan was to go home after he met with Edmund. I know that for a fact. He wants to get back to Nadia and Dmitri as fast as he can. He could be on Edmund's spaceship heading for Earth right now."

Her lips quirked, and a hint of a smirk took root. "He's not."

Damn.

"And he needed to be there yesterday," Ida added.

"I was supposed to take him back weeks ago," Max said, not sure why he felt the need to confess. "He was going to speak with Edmund, and then he'd reach out to me, and I'd come back and take him home. That was the plan, though now I can see it wasn't a very good one," Max said, wishing he didn't have to admit this to a superior, especially one like Ida. "But he never contacted me, so I figured he may have found another way."

"Max," she said as if his naivety amused her, "you know how random this world is, how often human beings change their minds, alter their plans."

"Yeah, but, Evander's not the usual human."

"In spite of that, I have word that he is not yet on his way home. Both Elsa and his daughter are still on Io. I need you to go there," she said, her voice rising in volume. "I need you to make sure Evander gets home. You must take him there yourself."

He sat up straight, the urgency in her tone instilling a rush of nerves. "Okay. I hear you."

She lifted the shot glass and downed what was left. "Good," she said.

"What will happen if he doesn't go home?" Max asked fearfully.

She grumbled. "That absolutely can't happen."

"I know, I know, I just—"

"The way things are right now with the balance of power," she said, riding over his words, "the chaos that's eager to rear its ugly head . . . anything can happen. Evander's cool, even ways are needed to settle the rift between

Jovian royalties. To ultimately bring peace. That's all I know."

How many times had Max been given a mission and not been told of the consequences that might result? *Just do it* was the Jovian way. Even if Ida was human and not Jovian, which he didn't see how that could be considering how ancient and skeletal she looked within her cavernous hood. How was she able to safely space travel—and time travel if she was human?

"Consider it done," he said. "Evander's one of my favorite people. I'd do anything for him."

When she smiled, he saw into her mouth, each tooth decorated with a golden clasp that held it in place. "The last time I spoke with your father, he was worried about you. He still thinks you're that kid who took off, what is it now, five years ago?"

"Three. I think. Or has it been five?"

She didn't answer his question. Instead, she said, "You've come a long way, kiddo."

"Yeah." He bowed his head and suffered the wave of embarrassment that came with remembering how lame he'd been not long ago. "I know."

"I'm glad to have a capable young man like yourself on my team. You're in it for the long haul, am I right?"

"The last thing I want to do is to settle down," he said, "so I guess you could say that."

She pushed off from her chair and stood. "I'm with you there."

"When was the last time you set foot on native ground?"

She tilted her head and stared across the room. "No one's asked me that in a long while." A light sparkled in her eye. "Fifty years, I think. Maybe the 1990s. Or, no, it wasn't as long ago as that. I was there around 2020 for a short time."

"Do you ever get tired of all this? Being out here all the time. I mean, I know you love your job 'cause you've been doing it for so long, but do you ever miss home?"

"It's more than a job, Max."

"Yeah," he said. "I realize that."

"It's a commitment. One that has no beginning and no end. Like life itself. Like the universe itself."

He stepped down from the stool and straightened his jacket. Something about what she was saying—or not saying—worried him. "It will all work out in the end, though, right? The universe will sort itself out for the good of all? That's what the older, wiser beings like you usually say."

She raised her chin and made an *Mm* sound.

But he couldn't let it lie. He wanted an answer. "I can rest easy knowing people like you are on the job?"

"Please don't rest easy. Find Evander. Take him home. I'm afraid he may be the only one who can mend the trouble between Jovians."

Shit, Max thought, *it's always life or death with these people.*

He snapped to, military style, and gave her a good, loud, "Yes, ma'am."

Then he turned to leave but suddenly remembered he'd wanted to ask about the story one of his passengers told him a while back. The one about the lost sister. When he turned around, Ida was already gone.

Chapter 6

The Jupiter System

Natasha had never seen her father's mood go from good to horrible so quickly. He wasn't a moody person, first of all, and second, he was well practiced in the art of keeping whatever strong emotions he did feel in check. The position of President of the United States had required the kind of serious calm most humans didn't possess, and her father, Evander Peterman, had practiced that levelheadedness for twelve straight years.

A Jovian individual—black as onyx, smooth as ice, the size of a skinny ten-year-old—had met them in what the natives on Io called an "entry room," a small windowless space, maybe ten-by-ten feet, only an elevator ride from the living spaces they'd inhabited for the past few days. Jovians in their natural form spoke a language strange to human ears. It sounded almost musical, like electrified violins. Natasha had heard it only a few times before. The most unforgettable was when she woke from surgery—a tiny Jovian that could have fit in the palm of her hand had told her the story of The Lost Sister, a Jovian prophecy—but Natasha still wasn't sure how she'd understood what they had said, and whether the meeting had been real or a dreamy side effect of whatever galactic pain medicine the doctors gave her.

Most Jovians spoke in Earth tongue when in the presence of humans. At least, that had been Natasha's experience. But the individual standing before her and her father had spoken in their native tongue, and Natasha was even more surprised when her father responded in kind. He did not sound like violins, but a cross between humming and muttering words that ran together like a song. She'd never heard him speak like that before.

The conversation between her father and the messenger went back and forth at a quick pace. Natasha interpreted the name Edmund and the words *moon children*. At mention of the Moon Children, her father had bowed his head as if in serious mental distress. He whispered through clenched teeth, "How could Edmund do this? How could he leave before we had a chance to talk?" Then he looked up, eyes blazing, his voice rising in volume. "Edmund said he would meet me here!"

The Jovian messenger startled and stepped backward on its slender black limbs before turning and leaving the room.

"What just happened," Natasha asked. "What did the messenger say?"

Her father drew a jagged breath. He seemed overwhelmed with anger. His neck and face grew mottled and red, and the tips of his ears glowed crimson. Natasha thought he might be having an aneurism.

"Dad? You're scaring me," she said.

He closed his eyes and clenched his jaw, then blinked a few times as if something snagged the inside of his mind. "I'm sorry," he said softly. He cleared his throat and with obvious effort spoke normally. "It seems that Edmund isn't going to meet with us after all. He left Europa on a ship with the Moon Children's leader."

"He left without seeing us?" she said. "But we've been waiting for weeks. We came here just for him."

Her father pursed his lips and glared at the wall. "He knew I would stand in his way."

"Stand in what way? What's happened?"

"Edmund is using the Moon Children to diminish the clone population on Earth, to take away Caroline's power. They're going to decimate her army. It's already begun."

"Already begun? How is that possible?"

"He must have sent a small group of them ahead. They're extremely elusive. They were probably living in the ocean for who knows how long." His brow scrunched as he considered this fact. "It could have been years."

Natasha put her hands on her hips. "But, wait, you agree that Caroline is too powerful, so why isn't that a good thing?"

"The Moon Children are killing clones because they're the most susceptible to their toxins," he said, "but what's happening on Earth will likely escalate."

Natasha had never seen him roiling under the surface like this, looking like he wanted to punch someone.

"The Moon Children belong on Europa where they can't hurt anyone," he continued. "No one knows what they'll do once they fully invade Earth. Eventually humans of all kinds will die a horrible death. Others will become sick. The Moon Children can poison the water, decimate the land. They're a nonnative species and shouldn't be there."

"Jovians are a nonnative species too," Natasha said.

It was a bold statement that probably should have been delivered with care, but she'd been swept up in her father's show of emotion and holding back had never been her way, so out it came in all its raw glory.

Besides, why adults suffered from blindness, she didn't know. But it was clear to her that they did. Even the great Evander Peterman occasionally didn't get it.

For a second he gazed at her with weariness, and she could see that what she said had not dawned on him before.

"Jovians don't belong on Earth," she continued, "and yet, there they are, at the helm of all things. Pulling the strings, as we Earthlings say."

"That's . . . not the same thing," he said, scrambling for an answer. "Jovian intentions have always been honorable. They've always wanted to help. And Earth needed help. It was dying. Our goal has been to get the planet back on course —"

"You've already done that," she said, her shoulders and brow rising simultaneously. "Jovian intentions may have once been honorable, but right now Caroline's gearing up for battle. You said so yourself. And Edmund's introducing a nonnative species. They're not just influencing or guiding anymore. They're not 'staying in the background' like they vowed to do."

"You're right," he said, his upper body deflating. "I can't believe it's come to this." A look of surrender crossed his face. He appeared even older than when they'd left Mintaka. Grayer. As if he'd been drained of his once-high level of energy.

"I've failed them," he said.

"What, no!" she said with a small jump. "Who have you failed?"

"The people of Earth. The planet itself. *All* of life on Earth."

Damn it, she'd gone overboard again. "This *problem* is

certainly not your fault. You're the only one who ever helped Earth. *You're* the only Jovian who ever made a difference in a good way."

"It doesn't matter. In the long run I couldn't protect them. The Moon Children will wreak havoc, and Mom and Dmitri will experience it firsthand."

His eyes filled, and Natasha remained fixated. Was he about to cry? She'd never seen him shed a tear and couldn't remember the last time she'd shed one herself.

"What will the Moon Children do, exactly?" As soon as she spoke the words, she didn't want to know. "They aren't nonviolent?"

He'd already told her they'd killed some clones and intended to kill more, so she knew how stupid that question was.

"Life on Earth will never be the same," he said. "If they're already there, we've lost. We've lost everything."

"Dad, no. It can't be that bad. I can contact Edmund. Let me try. I once reached you without the oneness. It might work. You can tell him not to do it. Tell him to at least wait until we can join him and talk about it. I'll figure out a way to get through to him."

"You've never met him. It's impossible for you to contact someone you don't know. And even if you somehow manage to do it, he won't acknowledge you. He knows you're with me."

He looked so distraught. So defeated. Like this was the last straw. And she had put him there. Her and her "Jovians are nonnative too." Why did she always say the wrong thing? Why did she feel compelled to shine a light on people's weaknesses?

Her father had told her time and time again to speak more sensitively to others, to hold back and consider how they will receive the thoughts she expressed. She had promised to try, but to this day she could not understand why she had to hide the truth or gloss over the facts. If they were unpleasant or "bad," why pretend otherwise? Wasn't it better to accept the truth than to hide from it?

"When did Edmund leave?" she asked.

"A few days ago."

"Do you want to try to catch him? We can summon Max and the *Sparrow* right now."

He rubbed his head in an old man way, his thinning hair so easily flustered. "Impossible," he said softly. "We'll never catch up. Besides, I'm not ready to get back onboard just yet. And neither are you."

He was right. She hadn't felt great since she'd woken in the pod. And he was as pale and pasty as flour. He had warned her that Io's atmosphere may affect them negatively, just like space traveling did. How ironic was it to be part Jovian and not fare well on one of Jupiter's moons?

"There must be something we can do," she said. "You shouldn't give up. You never have before."

"I know I shouldn't. But I'm not the same person I was before," he said with a guilt-laden grimace.

He was talking about what the traveling had done, the age he found himself to be. Something Natasha tried not to think about or notice, and not only because space travel affected her the same way. "You're still Evander Peterman. You're still the most brilliant human who ever lived."

His eyes glazed over, and she could tell he wasn't listening. He lifted his pack, slung it over his shoulder, swayed slightly as it settled.

"I need to think," he said, his voice gravelly. "Go back to your room. I'll come for you in the morning."

"Okay," she said, still grappling with the remorse of making him feel bad. "Call me if you want to talk. I don't care if you wake me up."

"I will," he said, forcing a smile that only made him look weak.

Natasha slept the morning away. She hated when her father let her do that. She didn't want more sleep. If anything, she wanted to be up earlier. She wanted to be present when he figured out what they would do next.

She rose from the bed. Inserted a clean NOxygen piece into her nose and tossed the old one, then went into the bathroom and turned on the shower. By now she'd grown accustomed to washing in her electric skin, which truly had become a second layer of epidermis for her. The doctors said she'd have to wear it her entire life and never take it off. It wasn't like the e-skins other human travelers wore— it was medical grade. The kind that assisted her heart and vascular system. It was, in a word, *special*.

She'd heard the word *special* (not to mention the word *vascular*) more times than a kid ever should.

But, then again, she was as special as the e-skin she wore, wasn't she? A child who, like her father, had not been a child for long. She was born only eight years ago and had already grown into the body and mind of an eighteen-year-old—or so Elsa, Dad's trusty AI assistant-slash-bodyguard estimated.

Eighteen years old and never been kissed. Wasn't that one of those humiliating ancient sayings? Where had she heard it, and why was it funny? Who cared to be kissed? And by whom? Whatever the answers, the saying didn't make her laugh. Then again, not much did.

Natasha hated the word *special*. Special meant having heart surgery on Mintaka even though you were born on Earth. It meant leaving her brother, Dmitri, with her dear mother on Earth without so much as saying goodbye. She sometimes wondered if Dmitri had grown at an accelerated rate as well. So far her special talent of breaking into the oneness without any network to support it didn't work with Dmitri the way it had worked for her and her father. She wished it did. She missed him. She often thought of him and his beloved keys. The way he used to stare into them all the time.

Dmitri would be at least eleven years old now, so he should have come to the oneness, not that it was working the way it was supposed to—or at all at this point.

"Everyone comes to it in their own time," her father insisted whenever she brought it up, as if her reason for doing so were to put her brother down.

She stepped under the shower's spray and let it cascade over her head. It felt slippery, a little oily. She lathered her hair with soap that smelled like wet volcanic rock (everything on Io smelled slightly of rotten eggs). She hadn't bathed in Earth-pure water since she'd left home. This was no one's fault—the Jovian community did its best to accommodate humans—but she still longed for clear, odorless H_2O so much that every time she dreamed, the dream included drinking water from home.

Being special meant bathing in smelly, oily water.

And it meant space traveling halfway across the solar system before the age of six. Something no other human on record had ever done because it was extremely dangerous to do—or so that's what she'd learned after she'd already done it.

No, *special* was not something she'd ever wanted. Trees, wind, atmosphere, gravity. Clean air and water. That's what she wanted. Of course she'd taken those things for granted when they'd been available in abundance.

Edmund had left for Earth without meeting with them, so maybe they'd be able to go home now too. They'd wasted a trip to Io. No big deal. She'd tell her father it had been nice to see where the Jovian side of the family originated, and then hopefully they'd call it a day.

She let the water bead up on her e-skin. Sometimes she very carefully broke the seal at the neckline, thinking, *Ahh, as* a few drops slid inside, though it was a pretend refreshing surge. In reality, the few drops that seeped in didn't do anything to quench her craving for seriously drenching her body. Instead, she found herself tamping down the urge to strip to her naked self.

In the middle of the day, for no reason at all, the e-skin became itchy. It lacked the softness of her natural skin. When they'd given it to her on Mintaka, the doctors raved about how the color match was perfect, but the texture? Not even close.

As soon as she arrived back home, she would guzzle gallons of Earth water and jump into every neighborhood pool, lake, waterfall, or sea that she came to. Never again would she take water for granted. And maybe, just maybe, she would risk pulling off the second skin for a few minutes just to let the water flow all over her actual body. It couldn't be that dangerous a thing to do. It wouldn't kill her, most likely.

She turned off the shower, grabbed a towel, and dried herself. When she faced the mirror, which hadn't fogged at all the way real water caused a mirror to fog, she met her own gaze and thought of her grandfather, Andrew. She didn't want to think of him, but whenever she and her father met other Jovians—lately they'd done a lot of that— the first thing those individuals said had to do with Andrew's eyes and how she'd inherited them. Or his smile, even though she didn't smile often. She'd seen photos of Andrew, so she knew it was true.

Her grandfather hadn't lived long. Only thirty-one

years. That's what everyone remembered about Andrew Jovian: his interesting eyes, weak heart, and early demise. And now they knew about her heart, too, and how she wasn't going to live long, either.

She wouldn't live long, but her life would have meaning. And that was good. Uncle Jimmy wasn't afraid to talk of such things the way her father was. She would not live long, and it would not be due to her weak heart. She had a new heart, and as far as all the genius doctors on Mintaka were concerned, it worked a lot better than the one she'd been born with. Her heart would live as long as she did.

But only if she remained outside of Earth.

In other words, she could visit Earth, but not for long. She couldn't be an inhabitant the way she had for the first five years of her life. The only place safe to her, really, was Mintaka.

And that was a problem because Earth was her home and exactly where she wanted to be. Her mother and brother lived there. Where else would she live? Certainly not on Io with its stinking rocks and oily water.

Since she wasn't going to live long, why not live on Earth despite the doctors' assurances that living there would guarantee her early demise?

That's how she rationalized it, anyway.

She grabbed her hairbrush and began to pull it through her tangled, wet hair.

Her life would have meaning. So, not all human lives did? That was the assumption, right? When someone said to you, you won't live long, but your life will have meaning, it was the same as saying, "You're lucky. You're special."

She had to accept it, she supposed: she was special. Destined to do something great—so great it would kill her.

Whenever she brought this up to her father, he insisted it was not necessarily true.

"Destiny is not written in stone," he argued. "Our lives are not written in the stars, even if Uncle Jimmy says they are."

Her grandparents' story proved that, right? Andrew was destined to die young, and so he did, but then Svetlana defied destiny by traveling to a different universe so they could continue to live together. If Andrew and Svetlana had found a place to exist in peace, then couldn't she?

If destiny was not set in stone, the answer was *maybe*.

As she wrapped her damp hair in a towel, she thought she could believe that much. But her father may be the reason she believed it, she realized. He possessed the talent of persuasion, an enchanting ability that had helped him guide the Earth and its inhabitants to recovery throughout his three terms as president.

So it was hard to know what to think.

Natasha liked facts, in general, and she always tried to stick with them. No matter how long she lived, the fact was that right now Earth was in trouble.

And so was she because Uncle Jimmy told her she would give her life for it. She knew that. That was not a question.

No one needed to tell her this was something she had to do. Somehow, some way, she was born with an unrelenting loyalty to Great-grandmother's bright blue planet. Even as a little girl entertained with her dolls in the playroom while her brother lay mesmerized by the tinkling cluster of his special keys, she loved Earth and knew that it would require her assistance one day.

"You should be proud that you look so much like your grandfather," Uncle Jimmy had told her before they met up with her father and Elsa, and the new pilot named Max. "He was a great soul. A kind soul. And now we know that you were born with his heart. The two of you are undoubtedly connected."

"Even if I don't have that heart anymore?"

"Yes, even so," Uncle Jimmy said.

She shook her head. "I've never spoken with my grandfather."

"One day you will."

"Do you mean in person?"

"That depends. Do you understand the multiverse?"

Of course she understood something as basic as the multiverse. What did he think she'd been doing in her studies for the past year?

"What does my understanding have to do with meeting my grandfather?" she said.

"Everything." Uncle Jimmy's voice deepened with seriousness. "Understanding has everything to do with it."

"Okay, well, whenever Grandfather reaches out to me, I'll be listening."

Uncle Jimmy chuckled. "I think you might be my favorite, kiddo."

"You don't have favorites," Natasha had said, and he patted her head because she knew that to him she'd always be a little kid.

A knock at the door of her room pulled her from this memory. Her father's gentle voice followed with a, "You up?"

She tossed the towel she'd wrapped around her hair. "One second," she called. She jumped into her black unitard before meeting him at the door.

EVANDER'S HAND trembled when he raised the small glass of dark green Nutrition to his colorless lips. Natasha hated that she noticed this quiver. Signs of progressive aging showed in his deepening eye sockets, sloped back, the pale paper-thinness of his complexion.

Evander Peterman, the charismatic middle-aged man who only a few years ago led Earth to a peaceful, environmentally friendly place had sped into old age with inhuman velocity.

"Did you sleep okay?" he asked.

They sat a table for two. His voice sounded a little gravelly, but normal enough. She tried not to frown. "You don't have to ask me that every morning."

"I know," he said. "I'm just making small talk."

"Don't we have something pressing to discuss?" She lifted her comm from where she'd laid it on the table, then shoved it into the thigh pocket of her unitard.

He leaned back and said, "Yes, actually. I've made a decision."

Something about his confidence in that statement took her off guard, and she wasn't ready to hear what he would say next. She broke eye contact to survey the spacious room dotted with empty tables and chairs. "Where's Elsa? She's still not back?"

They were alone, and that didn't happen often; Elsa was almost always nearby. The fact that no other travelers gathered here had to do with the Mars program. Most of Earth's travelers had jumped at the chance to establish a settlement there.

"She's still at the med clinic getting an update," Evander said. Her father crossed his legs and turned to look out the window at the rocky, mountainous landscape and sulfur haze. Between the dampness and the cold, a prevailing mist lingered in the atmosphere, not quite as thick as fog but noticeable enough: another reason Natasha would not want to live there.

"The mist is pretty, isn't it?" he said.

She didn't want to tell him she didn't think it was, so she tossed back the meal of the day—two shot glasses of liquid, one green, one yellow. She drank the little glass filled with green liquid first and pretended it didn't taste like the algae it was derived from. She followed with the yellow one, which was slightly sweet but nothing to get excited about.

"Are you going to tell me what you've decided?" she said.

He grinned. It was amazing what a genuine smile could do. This one took him from seventy to sixty, looks wise.

"Now that we will not be meeting with Edmund," he said, "an opportunity has presented itself."

The way his brows rose, Natasha supposed he was asking her to keep an open mind. Or maybe he expected her to show excitement at the idea of an unplanned adventure? He should have known better considering she'd made no secret about wanting to get home as soon as possible.

"What is it?" she said.

"I know we're supposed to head home, and we will, of course, but there's something I have to do first."

He didn't often hold back like this, and his hesitation struck a nerve in the back of her neck. "Please tell me what it is. We can do whatever you like."

He stared at her in a vacuous way. A very Jovian way, it occurred to her.

"I need to take a time trip." He placed his chin in the palm of his hand and anchored his elbow upon the table as if to steady himself after making an announcement he expected her to resist.

She exhaled a choked laugh. Time tripping caused all kinds of physical trouble for humans—the doctors believed it was one of the reasons Evander had matured so rapidly.

Both space travel and time tripping compounded his natural propensity to develop at breakneck speed.

"You can't be serious," she said. "Have you run it by Elsa? What did she say?"

He reached out with his hand, placing it just in front of her on the table. "I am serious, and time tripping is a lot safer these days than it used to be."

"I know it is. For most people. Not for you—or me, for that matter. Why exactly do we need to do this?"

"I have to see my mother."

"Your mother?" She held back a laugh. She'd always thought of Caroline as his mother. Then it dawned on her. "You mean Svetlana. But why?"

She watched the tension creep into his expression and tighten his already sloping shoulders. "Because I want to speak with her. It's important. And I've never met my father, so that's something I'd like to do too." His eyes met hers for a second, then darted away. "This is likely my last chance."

Her heart began to thud, and she wondered if that were normal. "No," she said. "You really shouldn't. Can't you just send her a message? Or maybe someone else could make the trip for you?"

"You know there are no messages between universes. And who would I send? Time trips are granted to a numbered few."

"Uncle Jimmy can do it."

He tilted his head in a disappointed manner. "*I* want to go. I need to speak to her in person. It can't be someone else."

The gravity of his words sent her to a dark place as his overall urgency to make the trip bubbled up dangerously around him. But she supposed his feelings were normal. He was half human, after all, and he hadn't seen Svetlana in many years. Rumor had it, he'd sent her away, but when he'd told Natasha the story, he said Svetlana made the choice to leave and that Caroline was more than happy to grant it.

"You'll have to come with me," he added. "I'm not going to leave you here."

"I really want to go home," she said. "I'm sure Mom's angry that we're not back yet—"

"Yes, you're probably right. And I am sorry about that. But I don't think I'll be able to make the trip home and then time travel from there. It's too much." He looked down as if ashamed. "For me. Realistically speaking."

His hands, with their age spots and wrinkles that ringed each knuckle, rested upon the table. Natasha covered them with her own hands. His fingers felt brittle, cold. He needed to make this trip before he became ill, before it was unsafe to do; she understood that. They would have to go. Home would still be there when they were ready to go back—if the Moon Children didn't decimate it.

"It could be fun," he said in a feeble attempt to convince her. "And you'd finally get to meet your grandparents."

She pressed her lips together to prevent telling him she'd rather see her own mother and brother than meet his parents.

"So, what do you think? Are you ready to time travel with me? I'm going to try a new preventive medication the lab came up with, one that should help with the aging."

That was a surprise that sparked a bit of hope within her. "Maybe I should take it too."

"You can't," he said with surprising abruptness. "It hasn't been tested on young people. We don't know exactly what it will—"

"If I don't take it, I'm going to keep aging like you do," she said angrily. "So far we seem to have that in common."

He shook his head. "There's no guarantee it will help. The drug comes with risks. If you age on this trip, you'll still be plenty young when you get home."

She held back what she really wanted to say and came up with a limp "okay," as if she didn't care, though frustration hummed below the surface. "I'm not going to live very long, anyway," she muttered.

At that, he erupted. "No parent wants to hear their child say that."

She raised her chin. "We both know it's true."

"Destiny is not set in stone." He was speaking a lot louder than he usually spoke. "Don't make me go through this again."

His reprimand made her wonder why she said things to upset him. She didn't *want* to upset him, but it always seemed to happen. It was the human adolescent inside her. Humans were so emotional. Then again, Dad always said she was more Jovian than human when it came to her emotions. Still, she often envied her great-grandmother and the other Jovians for not having any emotions at all.

"I'm sorry to tax you with this," he said. "It's just that I'm running out of time."

"I understand," she said.

That was twice in two days that he'd lost his temper. Very unlike him.

"If you're not willing to take the risk, I'll take you home," he added. "I don't want to make you do something you're not comfortable with."

"Of course we can go," she said, trying to make up for her unpleasantness. "I'd love to meet my grandparents."

He sat back and released a long, relieved breath. "And they will love meeting you."

"How long will it take to get there?"

"Time travel isn't like space travel. It's an elusive concept to understand, but in basic terms, it doesn't take any time at all. We'll be going backward a decade or two."

"But I wasn't even alive back then."

"Yes, I know. It's okay."

"Who will I be?"

"You'll be you, and I'll be me. Just in another place. In another time. We won't stay long."

"Isn't this going to screw up the history of the world?"

He chuckled. "You've been watching too many old movies."

Chapter 7

Cape Canaveral, Florida

At the third Mars liftoff in Florida, Caroline, Miranda, and Leo entered the public observation site surrounded by a detail of a dozen hulking Leonards.

The bustle and clatter of the crowd tamped down as soon as their group of Jovian royalty exited the Velostar, a spacious, autodriven luxury bus that had delivered them from the private airport.

A large buffer divided Caroline and her group from the civilians allowed to congregate on the ground—behind fencing—and those who took seats in the surrounding bleachers. Some of the giant viewing screens displayed the Jovians' royal entrance, and others showed closeups of the rocket or NASA's many-peopled control center. As the royals and their security took to the path that would lead them to a temporary stage built a safe distance from the launch, a drizzle of polite applause materialized.

Caroline scanned the crowd, noting the many Andrew, Evander, and Miranda clones that made up the nearest members of the audience.

Miranda said, "We've provided the family clones better seating. They've all been vetted. No resisters or Coalition members allowed."

Caroline expected nothing less of her security team.

"Death threats have been down since we started the Mars program," Miranda said, and Caroline sensed her attempt to take credit for that as head of the program.

"If they want to kill us, I say let them try," Caroline said, resorting to her usual show of strength.

Miranda laughed. Caroline didn't join her.

Weeks before, the two women had decided the time was right for the Jovians and Starbright International to claim responsibility for the Mars program's enormous success. During the ride to the liftoff, Miranda mentioned needing to brand the family in a positive manner. Caroline didn't care to know what that would entail. The fact was, she was in charge. *Of everything.* Whether the rest of the world saw her in a positive or negative light mattered not at all. With a mere shake of her head, she'd shut that part of the conversation down.

On the other hand, reminding humanity that the Jovians were responsible for the program that allowed them to travel to a new world appealed to her. Approximately 62 percent of adult citizens worldwide had entered the lottery to earn one of the fifteen hundred seats on the latest vessel traveling to Mars—the Celestial Quest, a ship powered with cold fusion, as Leo had promised it would be. No more antiquated fossil fuel engines with the possibility of explosions.

When given the keys to the necessary technology, the humans had finally embraced cold fusion and its zero radioactive waste. It had only taken them two millennia to get there. They really were a race resistant to change. In fact, Caroline couldn't believe their tiny minds accepted all they would have to do to make Mars compatible. All the work needed to create recycling systems of air, hydroponic food, water, interplanetary communications. The wearing of e-skins, NOxygen breathing devices, gravity boots. So much to think about and accept.

And yet it was happening.

Maybe that's just how much the six-story Jovian who'd showed herself at the Battle of Philadelphia had frightened them—so much that they wanted to flee from their native planet.

To Caroline, it was a ridiculous response considering Jovians had been on Earth since their race's very beginning. Of course, humanity didn't know that.

Remembering the enormous amount of power she had brandished when she was able to take her true form, she held her head a little higher.

Then again, maybe the Mars project appealed to humans due to, as Miranda suggested, good marketing: the images of the futuristic community coming together appeared on billboards and buildings (and the screens at this launch). The impressive metal-framed homes, community buildings, and farming facilities. The smiling faces of hard-working humans wearing cutting-edge e-skins and spacesuits. Resting in comfortable space dwellings. The motto *What an adventure it will be!* in bright red letters cutting across every brochure and wristcomm screen. As if humans left to their own devices could help themselves to whatever planet they were able to reach *and* be successful in doing so.

Pictures really were worth a thousand words.

Little did humanity know, the mortals who made the trip weren't in charge of anything once they arrived on the red planet. Just like on Earth, Jovians were. Miranda clones, mostly. And Miranda clones took their orders from Miranda, who took hers from Caroline.

In just a few minutes, Caroline and her entourage had reached the entrance to the stage. Once up the stairs, Miranda took her place in front of the microphone, and Caroline and Leo joined her at either side. Four Leonards stood guard a couple of feet away. Behind them, in the distance, the rocket rested upon a metal structure that resembled the lengthy column of a tree trunk. A curved holder at its top, like cupped hands drawn together, cradled the vessel, an enormous silver coin waiting for the late-autumn sun to rise. Beyond it, the dark-blue sea and mottled dawn of a sixty-five-degree morning made a shadowy backdrop.

Miranda cleared her throat as the spectators cheered, "Lift off! Lift off! Lift off!" Many in the excited crowd stood on their toes and raised their hands in the air and clapped, smiling gleefully. So many human smiles. Seeing them didn't make Caroline feel any happier than usual.

Miranda spoke into the microphone: "Thank you. Thank you all for coming to Mars Operation Liftoff 3.0. This, my friends, is the most successful space program in the history of mankind. And it's sponsored by none other than Starbright International." She paused for applause, which the crowd granted in droves. "If you don't mind settling down a bit, we're going to get started. I have the great honor of taking you fine people through the countdown, and the ship is on a tight schedule, as you can imagine, so we have to keep up."

The crowd settled into murmuring silence.

"Good, great. Thank you. So glad you could all be here in person on this beautiful December day to experience this momentous occurrence in person." She checked her wristcomm. "Oh my gosh, it's time. Without further ado, I say, ten! Nine! Count with me, people . . . Eight! . . . Seven . . ."

Surprised by her second-in-command's vigor, Caroline remained blank faced in response to Miranda's rallying display. Was it possible Miranda's DNA contained a large dose of human compatibility? Or maybe living on this planet for so long had made Miranda more human-friendly. She seemed to truly enjoy being in front of the crowd and growing their excitement. Caroline grimaced. Was Earth to make humans of them all?

Either way, Miranda certainly knew how to inspire the public.

A powerful, low hum vibrated in Caroline's ears and tickled her molars. In the distance, the ship lifted, rising from the ground as if it weighed nothing at all. A sudden cloud of vapor billowed below its wide, narrowly domed body and settled like a thin halo below the ship. The fusion engine glowed light blue.

Slowly the behemoth floated upward, blotting out the early-morning sun so that a cool shadow covered all in darkness. In that moment, Caroline anticipated something dreadful and dark, as dark as the shadow that covered them. Would the first cold fusion engine fail? Would the ship come crashing down in an epic Jovian family disappointment?

Of course not. It continued steadily upward like an enormous, 2,000-ton flower head reaching toward the sunlight that nourished it. Slowly it rose, higher and higher, and when it had climbed as high as airplanes fly, it cast into the distance and disappeared as if it had never been there at all.

The humans who watched shut their mouths. An elongated moment of awed silence spread like a low-hanging cloud over the observation site.

"And it's up there!" Miranda's delighted voice pierced the silence. "Wasn't that the most beautiful takeoff you've ever seen? Farewell, fellow humans!"

Caroline eased back mentally with relief.

The crowd cheered, "Beau-ti-ful, beau-ti-ful!" and Miranda readily joined in as if she were one of them.

"Well done, Leo." Caroline spoke the words though she'd meant to keep them to herself.

"Thank you, Ma'am." He lowered his chin in modest acceptance of her rare compliment.

A moment later, the usual human fanfare ensued. A shower of applause fell from the crowd followed by a marching band playing in the stands. Caroline detested band music. She wanted to leave.

The Jovian work was done, but Miranda continued to speak, casting compliments for the Mars program into the crowd—and enjoying their attention more than Caroline could fathom.

Caroline stared out to sea. The vapor that came from the liftoff hovered over the water, stagnant though a sea-to-land breeze persisted. That was unusual.

"Leo," she said, "the vapor."

He squinted into the distance, then raised a pair of small binoculars from his pocket. "More than the usual. Not sure why. Must be something about the humidity. I'll look into it."

"Please do."

Someone beyond the fence began to cough, an ugly sound. Then another person, higher up in the stands, did the same. Several people had begun to clear their throat.

"Wait a minute," Leo said, frowning as he continued to look though the binoculars. "It seems to be rising from the water like steam."

"Steam?" Caroline didn't need binoculars to see that he was right.

The audience continued to cough.

Caroline told Miranda to wrap up, then pointed at the Leonards standing guard. "We're leaving."

The security detail plunged into emergency-escort mode, ushering Caroline down from the stage, where three more Leonards, including Head Leonard, joined them at the base of the short staircase. The seven of them formed a circle around Caroline as if she were the pupil at the center of an iris. In high heels, she managed an uncomfortably quick pace to keep up with them, the group winding down the path that led to the parking lot where the Velostar waited at the entrance, ready to whisk them away.

Caroline's detail had made it halfway to the bus when Miranda, through the loudspeakers, finally said, "Have a wonderful day, everyone, and get home safe! Leo? What's going on w—" The thought was cut off along with what sounded like the loss of power to her microphone.

Beyond the fence that held the public at bay, an Andrew clone had fainted, and others rushed toward him. A high-pitched scream rose above the crowd. Someone shouted, "We need help over here! He can't breathe."

Caroline stifled her next breath, laced with the foulness of ammonia. In the audience above, many of the Andrew clones hacked horribly, their faces bright red, some of them bloating. One of them fell from the bleachers. His body tumbled down the steep slope and crashed into the security fence, which stopped his fall. Another Andrew collapsed and ended up doubled over the barricade, unmoving.

"What the hell is going on?" a woman shouted.

"Hurry," Caroline told the Leonards.

"What is this, Ma'am?" Head Leonard asked.

"The Moon Children."

As more and more clones fell to their knees, complete chaos broke out and some of the audience began climbing over the fence and running for their lives. This only created yet more danger and chance for injury. Head Leonard punched a man who came too close to Caroline's detail, then pushed a hacking Miranda clone off her feet when she attempted to cross their path. The other Leonards followed suit, blocking anyone who came near.

"Velostar in range," Head Leonard announced. "Prepare for lift, Ma'am."

Two of the Leonards put their hands on her, raised her off the ground and hoisted her through the van's sliding door while two more entered the vehicle directly behind her. In the next pulse of her coursing veins, the remaining eight Leonards had leaped into the vehicle and found seats as well. Caroline claimed one of the benches in the center of the bus.

"Lock down," Head Leonard said from the auto-driving command center. The door swooshed closed with shocking force. If anyone had tried to follow, they would have paid with a lost limb, or worse.

Caroline panted—something she was not used to doing. Sweat from her forehead seeped into her hair, and her clothing hung damp and uncomfortable around her. She took a breath and gazed out the window.

"Air purifier on," Head Leonard said. "Say the word, Ma'am, and we'll get out of here."

Through the window, Caroline sighted Leo and farther back, Miranda, caught in the pack of wild-eyed humans frantic to get away.

"Not yet," she said.

The mayhem came on like a tornado spinning through the fog. Suddenly bodies were everywhere, some stumbling over their own feet or the feet of others. Others crashing into signs, garbage pails, whatever blocked their way. An Andrew clone fell into Leo, taking him to the ground. Leo struggled to unwrap the desperate man's arms and push him back. Once free, Leo stood, but then tripped on the ungainly Andrew clone once again and fell face-first, his sunglasses flung through the air.

A few steps behind Leo, Miranda coughed in dramatic form, doubled over with her hand in front of her mouth. She stared into the distance with bleary confusion as her palm came away splattered with blood. In a slow circle, she turned, disoriented, and gazed at the sky. She grabbed her forehead in distress and left behind a red smear.

Then, as if all at once remembering the way to the Velostar, Miranda spun around.

Through the window, Caroline met her gaze and considered what to do next. Should she help Miranda by sending a Leonard to escort her to safety, or should she allow the number-two-in-charge to help herself, becoming weaker and sicker by the second. It occurred to her that Miranda could die out there, though that outcome was not likely. Either way, Miranda would become weak and incapacitated, similar, Caroline assumed, to how she felt whenever she remembered she could no longer take her true form. Best of all, Miranda would no longer pose a threat to Caroline's bright blue throne.

How convenient that would be.

The longer Caroline stared, however, the more the sight of Miranda's suffering made her uncomfortable. Some part of her wanted to do something to stop it. She remembered how awful it had been to watch David's end —she did not want to watch Miranda's as well. A sudden rush of fear coursed through her body, and she found she couldn't hold back any longer. "Head Leonard," she raised her voice above the murmur of activity. "Retrieve Miranda and Leo."

The fog had arrived in full force, rolling over the area and settling in, wrapping its tendrils around the panicked assembly like a nest of anaconda. Miranda sank to her knees.

Head Leonard appeared at Caroline's side, his hand displaying a screen he offered as he would a gift: a message concerning the air quality, written in large white letters. "Unsafe at this time," he read. "It is believed clones are more susceptible to ammonia poisoning than Jovian royalty and humans, Ma'am."

He'd never said no to her before, and his words turned her human face to steel. "Outfit one of the Leonards with a NOxygen clip and send him out there," she said. "None of you have been affected by the ammonia as far as I can tell."

The Leonard in the seat in front of hers, the one who was thinner, not quite as muscled as the others, raised his hand. "I'll do it."

Yet another Leonard passed him a NOxygen clip, and he inserted it.

Head Leonard moved back to the Velostar's seat of command. "Door opening in three, two, one."

The Leonard leaped out; he seemed to fly through the air.

The door slammed closed.

"How long until this passes?" Caroline asked.

Head Leonard tapped his wristcomm. "Checking satellite image now."

A bird's-eye view of the scene popped onto the Velostar's main screen. The end of the blanket of fog neared.

"Not much longer," Head Leonard said. "Three to five minutes."

Beyond the parking lot lay a forest of long-leafed pines. The cloud that was the Moon Children would consolidate at its edge before they took their physical form and fled on foot. By the time their fog of sickness and death had reached the wood, the media's cameras would have stopped filming, Caroline presumed, and the humans would not capture their metamorphosis from vapor to solid. They would remain focused on the chaos and miss what was most important.

The thin Leonard approached the Velostar, one hand dragging Leo behind him, the other securing Miranda's limp body over his shoulder. The Velostar's door eased open, and the Leonard pulled Leo to his feet. Leo stood wearily on his own and staggered up the vehicle steps. A desperate Evander clone tried to use the Leonard's leg to pull himself to a stand and enter the bus as well, but Head Leonard leaned his long body and arm out of the entrance and punched him in the face. The man collapsed and the thin Leonard carried Miranda inside.

The doors briskly closed.

Miranda moaned gently as the Leonard deposited her in the back-most seat, a bench that spanned the full width of the bus.

"Thank you," Caroline told him as he returned to the front of the bus.

He saluted her.

"Take us home," she commanded Head Leonard.

"Affirmative." The Velostar drove off, leaving dying clones in its wake.

Thrust back in exhaustion, Leo's head bobbed in the seat behind driver command. His suit was covered with dirt and debris, his complexion ruddy as a sunburn.

From the center of the Velostar, Caroline observed Miranda, resting as she stared dully at the ceiling. Her face resembled the skin of a pomegranate or beet, singed brighter pink at the peaks of her cheeks. The blood smeared across her forehead blended into her deeply flushed complexion.

Caroline stood and slowly stepped to the back of the bus, sitting directly in front of her.

One of the Leonards approached with a bottle of water and handed it to Miranda. She accepted it with wonder, as if unsure of how it came to be in her hand. When she brought it to her lips and tipped it back, a small stream meandered down her chin. She cringed and rubbed her fingers over her neck. "My throat . . . it's on fire," she moaned.

"You'll be better soon," Caroline said.

Miranda's eyelids fluttered as if rattled with confusion. "You left me out there," she said in a strained whisper.

"No. I sent a Leonard for you. He brought you to safety."

Miranda reached blindly for something to pull herself up. An approaching Leonard grabbed her outstretched hand and pressed a vitals checker to the underside of her wrist. Then he pulled a cold compress from his pocket and laid it across one of her cheeks.

She lay back and tears emerged from the corners of her eyes. With a rough hand, the Leonard removed the vitals checker and read its results. "Fine," he said, and left her alone with Caroline.

"The Moon Children can't kill Jovian royalty," Caroline said. "They're not powerful enough. What you're feeling is temporary."

"In our human form," Miranda rasped.

Caroline raised her brow in question.

"We're in our human form," Miranda said softly. "Leo and I could have died."

The Leonard returned with a NOxygen clip that he pressed into Miranda's nostrils.

"But you didn't," Caroline reassured her. "You're still here. None the worse for wear."

Miranda adjusted the clip in her nose and spoke through a frown, her chin quivering. "They only cared about you. They *left* me. They saw what was happening, and they left me behind."

Caroline forced a small smile. "It was a Leonard who came back for you."

Miranda grew quiet, puddling into her own weakness. She breathed an erratic rhythm and eased back as if giving into hurt feelings.

"The first report has come in." Head Leonard's voice easily reached the back of the Velostar. Glad for the excuse to turn away from Miranda, Caroline gave him her full attention.

"Ninety-eight Andrew clones dead or dying. Twenty-four Mirandas dead or dying. Thirty-five non-Jovian humans seeking various types of aid."

Miranda's small voice drew Caroline back. "You were always meant to be queen. I know that. I've always known."

Caroline didn't answer at first. Was it necessary to state the obvious?

"So, nothing has changed, then," she said.

Once again, Miranda struggled to sit upright. Her hand grasped the top of Caroline's seat back, and with some difficulty she pulled herself up, then muttered something indecipherable and fell back, clutching her middle.

Caroline scowled. "What is it you're saying? I can't hear you."

Miranda closed her eyes as she drew a painful breath, then hunched into a cough. She made a big to-do of swallowing and clearing her throat. "It's not like it was before," she said through a rasp. "It's not like when we were back home, in the Jupiter System. A lot has changed."

Caroline turned away. "Can someone bring her an oxygen tank? I don't think she's getting enough air." To Miranda, she said, "Rest. You'll feel more like yourself soon."

"I'm not willing to sacrifice everything for you anymore," Miranda said, meeting her eye.

So, it finally comes out.

A Leonard brought the oxygen tank and placed the clear mask over Miranda's nose and mouth. He pulled the elastic tight behind her head.

As he returned to the front of the bus, a newscast came over the vehicle speaker. Head Leonard must have put it on as a way to give them privacy, though Caroline had never known him to be thoughtful.

"Sometimes I wonder," Miranda said, pulling the mask down so she could speak, "what if I were meant to be queen?"

Perhaps for the first time in her Earthly life, Caroline put on a real smile. "I know you do, but you shouldn't because that's not how it is."

"I also wonder what you would do if I were in charge, and you weren't."

Why wonder? Caroline thought.

Miranda waited for an answer.

"We work together," Caroline said. "Lead together. That's how it has always been. We've been together every step of the way. What good is it to ask such a question?"

Miranda glanced at the floor. Her split cheek yawned in Caroline's direction. "I have been with you every step of the way, but would you remain by my side if our places were reversed? If you had been left out there to die instead of me?"

Caroline did not see the value in considering this scenario.

Miranda reached for her with a hand soiled with dried blood. A wounded look of sadness pulled her face long.

Caroline swatted her hand away, and Miranda flinched. She replaced her oxygen mask over her nose and mouth and lay back.

A moment later, she pulled the mask down again. "I don't think I want to live on Earth while the Moon Children are here."

Caroline straightened her spine. She could not afford to lose another Jovian ally. She tilted her head and softened her gaze. "I understand," she said.

"I would like to go to Mars, and I would like to rule there."

This was not the same as Evander's departure. She was not losing Miranda. The two women were far more powerful together than they would be on their own. Miranda knew that. She might need some time to accept Caroline's dominance, to recover from this attack of the Moon Children, but that didn't mean she wouldn't continue to respect her queen and bow to her.

"That can be arranged," Caroline said with a nod.

"I'd also like permission to bring weapons—or build them."

Caroline leveled a punishing glare in her direction. She meant bombs. Weapons of mass destruction.

The urge to lash out flashed through Caroline like lightning. Evander had rid the planet of such dangerous, ruthless things, and there was no way she'd bring them back. But the strong didn't need to lash out, she reminded herself. The strong settled into their power and wielded it subtly.

"If you want to go to Mars," she said, "I will agree to it. But no weapons."

Miranda pursed her lips, hinting at her disappointment. "They would be a precautionary measure only, of course. Protection."

Caroline wouldn't hear of it. The Jovians would never stoop so low, would never resort to munitions. Weapons certainly weren't the answer when it came to adversaries like the Moon Children.

"I'll protect you just as I have today," she said, placing her hand on Miranda's shoulder. "You don't need weapons. And you can come back to Earth anytime you like."

Miranda observed Caroline's hand sitting upon her shoulder, and her lips trembled. "If you get those scoundrels out of the air, I just might." The smile she put on dissolved into a rocky hack that left her wheezing for air.

Caroline patted her shoulder and said, "I'm glad to hear it," as if her relationship with Miranda wasn't tattered, and the problem with the Moon Children was just steps away from being solved.

Because that's what she had to do: feign control and confidence even when she didn't know how she would remove the Moon Children from the air, water, and land— how she would expel them from the planet. They were more elusive than the tarantulas that hitched rides in bananas, more suffocating than the kudzu that snuffed out entire forests, more plentiful than the common starling. Once they entered a new place, they spread like a plague. It was nearly impossible to eradicate them without killing everything else.

Weapons would not be the way to do it.

The only way to win against the Moon Children was to convince their monarch that it was in her best interest to settle elsewhere. Caroline wasn't as good at convincing as she was at commanding.

Long ago, Edmund had made the treaty that sent the Moon Children to Europa. So it made sense that he assumed he could orchestrate the manipulation of their species on Earth as well. He wanted to nullify the clones, Caroline understood that. But didn't he care what happened to Earth in the process? Was he willing to risk the entire planet to relieve her of their support? That couldn't be.

He must have an exit strategy, a means for banishing the Moon Children and preventing the complete annihilation of the Earth.

Mustn't he?

Chapter 8

Kirksberg, Pennsylvania

F ran met the Petermans in the old, neglected farm field that surrounded and concealed the bunker. The Jovian couple came alone, as instructed, acting even more personable than he'd remembered. Even more human, except for the fact that they hadn't aged at all. At fifty-nine, Fran was catching up to them in that vein.

"Thank you for having us," Dana said. "John and I are so happy that you want to keep the lines of communication open."

"Yeah, well, I'm afraid Drew isn't quite as happy as we are. Though, after what happened at the launch last week, he doesn't have much of an argument to stand on."

"It's important that we share information," Dana said. "Don't worry about Drew. He'll come around."

"I'm sure he will," Fran said, though he wasn't sure at all. Drew was tough. You either dealt with his abrasive personality or you steered clear of him. Fran often wondered if the only one capable of convincing him to do anything was Queen Jovian in alien form.

John chimed in: "Haven't you heard? Dana's charm is hard to resist."

Fran replied with a polite chuckle as he drew back the bunker's door and waved them through. They stepped down the steep staircase and didn't comment on the bunker's unusual interior, which made Fran think they'd been there before. Connie and Lisa sat at a table for six in the pubspace and voiced their welcome as Dana and John approached. Drew, who remained on a stool closer to the far wall, said nothing, his impassive face reflecting unspoken consternation.

Lisa offered the coffee and cookies they'd put out, which the couple turned down. Fran wondered if the Jovian royalty needed to eat. Then he remembered Dana's home-cooked meals. He'd had dinner with them a few times when Svetlana lived with them—though that seemed like a lifetime ago.

"So," Drew said in a gruff voice, "fill us in on the situation. The first attack, which you witnessed firsthand, occurred about six months ago? And at this point, clones seem to be dying on a regular basis?"

"Yes, they are," Dana said through a veil of concern, "and it's not going to stop soon."

"Mostly Andrew clones," Drew added, "which doesn't bode well for me, for obvious reasons."

"Of course." She gazed at him with what appeared to be empathy. Fran wondered if this was the acting Drew had spoken of.

"First of all," Dana began, "however it may appear, and whatever the media tells you, the five or six instances that you've heard about are not a random rash of chemical reactions or clouds. It's a species called the Moon Children. Are you familiar with them?" She directed the question to Drew and Connie.

"No," Drew said, before glancing at Connie.

"I'd never heard of them until Miranda said something in a meeting after the first attacks occurred," Connie said. "But she also said they'd been banished to Europa long ago."

"Neither of you have lived in the Jupiter System—or even visited?" John asked.

They both shook their head. "Earth born and raised," Drew said proudly.

"The Moon Children are a native species of Io," Dana continued. "But about two millennia ago, Edmund struck a deal with their monarch that sent them to Europa."

"Edmund convinced her to lead her people away from their native planet?" Fran asked.

"Correct. The problem is, they have never liked Europa. And now it seems Edmund has made a new deal with the monarch."

"Please don't tell me he promised them Earth," Fran said, doing his best to muffle the wail of alarms sounding off in his head.

"Not exactly," she said. "Whatever deal he made, though, includes relocating them to Earth for the purpose of 'righting' the clone population."

"How many are here right now?" Fran asked.

"They're a hive mind, so there are as many as they want to be here. Only one has to be present in order for many to be present."

"A hive mind is a being made up of many individuals," Connie explained. "I studied them ages ago."

"Yes, and that's hard enough to deal with on its own, but this species can also change from solid to liquid to vapor and back again," Dana said.

Fran rubbed his chin. "So you're saying that even if we

somehow manage to get rid of a whole bunch of them, they'd just keep coming."

"More or less," Dana said gently. "There's no way to 'get rid' of them all. They're liquid when they want to be. Or they're fog. Even when they're in solid, bodily form, they're difficult to see—unless they want to be seen, of course," she said, concern sapping her positive tone. "Anyway, you'd have to drain the ocean, alter Earth's atmosphere, and chase every solid being off the planet. Or kill their monarch—and no one knows how to do that."

"And Jovians don't kill," John reminded them.

"Negotiating with the monarch is the only option," Dana said.

"Where is she now?" Fran asked.

"On Europa, we assume."

"The Moon Children are on Earth," Fran said, voicing his confusion, "and their leader is on Europa?"

"She could be anywhere. She and the hive don't have to be in the same place."

Fran scratched his head.

"I know it's confusing," Dana said. "The really interesting thing is that the Moon Children aren't built for distant travel. If Edmund met with the queen, he would have brought her to Io for negotiations, I'm quite sure. He would have treated her to a nice time."

"What do you mean?" Drew scowled. "Are you saying Io is nicer than Europa?"

"Wow," John said, "you really don't know much about your place of origin, do you?"

"As far as Jovians and humans are concerned, it's far nicer," Dana added before Drew could respond. "Europa is basically an undeveloped crust of ice. The opposite of luxurious."

"And Moon Children want luxury?" Fran raised his brows.

"What they want is *land*. Something they don't have much of on Europa because it's 95 percent frozen saltwater. They're forced to reside underneath, in liquid form."

Fran blinked a few times as he tried to make sense of the whole thing. "Okay, okay, so where is Edmund now?"

"I don't know," Dana said. "He may be on Io. Or he may have left by now."

"Meaning he may be on his way back to Earth? And why don't you know for sure? I thought all Jovians knew everything about everyone." He caught himself scowling and purposely relaxed the muscles in his face. "Excuse the question, but why would one of the royals, such as yourself, be out of the loop?"

"Not too long ago, David died," she said. "He was the only thing keeping the oneness together. It hasn't been right since Edmund left. I believe he found a way to compromise it as part of his plan to relieve Caroline of some of her power. So unless he wants us to know where he is and what his plans are, we have no way of knowing."

"Right, right, but that's what I don't get. The oneness is down, but when Caroline did her thing in front of the whole world, when she became . . . the, uh—" He stopped there.

"When she took her natural form," Dana said soberly.

"When she did that, every clone, every hybrid fell under her control again. Drew says she was in every Jovian's head."

"She most definitely was," Drew said with a cough, as if remembering tangibly the discomfort of that situation.

Dana gazed at the table. "I'm sure Drew and Connie have already told you that Caroline wields power over all

Jovians. And she can turn the oneness back on in that manner, if she chooses to do so."

Fran rubbed his forehead and reached for one of the bottles of water clustered at the center of the table. The idea of Caroline's power always made him sweat. "Is she the only one who can do this?"

"We can all take our natural form," Dana said.

"But you can't all kick the oneness back into place," Fran said before taking a quick sip of water.

"No."

"Can anyone outside of Caroline do it?"

Dana considered the question. "It's possible there's a Jovian out there who can."

"You don't know for sure," Fran asked.

"I don't. Edmund might be able to. Uncle Jimmy, perhaps." She turned her head and gave Connie the once-over.

"Don't look at me," Connie said. "The oneness isn't Constance's thing."

"What *is* her thing?" Lisa asked. "I've been wondering."

"She's a supreme being," Connie said. "A stealthy one."

"There's more than one supreme being?" Fran said. "Why haven't you told me before?"

"David was a supreme being," Connie said, crossing her leg over her knee, her black boot bobbing. "And some think Uncle Jimmy is one too." Then she added, "You never asked."

Fran said, "And what does it mean to be a—"

"They have certain abilities outside the norm, but this isn't the time for this conversation, I'm afraid," Dana said in her usual kind manner. "We need to focus on the problem at hand."

Fran returned his attention to her and nodded.

"If it's security you're seeking for your coalition, there is none that I can give you. The oneness could snap back into place at any time, and Caroline could demand all clones and hybrids report for duty. The more pressing dilemma Earth faces right now is the Moon Children. They possess the ability to send this world back to the Stone Age. Complete societal breakdown followed by extinction of Earth's living organisms. And Caroline's clones won't be able to do a thing about it."

The news was indeed shocking. "In other words, it's far worse than we thought," Fran said.

Some shifting occurred behind them, and Lisa gasped. Fran's ears perked at the sound of it.

"Fran, get over here," Lisa shouted. "Something's wrong with Drew."

Connie leaped out of her chair and lunged to the ground. Fran followed her. Drew was on the floor. What Fran could see of his face looked an awful shade of gray. "What happened?" he said.

"He slipped right off the chair," Lisa said. She rolled him onto his back and took hold of his wrist. "He's unconscious."

"Drew!" Connie gripped his other hand. "What happened, what's wrong?"

Fran glared at Dana. "Is this them? Is this the Moon Children?"

"Are you trying to poison us?" Connie growled.

Dana shook her head. "It can't be. We're indoors. I don't smell ammonia." She came closer to observe Drew. "That is not what ammonia poisoning looks like."

"That looks more like fainting," John said. "Has he been overworked, maybe he hasn't been eating. He could be dehydrated. Or—" He stopped himself.

Connie patted Drew's face. "Wake up, please wake up."

"He's not breathing," Lisa said. "I have to do CPR."

Connie continued to hold Drew's hand while Lisa began compressions, her game face on. Fran hoped her nursing skills would be enough to see him through.

"Come on, Drew, breathe," Lisa begged him before dropping down and giving him two breaths of air.

"Drew, stay with us," Connie said. "You can't leave us. You can't leave *me*."

Fran had always wondered if they were more than just co-leaders.

"How old is he?" John asked.

No one answered, so Fran said, "Connie, how old is Drew?"

She shook her head. "We're Jovians. We don't keep track of age. We've never even discussed it."

"Andrew Jovian died at thirty-one of a heart defect," John said, raising his brows. "And several Andrew clones have recently died of heart failure."

Lisa looked up, continuing to press rhythmically upon Drew's chest. "He isn't going to die. Somebody call an ambulance."

"We can't do that," Fran said, feeling the pain of that truth in his chest.

"John's only trying to say that there's a good chance Drew inherited Andrew's heart condition," Dana said. "And if so—"

"Please shut up, all of you," Lisa said, breathing hard. "Connie, keep talking to him. Someone grab the crash cart I put together," she shouted over her shoulder.

One of the Miranda clones standing in the wings ran into the main corridor.

"Drew, you stop this right now," Connie said, bringing

his hand to her lips and kissing it. "You are going to live. You will lead the clones to freedom." Her eyes filled with fear, but she blinked it away. "*I* need you. We all need you," she begged him.

Drew's body lurched to the beat of Lisa's compressions.

Was this how Andrew, Fran's best friend, looked when he had died? Did someone, a paramedic maybe, attempt to bring him back, pressing on his chest over and over again? Fran couldn't have watched Andrew die back then, and he fought the desire to run now. To spare himself the trauma. The room spun around him, and he stood and reached back for a chair, then dropped into it.

"Fran, we need a doctor," Lisa said in her I'm-about-to-lose-it voice. "He's not responding, and someone's going to have to shock him."

"You know we can't call anybody," he said softly as he hunched over his own lap and rubbed the top of his head.

She rose to her knees and gazed intently in his direction. He knew what that steely look meant: *We can't sit back and let him die.*

The Miranda clone who'd run down the corridor appeared with the trunk labeled "Crash." More than just a First Aid kit, it was a box the size of a suitcase, and a defibrillator materialized in seconds. Soon Lisa was shouting, "Clear!" There was a thud, and the Miranda clone checked Drew's neck for a pulse. Lisa shouted "clear" again, and the following string of words passed through Fran's mind like an unwanted omen: *It's written in the stars.*

Uncle Jimmy's words.

Fran hated that saying almost as much as Svetlana had back in the day.

He looked to Dana and John. "Any advice?"

The sad way they'd bowed their heads affirmed what he already knew.

"Keep trying," Fran told Lisa. "You're as good as a doctor. Better than most."

"Resuming compressions," she said.

Fran swallowed his fear and rejoined the women on the floor. Drew's complexion resembled that of every dead body he'd ever seen. He took over CPR so Lisa could regroup. "Come on, Drew," he said. "Stop screwing around and wake up." Then he asked Lisa, "What else can we do?"

She breathed in and shook her head, at a loss.

Connie, who'd been quiet, let go of Drew's hand without warning and shouted, "I can't do this," seething with anger. "He doesn't deserve to die!" Then she phased out, becoming undetectable the way Fran had seen her do plenty of times.

He met Lisa's eye as he continued to press on Drew's chest. After a few minutes, he said, "I think we're gonna have to call it."

She nodded as she slumped back in surrender. A sheen of pink rose in her tawny cheeks and heartbrokenness muddied her expression.

Fran reached out and touched her knee. "I'm sorry, babe," he whispered. "We tried our best."

Chapter 9

Metka, Russian Federation

Dmitri knew the saying "third time's a charm." Where he'd first heard it, he wasn't sure. It was just there, in his brain, waiting for him to use it. And that day, he decided, had finally come. If three times was the charm, this time he'd get away, out of Russia, into America. No one on the planet knew of his plan to leave.

Better to be on my own.

He and Alexandria tried to make the trip the day after her birthday. That was the first time. Mother had an appointment with the lady who colored her hair so no one in Metka would recognize her as the former first lady, but the appointment didn't last very long, and she happened to drive home past the bus depot where he and Alexandria waited for a ride to Moscow.

The second time, Aunt Helena caught them at the train station. Her friend, Alyona, had lost her dog, Kolya, and Aunt Helena had gone out in Uncle Ivan's old truck to look for it. She hated to drive that truck and rarely did, but there she was, creeping along, eyes peeled for a dog she'd never find.

Both occasions branded Dmitri's memory with lots of disappointed shaking of his loved ones' heads, and their shouts of *How could you do this to us? The Jovians do not love you, the Jovians are dangerous, the Jovians cannot be trusted,* and other things like that.

It was unpleasant to say the least. Which only made Dmitri more determined to make the trip to see Great-grandmother. *She* was Jovian, and she *did* love him. Before the oneness had broken down, she'd made it clear that he was important to her, and to the rest of the world.

He liked being important.

The second time, when Aunt Helena caught them, he had begged his mother, "Just take me-ah to America. We won't stay forever."

"Never," Mother had said. "I will never take you to see that witch."

"She is my great-grandmother. And you can't hold me prisoner forever."

"Is that so? Maybe I will install iron bars on these doors. Or better, I'll get fingerprint door locks that don't include your fingerprints. How would you like that?"

At that moment he'd experienced a sudden surge of David's strength and when he wheeled himself out of the living room, he crashed into the wall in the kitchen, knocking over a chair as he went.

He'd bumped his head in the process, and after that, Mother treated him nicely again.

Six months had passed since he'd heard Great-grandmother's *help-me* plea, and he figured he'd better hurry up and make a plan that would take him out of the country. Mother had a doctor appointment, and Aunt Helena never went out this time of year, as the threat of colds, flu, and the stomach bug convinced her to remain safe at home.

Alexandria was coming over to watch him. His small

backpack of clean clothes and supply of medications waited in his bedroom. Other than that, he had packed his essentials in the pockets of his wheelchair: passport, cash he'd stolen from the suitcase in Mother's closet, a few crackers and boxes of raisins. Also, his cluster of keys, which he kept forever at his side. With any luck, he'd experience one of his surges of power just before he left, and it would fuel him all the way to the bus depot.

That would be nice.

Except he never knew when a surge would occur—or how bad he'd feel afterward.

Finally a tap-tap-tap sounded at the front door. Alexandria stepped in. She closed her umbrella and shook it. Her long hair appeared shiny with raindrops, and she wore tall black boots, which she removed and left to drip on the small rug just inside the door.

"Sometimes I wish I knew how to drive," she told Nadia, who came from the kitchen to greet her, "not that my mother would ever let me take the truck."

Dmitri had hoped the rain would have stopped by now. It had been days of unseasonably warm gray skies and winter downpours.

"Cousin," he said like always.

Alexandria smiled, her cheeks plump with cheerfulness. "You're looking good, kiddo."

"Thank you," he responded.

Mother gave him one of her serious stares, eyebrows arched like mountain peaks. "You two will not go anywhere, correct?" She opened the closet door and removed her long, lavender raincoat. "You will stay put, in this house. . . . in this *country*. Do you promise?"

"Ha ha, yes, of course," Alexandria told her. "No worries. We have zero plans to go out. It's a dreadful day."

"Okay." Mother put her arms though the sleeves of her coat. "Then I will leave. You call me if he tries to get away." She pointed at Dmitri, who smiled one of his loose-noodle grins.

Alexandria bit her bottom lip, showing regret for earlier times, he supposed. "I promise I will," she said.

Dmitri took a good look at Mother, her pretty face glowing within her lavender rain hood. It broke his heart a little to think of how kind she was, how much she loved him—and he her. He would not see her for a while, and he would miss her. The loss reared up within him, threatening to come out the tiny ducts of his eyes, but he couldn't cry. Not now. He would see her again. He just had to visit with Great-grandmother and then he would be back.

"Goodbye, Mother," he said.

As soon as Alexandria closed the door and locked it, he said, "I'm leaving," and took off down the hall, toward his bedroom.

"What?" Alexandria yelped. "No, you are not."

Her socked feet thumped after him.

"Yes, I am."

"You just watched me promise I wouldn't let you get away. I told her I would call—"

"No-ah you won't."

"Mitya! You can't go. Not while I'm here. Please."

"I have to." He reached the bedroom and took a sharp turn inside.

She was right behind him but stopped at the room's entry. "Well, I can't go with you. It doesn't work. We always get caught."

"I am not asking. I am-ah going alone."

"Fine. Go." She pulled her silver flask from the front pocket of her sweatshirt, the one with the dent he'd put in the bottom, and popped it open. "What do I care?" She drank.

"Yes," he said, rolling himself toward his dresser. He pulled out a wool sweater considering how wet he'd be when he reached the bus depot. Then he swiped his black backpack from the floor, bonking his cheek with it as it made its way onto his lap.

"Hook these in back," he held out the straps of the bag, "and help me out the side door, please."

She seemed to deflate with the request. "Your mother just left. There's still car exhaust in the driveway."

"Bus will be here in an hour."

"And you think no one will notice the boy in the wheel-chair traveling alone in the rain. You'll never get away, Mitya. The whole town knows you've been trying to escape."

"I will do it," he said, the heat of determination warming his cheeks. "I-ah have to."

"Did you hear from the old lady? Did she show up in your head again?"

He wheeled his way toward the kitchen, grazing the trim that protected the wall. Alexandria raced up and around him so they were face-to-face. "You've heard from her?"

"No, I've not."

"So then you know it could have been a mistake. What you heard. What you *thought* you heard the first time. If she really needed you, she would have reached out again. She would have sent a spaceship to pick you up."

"Everyone is watching too closely."

"She's very powerful. She would find a way."

With Alexandria blocking his path, he pointed to the back door. "Oneness is gone. David is dead."

"Yes, I know about David. You've already told me."

His hand wavered once again as he pointed in the general vicinity of the back door.

Alexandria grabbed her forehead, and said, "Shit," then swiped her long hair from her face. "Fine. I'll push you to the bus depot. I can't let you struggle your way through this rain. You'll be drenched. You could fall and crack your head. I have a very big umbrella. It'll be fine. When your mother realizes you're gone, I'll tell her you spiked my juice with vodka, and I passed out."

"Perfect!" He wanted to jump up and give her a hug, but the best he could do was grin, his head bobbing.

DMITRI AND ALEXANDRIA passed only three cars on the walk to the bus depot. This was not unusual for the mid-morning hour. People went to work and stayed there. The last bell had rung for the neighborhood elementary school more than an hour before, so caregivers were already back home, and no one was out walking the dog. The rain pelted Dmitri and Alexandria without apology, but they stayed relatively dry beneath Alexandria's umbrella. If any neighbors saw them, they hadn't tried to stop them.

When they reached the bus depot, they took shelter below the overhang. Alexandria began to chew her bottom lip.

"Take me inside, please," Dmitri said.

She turned him around and pulled him, backward, up the three steps that led into the building. Without a ramp, it wasn't easy. Thanks to her size and strength, she'd always moved him easily in the past, but he weighed eighty pounds now. Mother had been feeding him well.

As they continued up the last two steps, the chair jostled side to side, and he feared he might topple over.

"Wooh! That was tough," Alexandria said, a pink sheen coloring her cheeks. "I wasn't sure we'd make it."

"You are strong," he told her.

"Not really," she said.

Inside the chilly, dimly lit depot, a few people loitered with small suitcases and backpacks. Alexandria rolled him toward a bench and parked him at the end of it. She took a seat beside him and extended her long legs straight in front of her.

"Listen," she said, "your mom and my mom would kill me if they knew I let you go to Moscow alone." She turned away, speaking more to the window beside her than to him. "I've decided to go with you."

"But-ah—"

"It's my duty as your caregiver," she said, ignoring his attempt to respond. "I've been wanting to move out of the house anyway, but I've, you know, been afraid. It's not easy for me to go out unless it's, like this, you know, like an emergency. After I take you to the city, my mother will probably throw me out. It's fine. I mean, if you're brave enough to travel to America alone, I should be brave enough to move out of my parents' house, right?"

"I *love* you," he said, wavering as he chuckled in a jerky manner.

Alexandria faced him and put her hand on his shoulder. "I wish you didn't feel like you had to do this."

"But I do have to."

"I know it's important. You're Jovian. And your mother doesn't want to deal with that. But Evander would, wouldn't he? Your father would want you to go."

Dmitri thought for a second before answering.

"Yes," he said, suddenly sure of it. "He would."

. . .

Dmitri woke to the squeal of bus tires and a shift forward as the vehicle came to a full stop. Beyond the window a large, boxy building loomed. A sign over its entry read "Moscow."

The bus terminal. They had made it!

After they disembarked, Alexandria helped Dmitri find a taxi van. The driver, an old man in a cap that had seen better days, threw around prices as if nothing were set—or legit. When it came to Dmitri, he pursed his lips and said, "One hundred."

"That's ridiculous," Alexandria said. "The airport's less than a mile from here."

"Because of the wheels." The old man gestured to Dmitri's chair, as if Dmitri wasn't worth acknowledging and was nothing but his mobility aid.

Alexandria bared her teeth like she wanted to bite the driver's head off. "*You* have a van. You provide transportation to people who have chairs! We will give you twenty-five. I will get him on board myself."

The driver shrugged and said, "*Da*," then moved on to the next customer.

Alexandria struggled her way inside the van, dragging Dmitri up the rusty ramp. "Why do people have to be so rude?" she grumbled. When she took a seat beside Dmitri, she placed her bag on her lap and grinned at him, as if to say, "All is well."

"You are coming with-ah me?" he asked.

"I can't leave you alone with this idiot."

"Oh, thank you. But you don't have to," he said.

"I want to," she insisted.

The airport appeared after ten minutes of creeping traffic.

"See?" she told the driver. "Quick trip. Easy for you. Here's your twenty-five."

The driver threw the gearshift into park, then turned and said, "No tip?"

"No. No tip." Alexandria opened the back doors, then guided Dmitri safely down the van's ramp. When they were on the ground, she peered at the driver through the vehicle's interior and said, "You get what you deserve!"

Dmitri laughed. "I will miss you, Alex."

"Yes, I know you will. And you should. I came all the way to Moscow for you."

She rolled him into the main building. He expected her to hug him and kiss him goodbye, but instead she said, "Hey! What's this?" and reached into her bag.

He couldn't believe it when she pulled out a red passport. "Yours?" he asked.

"I had a feeling you would try to leave today," she said, feigning smugness. "I know my Mitya very well."

"Oh!" he shouted as he thought, *How lucky can I be?*

"You never would have made it this far without me," she said. "What were you thinking? You know you need a strong woman in your life. Or at least an adult," she said, backtracking the compliment she had given herself.

"Was hoping my energy would appear."

"Your strength is unreliable. You know that as well."

"Yes."

"And you're eleven. It's not safe for you to travel the world by yourself. Who knows where you might end up?"

He tried to smile but was so excited that his lips twisted like the body of a tickled toddler.

"And if you're going to have an adventure at your young age, it's about time I have one too. Right? Even if I am scared shitless." She reached into her pocket, then pulled the fabric of her sweatshirt halfway over her head and drank something in secret. He saw the glint of her silver flask.

"Liquid courage," she whispered, followed by the metal sound of a cap twisting. "Now let's go buy my ticket."

For the first time that day, Dmitri relished a moment of utter relief.

Dmitri didn't mind flying. He enjoyed gazing at the Earth from an almost outer-space point of view. The rough and smooth textures formed a faraway tapestry, its straight and curved lines dividing swaths of green and gold dotted with tiny homes and abutted by broccoli forests. Like a painting the planet itself had created.

Soon after takeoff, he grew drowsy and must have fallen asleep. He woke only once or twice during the eight-hour flight. As they neared Philadelphia, the clouds below the plane grew thick. A dark-gray fog unfurled like a blanket as far and wide as he could see. The pilot's voice came through the speakers warning passengers to remain in their seats. "We will be descending, and turbulence is likely," he said.

Which was strange because turbulence didn't happen on planes anymore. The last time Dmitri flew with Mother, she'd explained how bumpy plane rides used to be when they came up against wind shear, but that modern planes had been constructed with special engineering that took care of that problem. Since then turbulence had become a thing of the past.

"Passengers who feel more comfortable breathing through an oxygen mask may do so," the pilot added. "Simply push the blue button beside your overhead lamp, and your mask will drop from the ceiling."

Alexandria turned to him with a furrowed brow. "Should we?"

Nearby passengers were doing it. "Yes," he said.

Alexandria pressed the blue buttons above their heads, and the white plastic cups dropped from tubes hung from the ceiling panel. She covered his mouth and nose, then pulled the elastic around to secure it and did the same with her own.

He laughed and told her she did that wrong, his voice muffled by the cup. "Yours-ah first," he said.

The descending motion began, and the lighting inside the plane grew dim. Soon it was as if they'd flown into a tunnel. But they hadn't. They were still in the sky. Alexandria grabbed his hand and squeezed it like she was frightened. He continued to observe the view out the window. They'd entered a fog. Thick and silvery. Dark, but also lined with glinting edges.

That wasn't normal for fog.

The plane jolted with a drastic thump, as if it had knocked into the trunk of a tree. Then it happened again. Alexandria's complexion grew white, and she whispered, "Holy crap."

"Is just the weather," he told her, but he worried as well.

More bumping occurred. Strange and violent thudding sounds. *Bam, bam, bam-bam-bam.*

Then the flight became smooth once again.

They'd crossed through to the other side of the fog, he supposed.

People around him removed their masks, so he did the same. The air smelled unnatural. Like a chemical. A little bit harsh. The masks and their tubes inched back into their compartments.

The plane rounded into a turn, and Dmitri gazed upward through the window, at the fog from which they had come. Its edges seemed to gleam. How could it be silvery and at the same time block out the light of the sun?

What was going on with the sky?

After the landing, Alexandria assisted Dmitri into his wheelchair. Then the two of them ascended the boarding bridge along with the rest of the disembarking passengers. Alexandria, who still wore her tall black rubber rain boots muttered something about buying a pair of slippers. As they crossed through the entry to the gate, where large bustling numbers of eager people awaited their flights, Dmitri raised his arms with joy, every wobble celebrating the victory. They'd made it.

Glancing up, he tried to high-five Alexandria, but she missed his erratically moving palm three times.

"Dmitri Peterman," a man's stern voice came from behind them. "Alexandria Novikov?"

A group of maybe a dozen people in suits accompanied by airport security rushed toward them, but Alexandria continued to push forward. "Those are not our names," she said without turning around.

Dmitri did his best to see what was happening behind them. Within the collection of people who followed, many heads bobbed this way and that—toward the gate, the podium, the arrivals screen. Murmurs of "Is this not the flight from Moscow?" rose above the overall din.

"Sorry, we've come from Glasgow," Alexandria insisted as she hurried down the crowded corridor with others who had recently disembarked. She was all but running, and Dmitri hoped with clenched fists that these people would let them go.

But then a man shouted, "Stop right there!"

A hush fell over the area. Travelers seated in the chairs of surrounding gates pulled up from whatever they were reading, closed their mouths to whoever they'd been speaking to, and turned to see what the fluster was all about.

As Alexandria came to a stop, she hunched over, close to Dmitri's ear. "Don't worry. I can handle this," she told him.

The shortest man in the group, with black hair and a crooked nose that must have been broken in the past, caught up to them and blocked their way. Alexandria would have to run him over in order to pass. "I'm going to need to see your passports," he said with intimidating firmness.

Alexandria put her hands in her pockets as if searching for hers. Then she overdramatically rifled through the pocket on the side of the wheelchair, her face collapsing as if she held back a cry. But pretending not to have passports or to have lost them wouldn't work, Dmitri knew. Before Alexandria could say a word, Dmitri said, "I am Dmitri Peterman. Please, we have to go-ah."

The man leaned toward him and spoke at a discreet volume. "Former President of the United States Evander Peterman's son?"

"That's definitely him." A woman very much like Father's AI bodyguard, Elsa, stepped up while the other security people stayed back. She wore all white and moved with robotic precision. Her inhuman crystal blue eyes scanned his face from top to bottom.

"Yes-ah," Dmitri said. "Please take us to—"

"Pardon our rough manner," the man who asked to see the passports said, "but your mother has filed a missing person report. We must make sure you are all right."

Alexandria whispered a stream of Russian curse words under her breath and put on an angry face.

Dmitri said, "I am fine."

The short man continued, "And you are with this

woman and *without* a security detail, so I assume your mother didn't know you were traveling internationally today?"

"Alex is here 'cause of me." Dmitri raised an arm toward Alex. "She's my detail."

The short man responded with a wide smile as if he found this information amusing. "Well, I am Lieutenant Canseco, and my partner is Javenport. You and your friend will please come with us to a private room, and we'll discuss the matter there. I'm sure there is a reasonable explanation for whatever has occurred." The swooping sides of his mustache fluttered as he spoke.

Dmitri supposed that wouldn't be so bad. His head lulled to one side in a nod.

Alexandria maneuvered him forward, joining the group of suited people, with Canseco in front and Javenport behind. It was then that Dmitri's legs began to tingle. Was it just a case of nerves caused by being chased down? Or was his power gathering? He tried to wiggle his toes, but nothing happened.

Behind him, Javenport told Alexandria that she would "take over from here." Alexandria's feet shuffled as if she'd taken a wrong step, and a sturdier grasp took control. Dmitri, affronted by a stranger grabbing his chair as if he didn't exist, felt protective of his personal space. He wondered if Alexandria would be left behind, but then she reappeared by his side, grabbing his hand, her palm hot and moist.

He craned his neck and saw the fear on her face. She probably wanted a drink, and he didn't blame her.

While they waited for the elevator, the airport's security detail caught up. Javenport pushed Dmitri into the lift and five or six security members followed along with Alexandria still clutching his hand. No one spoke as they plunged downward.

A melodic tone sounded, and the doors reopened. The group shuffled into a wing of the airport that struck Dmitri as too quiet, too confined. Like a basement. Buzzing lights made a backdrop for the group's collective tapping heels against an ungiving stone floor as they moved as a tight-knit group. When they reached the end of the hall, the sound of a bustling struggle occurred, and Alexandria yelped as her hand slipped from his grasp.

"Don't touch me!" she shouted right before a door slammed.

"Where are you taking her?" Dmitri said as Davenport whisked him further down the hall, into a small office without windows.

"It's okay, Dmitri. Don't be afraid," the woman said, as she moved him to the opposite side of the room. He wished people wouldn't just put him wherever they felt like putting him. They wouldn't do that if he wasn't disabled. The woman turned him around to face Lieutenant Conseco. "We only want to speak with you," she said.

"Why can't-ah Alex stay?"

"Tell us the truth. Did she take you against your will?" the Lieutenant asked.

"She's my cousin. She is-ah helping me—"

Dmitri doubled over in pain. His midsection seemed to be boiling, and the tingling sensation in his legs had become more like caterpillars with electric feet crawling up and down his shins, spiders spinning hot charged webs in his arms.

Is this David's power?

"It's all right," the man said, placing a cold hand on Dmitri's back. "No need to cry. No one is in trouble."

This time when Dmitri tried to move his toes, he could. He raised one leg slightly, then the other.

"We don't have to tell you how tricky kidnappers can be," Canseco said, "considering what's happened to your older sister. Perhaps Alexandria only pretends to be a relative?"

Dmitri closed his eyes and willed himself to sit upright. The heat pulsed through his veins and climbed the ladder of his spine. "She *is* a relative. Alexandria is my cousin. I've known her for a long time," he said, speaking as fluidly as he had the night the green glow came to him. "I convinced her to come with me to America, not the other way around."

Javenport tilted her head curiously in his direction. "What just happened to your voice?"

He didn't know how to answer that question as a second burst of electrified pain flashed through his middle. He wanted to move, to stand, to walk—to run. Instead, he stayed put, cringing as he bore the wild, spinning energy wreaking havoc inside his body.

"What's happening to him?" Canseco said.

Javenport grasped Dmitri's wrist. "Blood pressure 140 over 90. Pulse 98. Temperature 104."

"I'm fine." Dmitri grimaced. "Please, call my mother, so I can explain."

"Your vitals are not normal," Javenport said, "and we've already spoken with her."

Dmitri stood. He had to. The energy coursing through him demanded it. "I am not sick," he said.

"You can stand?" Canseco and Javenport said simultaneously.

When Dmitri didn't answer, Javenport raised one hand in an effort to calm him. "You have a fever. A high one," she said, pleading. "We can give you medicine."

The energy gathered like a cyclone of fire in his chest. He needed to do something to disperse it, to *use* it. He feared it might blow a hole in his body. The heat spread from his middle into his legs, into each of his arms all the way to his fingertips. His head began to buzz, a hive of ferocious, circling bees. He saw double and dropped his face into his hands. Sweat gathered at his hairline. What was happening? He didn't like this at all. How long would it last?

"I have to get out of here," he muttered through panting breaths. "Where have you taken Alexandria?"

Conseco cowered back. "Tell us how you are standing and speaking."

"Please unlock the door and let me go," Dmitri said.

The heat and electricity pooled in his hands, his fingers zapped and burned, held the energy as if it were a ball he might throw. The pain grew, became even hotter. It needed a way out. He feared his hands might burst into flames.

He staggered forward and reached for the handle of the door.

As if hit with a wrecking ball, the door and the surrounding wall blasted apart. Broken cinder blocks tumbled into the hall and crumbled to the ground. A hole the width of two doorways materialized. Frightened, Dmitri glanced back at his captors. The lieutenant, who'd taken cover behind Javenport, squatted beside her withered body. She appeared to have shorted out.

Instead of diminishing his own energy, the blast had left Dmitri energized. He leaped over the pile of rubble and entered the hall. "Alexandria! Where are you?" his voice rang out.

Her head poked out of a doorway down the hall, and he moved in that direction. When he reached her, he grabbed her hand and continued to run past, pulling her away.

"You're running now?" she asked.

His legs carried him without any thought or effort on his part. He imagined he could run forever. And Alexandria kept the pace beside him. It was as if the energy were coursing from his hand into hers. From his body into hers.

This time he would not let her go.

Chapter 10

Kirksberg, Pennsylvania

A week after the Moon Children rolled over the launch complex in Florida, Caroline, in her upstairs office in the executive wing at Starbright International, meditated on the whereabouts of Constance.

She hadn't visited her office outside of the tubes in months and thought a change in scenery might inspire her, or maybe renew some of her Jovian strength, if that were possible. Unfortunately, she was getting nowhere in her attempts, her brain much less equipped for the task since the loss of David and the oneness. While she sat steeped in frustration, Head Leonard and three other Leonard clones barged through the closed office door, and she wondered, *Do they follow no rules of etiquette at all?*

"A rogue FBI director and as many as one hundred agents are on the property with the intent to penetrate Starbright International and arrest all Jovians on the premises," Head Leonard reported. "The director, Howard Pratt, intends to use brute force to enter the building, the goal being to shut the company down once and for all."

"They're here? Right now?" Caroline rolled back in her wheeled office chair. She was surprised President Abela, or someone else from the government, had failed to warn her. Then again, Abela had phoned several times since the attack in Florida, and Caroline had yet to accept her call.

"Due to your rare public appearance and quick getaway from the highly publicized event, Pratt suspects you are to blame for what the media has dubbed the 'Killer Ammonia Cloud.'" Head Leonard offered a paper screen with a few headlines pulled up as evidence.

Of course the media blamed her. She was an alien and couldn't be trusted. But the FBI had known what she was for far longer than the public had, so it didn't make sense for them to show up now. Then again, Head Leonard had described the director as a "rogue" individual.

Caroline stared into the blue eye wedged into the black side of Head Leonard's two-toned skull. "And what would you suggest I do about it?"

"For caution's sake, we've gathered the Starbright staff in the basement. Pratt and his tactical teams are just beyond the parking lot, organizing as we speak. They have some heavy-duty hardware. How would you like us to proceed?"

She made a steeple of her fingers and brought the peak to her lips. "It was the 2020s, when the government first made an indisputable connection between the being that crash-landed in Kirksberg, Pennsylvania, and the Jovian family's DNA," she said. "They've been trying to learn more about us for decades."

"Yes, Ma'am, I am aware."

"They've never succeeded," she added, "and they

never will." She sounded bored with the whole thing because she was. Bored with her life, with the general sense of lack that had been weighing her down for years now.

Why was Head Leonard bothering her with this, anyway? He knew that a faction of the human government longed to get their hands on the wealth of knowledge they believed lay hidden within Starbright's walls. Every once in a while a trained operative posed as a candidate for employment and scheduled an interview for a position on Starbright's security squad. They landed the interview but never the job, turned away without so much as a tour of the facility.

The Jovian family shared some knowledge with NASA, but they would not be bullied into working with, or for, the American government. The only reason Caroline communicated with President Abela was so she could tell her what to do. The scientists at NASA understood how valuable Jovian information truly was. As a matter of respect, they had duly protected and worked with the Jovians in a hands-off manner since the 1970s, some departments even earlier than that.

Little did Howard Pratt and his rogue agents know, the only Jovian in the building at this point was Caroline. Miranda had spent forty-eight hours in the infirmary healing before she'd left for Mars, and Leo, also traumatized during the launch, had opted to go with her. David had passed, and Caroline had no idea where Constance had gone—most likely she traveled the galaxy in search of Edmund and Evander so the three of them, and James, could decide what to do about Earth and Caroline's power over it. How they might move forward without her. It even crossed her mind that they might want to punish her.

Except . . . Evander would never. On some level, he

still understood her. It would be beneath him to abandon her. More and more, she regretted sending him away.

Besides, Jovians didn't punish other Jovians. Or did they? Caroline had wanted to punish Drew and his clones that day at Independence Park—if punishment meant injury—and Edmund, she suspected, aimed to punish her now with his strategic use of the Moon Children.

Just like her, Edmund wasn't as Jovian as he once had been.

"They will enter the building if we stand down," Head Leonard said, interrupting Caroline's thoughts. "I await your instructions."

"I'm not worried about them breaching the tubes," she said. "And as for the rest of the building, the FBI will not find the family if they penetrate Starbright's walls."

The tubes offered every earthly luxury, even sunlight by way of the astronomical observatory. Caroline could live within the walls for decades. She could continue to conduct business and remain quite comfortably out of sight. Virtually untouchable.

"We will be on high alert," Head Leonard said. "As soon as one of them attempts to open a door or window, we'll blow their head—"

She glared at him, and he stopped talking.

How ironic that he, a person who'd lost much of his head in exactly that manner, would use that ruthless phrase. Caroline may have changed more drastically than she ever thought possible, but senseless killing would never be her way.

"Any further instructions, Ma'am?" Head Leonard asked, eyes downcast in a much humbler manner than the moment before.

The Leonards would protect her at all costs; that was the important thing.

"There is no reason to cause chaos at this time," she told him. "Even if the agents manage to enter the building, they will find only offices."

Offices without files, without catalogs, without computers that stored the secrets humans imagined Jovian computers stored. They would find the lab, which served as an infirmary at this time. It was the place in which Andrew, Caroline's son, had been conceived and then transferred into her human womb, the place in which the cloning program began with James and Constance at the helm.

They wouldn't find the clones themselves, nor the fledglings growing in their nascent pods, nor the DNA samples Jovian scientists had processed and manipulated. They wouldn't find the spaceships underground nor the fleet housed within a mountain in Alaska nor any of the other places Jovians secreted their vessels.

They wouldn't so much as enter the tubes or see the telescope, the greenhouse, the planetarium—it was impossible for ordinary humans to cross the threshold into those spaces without a Jovian to take them there.

Because humans were not meant to see these things.

Caroline gazed at Head Leonard with renewed conviction. "You may leave."

"And you will take to the tubes," he said, his voice rising in question.

She nodded.

He turned and left her, his team of three falling in behind.

Caroline departed the wing of executive offices and took the back staircase all the way up to the greenhouse. She entered the humid space, not her favorite environment to visit (though she did relish the scent of peat moss and soil) and stepped into the tubes through the garden exit. Instead of seeking her residential quarters, she descended the slope that led to the astronomical observatory. It was the first time she'd entered the space since David's death, and a part of her still expected to find him there, meditating on his stool.

Rays of soft illumination mixed with the bouquet of damp stone and cool, pure oxygen, and Caroline's angst and displeasure began to bead up and roll from her skin. Above her, the light of day entered through the opening in the ceiling and spotlighted the deep gray wall behind her. She had yet to ask the Leonards to replace the telescope to its proper site in the center of the room and so was free to stand there herself, to tilt back her head and take in the morning sky, to allow the room's serene atmosphere to surround and embrace her.

She closed her eyes and whispered, "I am the keeper."

The phrase entered her like light flowing through her eyes and colliding into a rich golden gong in the back of her brain. The reverberating phrase—*I am the keeper*—gave her the power she no longer possessed physically. She didn't ponder it often. It wasn't a moniker she wanted to share with the rest of the family, but now that the oneness had gone along with David himself, she could indulge in the truth.

I am the Earth's keeper.

She remembered the only time she'd spoken these words in front of another person. It was during a conversation with Edmund. The day before he left the planet. The day they engaged in the disagreement that had sent him away. She had spoken the words, and he had accepted them. To her surprise, he had agreed she was indeed the keeper.

"It is only natural for the keeper to become infused with feelings for the planet," he'd said. "Perhaps these feelings are leading you astray?"

"You are wrong," she argued with conviction. "I have no feelings. I am Jovian through and through."

"Jovians are nonviolent, and you have built an army that answers only to you," he'd said with a boldness that made her blink.

"This planet has changed you," he continued. "And me. Every one of us. You are not the same individual you were when we first arrived, and neither am I. You love this planet, as we all do. Do you also wish to possess it?"

"Don't be ridiculous," she'd said.

Interesting how denied words often ended up coming true.

After this conversation occurred, the clone protests flared, the Battle of Philadelphia took place, and Caroline showed her true self in the park. Then Constance made sure Caroline became far more human than she'd ever thought possible.

Now that she could not resort to the power of her Jovian body, she couldn't help but wonder if her connection to the planet was more than just her duty to watch over and protect it. Did she love it the way human beings loved? The way human beings wished to possess what they loved?

Through the observatory's cool, quiet atmosphere, these thoughts came with a flicker of desire that Caroline could not deny, and she resumed her search for Constance without concern for the rogue FBI director intent on entering her home.

It wasn't long before Head Leonard burst through the closed door and broke the blissful silence. She turned her head slowly in his direction. "Yes?" she said, making no effort to keep the annoyance from her voice.

"Howard Pratt and his team have ceased and desisted," he announced.

She hesitated before responding, worried the Leonards' guns may have been the things that had stopped him. "Yes, and how did it happen?"

"A small part of his own department stepped in and apprehended him, then escorted him from the property."

"There was no bloodshed, then." She breathed out with relief.

"You were worried," Leonard said, his curiosity beaming bright as the rays that spilled through the ceiling's oculus.

She hadn't realized he'd been watching her so intently. Jovians didn't worry, especially not their queen.

"Do I appear worried now?" she said, tipping her head back to observe the sky.

"The Leonards stood down as ordered, Ma'am. We follow your wishes to a T and always will."

"That goes without saying," she said gruffly. "You may leave."

Head Leonard said, "Yes, Ma'am." The door opened, admitting a spate of artificial light that vanished when it closed behind him.

THAT EVENING, Caroline took to her residential space in the tubes. Perched upon a high-backed armchair with an antiquated book about the precious stones of Earth spread across her lap, she'd paged to the chapter on Tanzanite, a gorgeous blue-purple stone that filled her with undeniable desire. Unfortunately Head Leonard pinged her wrist-comm as she reached the information on the Merelani Hills that produced it.

"President Abela to speak with you, Ma'am," he said.

Whenever Leonard informed her of a phone call, a duty formerly tasked to Miranda, Caroline was taken aback. She'd never get used to the rough baritone that greeted her in place of Miranda's familiar soprano.

"Should I put her through?" he asked.

"Go ahead," she told him, thinking it a good time to discuss worldly issues.

She placed the book on the table beside her and tapped her wristcomm, then looked down her nose at the live image of Abela.

"Thank you so much for taking my call," the President said through a breath of relief. "I apologize for the late hour."

She always looked like she'd been running from someone or something—her wavy hair untethered and breezing around her head.

"The FBI tried to enter my home," Caroline said.

The woman's mouth tensed, the lines to each side deepening. "As soon as I heard there were agents in Kirksberg, I demanded they stand d—"

"They will never get in," Caroline said.

"That's what I assumed, but you know you can count on the full extent of my power should you ever—"

"About that, I need no reassurance," Caroline said.

The president closed her mouth, and silence hovered for a moment between them. Caroline rendered a blank Jovian stare without mercy.

"The situation with the Moon Children, for instance," Abela continued, "the National Guard has managed to suppress a panic response for the time being, mostly because the public believes the offenders pose a fatal risk to clones alone, and not to original humans. But I don't know how long this will hold. For one, much of the National Guard is made up of clones. And for another, our citizens have seen the devastation that occurred at the launch. They've heard the reports of these mysterious poison clouds, and they're frightened. Rightly so, I might add." She paused and tilted her head in a pensive manner. "Frankly, Ma'am, the government wants to do more. We would like to be proactive in our protections, but we have little idea what we're dealing with."

"Meddling humans have no place in the fight against the Moon Children," Caroline said matter-of-factly. "They will support when their support is requested, and that is all. It's your job to see to that."

Abela lowered her gaze and answered with a succession of quick nods. "Understood. When and how can we support?"

"Ready your people. Alert the world leaders. Prepare to rebuild civilization. Expect great changes in the life as you know it."

Abela's image darted forward, a closeup of her brow overwhelming the small screen. "Are you saying it will come to that—the need to rebuild civilization?"

"You've seen what our opponent can do, and you've said yourself the humans are frightened. There is no illusion greater than fear, and I assure you, fear can tear down an entire society. As a leader you surely know this."

"Yes, yes I do. The armies around the world will be ready, Ma'am. I'll make sure of it."

"Good. You will need the tactical thinking of your armies, their organization, power, and presence but not their weapons. Their weapons will be useless."

"But . . . I don't understand."

"This will be a fight like none the human race has ever known."

Abela stared, her face twitching with confusion. "A fight without weapons?"

"Yes."

"May I ask, who are the Moon Children? What do

they look like? The footage I've seen showed only a thick fog. Are they individual beings? What do they want? We know ammonia poisoning is their weapon."

"They want whatever their monarch wants, and they will stop at nothing to get it. You cannot harm them. There is nothing you can do to stop them."

"Uh-huh. I hear you." She paused. "So please tell me, how can we predict the next attack? How can we prepare?"

Humans could be so tiresome. "You *can't* prepare. They rise like steam into the air and drop like the branches of trees onto the ground. Be ready for a new world."

"I don't under—"

"A new way of life," Caroline continued. "Make sure your people and all the people around the world agree to remain calm. They will have to work together for the good of the Earth if they want to continue to live here. Convince your world leaders to join forces."

"Of course they will. They'll do whatever is necessary to—"

"Good. The clones will not be able to win this one for them."

Tears emerged in Abela's eyes, her chin quivered as she outwardly struggled to remain dignified in her discomfort. Finally, she spoke: "If our weapons are of no use, and the clones can't fight them, and the humans are helpless, who will stop them?"

Caroline hated to state the obvious for anyone, let alone a human.

"Ma'am?" Abela said. "Are you there? Can you hear me?"

"*I* will," Caroline said firmly. "That is why I am here."

Chapter 11

The Jupiter System

The massive gas giant that was Jupiter, with its stripes of rust, beige, and orange that surged and surrounded the red swirling eye, dominated all Max could see through the captain's window, as it always did when in near proximity. Io showed up on his pilot screen soon after. Max was typing the coordinate numbers necessary for landing when the little pinecone he kept on the instrument panel rolled sharply to the left and flipped into the side window of the cockpit, as if intent on harming itself.

That's odd. Max scratched his head in wonder just as the *Sparrow* slid into a tailspin.

He struggled to regain control while the g-force sucked him into the pit of his chair. Somehow he managed to raise both hands to the control board, battling back the crushing pressure. Touching the board was as far as he got before he lost his lunch. Thankfully, what he'd expelled whirled into the size and shape of a baseball, and flung away from him, spattering the same window the little pinecone had careened into.

Man, he hated when unexpected stuff like this happened. Never in his three-to-five years of flying had anything like this occurred.

The spinning slowed, and Max gave in to it, resting back while he waited for normalcy to resume. Maybe he'd passed too closely to a large spacecraft. He hadn't seen anything, and nothing had showed up on his screen, but that didn't mean they weren't there—camouflage systems rendered ships invisible, not that this was a battle zone. Maybe Jupiter's massive gravity had wreaked havoc on his navigational controls. Sometimes it created weird space turbulence that he needed to practice navigating.

"Syndi?" he said, waking the agentive controls. "Are you going to tell me what just happened and why we're spinning in circles right now?"

"A disturbance has caused a third-degree spin. Subsidiary systems paused as a cautionary measure."

"Yup, that much is clear," he muttered.

"Seventy percent of systems rebooted. Normal flight recommencing in thirty seconds or less."

He closed his eyes, hoping to relieve the dizziness. He would not throw up again. He never threw up twice. He hardly ever threw up once.

A couple of long minutes passed before the *Sparrow* resumed a straight course of flight and Max resumed a proper, upright position in the captain's chair. *What were those numbers again?* Still a bit bleary, he retyped the coordinates to the destination. The *Sparrow* took a slow quarter turn to the right and brought into view a massive heavenly body. Io's dark and shadowy side, in all its glory.

Max sat back and gazed drowsily. Crisis averted. Life was good.

"Bring me in," he told Syndi.

"Are you sure, Captain?" the AI said.

He laughed. "Yes, I'm sure. I've got eyes on the destination now. Bring me in—uh." He forced back a gag, disappointed with his stomach for the trouble. "I think I better kick back and take a breather."

"Enjoy your rest, Captain."

Max pressed back in his chair, activating the extended footrest. He would just let the motion sickness ride out.

A BUMP AND A METAL-SOUNDING JIGGLE. The ship had landed? Apparently not too gracefully. He must have dozed off. Didn't feel like a docking-strip kind of arrival. Max opened his eyes to the surrounding terrain, covered in what appeared to be ice. Dark gray, like a storm cloud in every direction. The Io he knew was a lot lighter. Not to mention the lack of the docking station—or anything else.

"Uh, Syndi? This doesn't look right. What did you do?"

"I brought you in, as directed."

"Where are we? I programmed a landing on the moon right in front of us."

"That is what I have done, Captain."

Max pressed his fist into his lips as he stared at his screen. "Why's it so dark here? What's going on?"

"The dark side of Europa spends much time void of sunlight, both direct and indirect. It is not cause for alarm."

Max grabbed his forehead. "No, no, no . . . Oh my God, repeat what you just said!"

"I said, the dark side of Europa spends much—"

"We are not allowed to land on Europa."

"But we have. Those are the coordinates you entered."

"Shit, shit, shit."

"Coordinates 3-3-6-6-4-2-7 comma 4-4-6-7 . . ." she continued to spout numbers.

Max checked his controls. Had he made an error in typing? Damn, his bad typing skills! Mom always told him to take a class.

"Bodies approaching, Captain."

"Bodies," he whispered. "Where?"

"North, sir."

"I don't see them. North is through the Captain's windshield."

"Correct, captain's windshield. My viewer shows three bodies straight ahead," Syndi said. "They have approached, and now they have stopped in front of the ship."

"Your viewer is wrong. I have eyes on that area right now, and I don't see anyone. You know what? Never mind. Take off. We need to leave."

"My viewer shows three bodies in proximity. We will injure them if we leave."

"Crap." Max collapsed into a severe slouch and knocked his forehead with his fist.

"They seem to be waiting, sir."

He squinted into the dark. All he could see was a large, flat swath of ice-covered ground. Dark, for the most part, a bit silvery here and there, but no one standing on it. "I still don't see anything."

The terrain, though void of much of anything, glowed in a beautiful, eerie manner, but that didn't mean it was safe.

Then he remembered: Ida said the Moon Children, the ones forging an attack on Earth, lived on Europa. But she also said they lived underwater. So whomever Syndi saw couldn't be them.

He relaxed into this thinking.

"They are gesturing, sir. This is their method of communication. I'm translating. It means, 'Come out.'"

He stood. "Back the ship up, Syndi, and take off, please. We can't stay here."

"Chance of injury to bodies is 75 percent if we do."

He couldn't get away. Surely if he hurt them, others would chase him down. Evander had never told him what to do if he accidentally landed on the wrong moon.

"There are ten beings now. They are gesturing. 'Come out.'"

"What should I do?" he muttered.

"You should suit up, then open the airlock, and leave the spaceship to 'Come out' at their request."

"Okay, okay. I'll just . . . I'm sure they're friendly, right? . . . If anyone is actually there." He reached into the upper compartment for a fresh NOxygen piece and pressed it into his nose.

"Ninety-seven percent of the universe's beings are benevolent, so there is a 3 percent chance they will not be," Syndi offered.

"Thank you for doing the math," he said with sarcasm.

"You do not have a talent for math, so I make all calculations."

"Yes, I know. Very helpful." He sighed, then headed toward the back of the ship, careful to step around the puke that had dripped down the wall and pooled on the floor. The toe of his boot kicked something on his way to the exit. His little pinecone. He lunged forward and grabbed it, then dropped it into the pocket over his heart, safe and sound. He checked his spaceskin (a special e-skin for flyers like himself), which thankfully retained a charge of 90 percent and was oxygenated to 96 percent.

Just before the entrance to the airlock, he reached into his cubby and pulled out his helmet, then fitted it over his head with a click, click, click. In the airlock, he pressed his spaceskin's activate button, feeling the zip of energy from neck to toe.

The airlock whirred as it opened, and he stepped out.

Cold. Even through the spacesuit, he could tell.

Behind him, the door to the interior of the ship closed, but the airlock would remain open, just in case.

Once the bottom of his foot contacted ground, various metrics showed up on the helmet screen. Minus 260°F; Atm O_2, water vapor, hydrogen; saline solid ice surface.

"Just like the Europa I studied back in high school," he muttered.

Should he have grabbed a weapon? Something to throw at these beings that he couldn't see, should the need arise? Max was no soldier. The one time he'd tried to be one, he had nearly killed a man and all hell broke loose. So, no. He would approach whoever was there with nothing but his good intentions.

He rounded the side of the ship and gazed ahead. Sure enough, he detected a group of small beings that blended very well with their surroundings. Whatever the means of camouflage, they appeared to be the same color as the ice, their edges silvery and glinting, their bodies a subtle blur, possibly materializing and dematerializing over and again. *Strange.*

Now what? He'd come out. Would they continue the conversation?

"Syndi," he spoke through his helmetphone, "please provide information."

"*Luna Liberi.* Language of hands. They say, 'You cannot be here.' Reply message?"

Luna what? he wondered before telling himself it didn't matter.

"Tell them I made a mistake. And I'm sorry. I will leave now."

Through the spaceship's outside speakers, Syndi made a bunch of ticking sounds. After a pause, she said, "They say, 'Come closer.'"

Do they want to abduct me? No one knows I'm here. Not even Ida, who ordered me to go directly to Io.

"Tell them I'd like to, but I need to take off. I'm late for a meeting."

Would they even know what a meeting was? Doubtful.

Syndi's strange words came through once more. Then she told Max, "They reply, 'You cannot land here.'"

"Tell them I'm sorry. It was a mistake. My spaceship was caught in a spin. I thought this was Io.'"

Suddenly a chorus of *Io, Io, Io, Io* rose up like frogs congregated in a lagoon on a humid summer night. It was a pretty sort of alien sound and at the same time, a child-like sound. They were small creatures, and he assumed their faces would be cute if only he could focus on them.

"Group is approaching," Syndi said. "Twenty now."

"Twenty?" Max took a step backward.

"Individuals," she added.

Where were they coming from? He didn't see any in the distance near or far. Were they splitting like cells?

"What do they want?"

"They say, 'You need permission from the monarch to land.'"

How would he get that? He didn't have time to meet the monarch. He needed to board the ship and get the hell out of there.

Keeping his eyes on them as well as he could, Max stepped backward toward the spaceship, eventually bumping his head on it and stumbling sideways. He caught himself, but the jerky movement sent the pinecone from its perch at the top of his uniform pocket onto the icy ground a few feet in front of him.

Like a cloud pushed by a gust of wind, the creatures swarmed. Max watched as the silvery outlines of individuals melded together at the same time they came apart.

Weird, and amazing, he thought. Their strange, glassy brightness overwhelmed his eyes and made them feel numb. He fought against the urge to close them, and lost.

Syndi spouted a stream of clicking sounds—orders, Max assumed, spoken in their language. When he opened his eyes again, they'd backed up. One of them held the pinecone in its glossy three-fingered hand. Gently, it pulled off a few of the conifer's lower-most scales. The group sounded a simultaneous gasp that resembled wind rustling through tree branches.

They stared at the little pinecone pieces and made excited clicking sounds. Finally, the one holding the pinecone reached his hand toward Max.

Syndi interpreted: "They say, 'We want this.'"

Max hated to lose his father's pinecone, but Dad would understand, it was a matter of life and death. "Tell them they can have it, if they just let me go."

"Again, they say, 'We want this,'" Syndi said.

He'd already said they could have it. And why would they want a tiny pinecone, anyway? Could it be for the seeds? They'd pulled it apart and gasped when the seeds dropped out. There weren't any trees here. This was Europa, a big crusty saltwater sea. Maybe they wanted to try to grow trees?

"Syndi, tell them I can get more pinecones for them."

She clicked the words. Then she said, "They say, 'You have these?'"

"Not with me, not on my ship, but I know where to get them. I can get lots of them if they let me go."

"They say, 'We want this. We need this. To grow.'"

"Okay, good. Yes. Tell them I understand. Tell them I'll bring the pinecones with me when I return. I'll bring hundreds, or thousands. Large amounts. Enough to grow an entire forest."

He had reached the airlock and was tempted to jump in and get the heck out of Dodge, but he couldn't rush it. He needed them to believe him, to trust him.

"They say, 'We need these now.'"

"Yes, I get that," Max said, nodding as vigorously as possible in his helmet. "I just have to transport Evand—" He stopped himself from speaking Evander's name. "I have to pick someone up, and then I'm going to Earth. When I come back, I'll bring the seeds."

"Earth?" they said in unison moving toward him again.

"Yeah, it's a planet."

"They are making confused hand gestures," Syndi said.

"Tell them I'll be leaving now and that they need to back away from the ship."

"They say they will wait for your return," Syndi said.

"Thank them for me." Max leaped into the airlock. He smacked the button to seal the compartment as the tension ran out of him like a hot surge of pee down his leg.

"Let's get out of here."

"Yes, Captain," Syndi said. "Taking off."

Chapter 12

Kecksburg, Pennsylvania

A Universe Without Jovians

Before they left Io, Natasha's father had explained the concept of time travel as best he could.

There were, it turned out, various ways to do it. Sometimes it involved traveling pods and sometimes it involved stones or other natural elements. Sometimes it didn't involve either of those things. And that was something she simply had to accept, Evander had said.

Time traveling backward, for instance, differed from ordinary space travel and time traveling forward, in that at no point were you conscious on the journey. You boarded the spaceship, and you entered the pod, but instead of waking from your pod at a preset time, instead of sipping liquids and taking pills and surrendering to the usual IVs once you woke onboard, you simply arrived in your consciousness in another time and place. *In medias res*, as it were.

Which was jarring, and strange, but cool, Natasha supposed.

Though, it seemed too easy.

In this case they'd landed (was *land* even the right word?) on Earth. Kirksberg, Pennsylvania, fully dressed in 2020s attire: a pair of white sweatpants and a pink cotton sweater for Natasha (time had done her no favors in that vein) and a light blue cotton shirt with darker blue and white stripes paired with dark blue-gray carpenter pants for her father.

Was this what people on Earth used to wear? She'd seen pictures, but wow, it was like wearing a costume compared to her usual black unitard.

In a bedroom painted light gray with a pair of twin beds, twin night tables, twin lamps, and an antiquated analog-style clock that read 6:32 a.m., a bookshelf displayed paper books on two of the shelves (humans still killed trees here?) and various decorations—vases, candles, and wooden signs that made saccharin declarations like "Home is where the heart is."

A few photos in frames on those shelves drew her in.

She hopped out of bed and lifted one of them. She'd seen it before. Her grandparents, Svetlana and Andrew, with a child, standing in front of a ranch-style home. Natasha studied the image of her grandfather. The blue-green eyes she and her father had inherited from him. Her eyes were his eyes, just as her heart had been his heart, before she received a new one. She was very much descended from this man.

But that wasn't the most interesting thing about the photo.

The child that accompanied Svetlana and Andrew proved far more compelling. A toddler who wasn't Evander in child form, as it should have been. It was someone else. A child wearing a dress.

A girl.

"The Lost Sister," she whispered, her head buzzing with sudden understanding. Svetlana had left a world with Jovians to come to a world without Jovians, and when she gave birth to her first child, it had been a girl instead of a boy!

This was why the universe had brought Natasha to this place. It wasn't because her father needed to apologize to the mother he hadn't seen in decades (though surely *he* assumed that was the reason). They'd traveled through time for this girl, the key to the Jovian prophecy.

Or was she?

"Prophecies can be fickle," Uncle Jimmy had told Natasha not long ago.

Still, it couldn't be a coincidence. There were no coincidences in the universe.

Natasha's heart thumped like a leg with a limp, and then something—a muscle maybe—clenched in the middle of her chest. She imagined a lemon squeezed over one of those old-fashioned juicers, and for the first time, she doubted the strength of her new heart. A few breaths passed before the pressure released and the pain flattened. She put her hand upon her chest and stepped backward until she'd reached the side of her bed and lowered onto it.

The Mintakan doctors had warned her Earth would not be good for her heart. Something about its gravitational pull combined with the electromagnetic spectrum could wreak havoc on the organ's delicate timing, they'd said. Up until that moment, she'd thought their warnings erred on the side of caution or may even had been meant to scare her into keeping her special e-skin on forevermore; something she'd made clear she did not want to do. She'd also assumed they didn't want her and her father to travel back home, considering how travel affected their tendency to age.

But what if her assumptions had been wrong?

What if the gravity and the magnetic spectrum had already caused damage to her physically? What if the time trip had? Could this visit with Svetlana be the meaningful act she'd commit before dying? Meeting her father's sibling? Sharing the prophecy with the lost sister? Could death be so close when the surgery had gone so well?

"Don't crap out on me yet," she told her heart.

She had to get her father back home, back to her mother and brother. It was her fault he'd left them, and her responsibility to return him.

She looked for her NOxygen clip on the night table, but it wasn't there. She was breathing real air. Big, beautiful breaths of fresh air! She breathed deeply and rose from the bed. An indent in the pillow on the bed opposite indicated her father had shared the room, though he'd risen earlier. She headed toward the door in the corner and hoped to find, *yes!*, a bathroom. *A shower.*

She couldn't remove her clothes fast enough though her e-skin would have to remain—she wouldn't chance taking it off after the pain she'd experienced in her chest a moment ago. Still she'd step into the shower and run the water over her face and her neck. She'd let it enter her mouth and then she'd swallow it. Maybe that would be enough to satisfy her craving. If not, she'd pull up a corner of the e-skin and encourage a few drops to slide in.

And she'd wash her hair! She could hardly remember what it looked and felt like minus the oily residue of space water.

Standing in the tub, she smiled at the showerhead's perforated face as streams of clear, sparkling Earth water burst forth, splashing down on her and making her close her eyes. She'd missed this so much.

For just a little while, her concerns washed away.

. . .

"COME SIT, I'm so glad you and your father are here," Svetlana said in a Russian accent so much like Natasha's mother's that Natasha experienced a cramp of homesickness. Svetlana held a coffee pot in one hand, a dishtowel in another. "Would you like some?"

"Oh no, she can't," Evander was quick to say. "Just water for her."

Normally Natasha would scowl at her father for the offense of speaking for her, but at that moment she couldn't free herself from the sight of Svetlana. Her grandmother, the one she'd heard so much about, stood in front of her in the flesh. The legend in a black, fuzzy bathrobe. The human who'd rebelled against the Jovians and lived to speak of it. She'd beaten them. At least for the moment. Though, who knew what the future would bring.

There was no winning or losing in the universe. The best a person could hope for was to temporarily move in the right direction.

At the moment, Svetlana's smile tried too hard. It didn't light her face. Was she sad? A long-overdue visit like this between mother and grown son had to be what human beings called "bittersweet." Both happy and sad at the same time. This was a new emotion for Natasha, one she had yet to figure out, but she learned as quickly as she aged, so no doubt she'd understand soon enough.

"Come in, sit down," her father told her. "Are you hungry?" He gestured to a group of sticky-looking Danish, brown and shiny with cinnamon sugar. She hadn't eaten Danish since she was five years old and doubted it would be good for her heart.

"You don't have to eat just yet if you don't want to," Svetlana said, taking a glass from the cabinet and filling it with water. Beautiful, crystal clear, like diamonds in liquid form. "I know it's early. I hope we didn't wake you."

Natasha took the glass and drank it down, water spilling over her chin. She felt her father's attention on her and stopped short of guzzling the entire glass.

From across the circular table, Svetlana observed her with what seemed like interest. She lacked the grandmotherly gray hair and soft, wrinkled complexion of the older-lady stereotype. Her wide cheekbones and squarish face with deep blue eyes brought words like *pretty* and *youthful* to mind. Maybe Svetlana looked young because she'd traveled backward in time, to an earlier part of her life. Natasha would try to remember to ask her father.

She also wondered if Svetlana knew they'd time traveled. Or did she think they merely hopped a plane from their busy lives in California, or some other faraway state, and now nursed a bout of jet lag? Either could be true.

Natasha eased into a chair and looked to her father to provide a clue.

"She knows," he said with a nod. "You can speak freely."

"I'm so glad to meet you, Natasha," Svetlana said. And now it became clear: Svetlana had been crying. Her swollen eyelids and stuffy nose gave it away. "You're beautiful and smart—and *talented* from what I've heard."

"This whole thing feels surreal," Natasha said. She paused to examine their surroundings, scanning the kitchen, the connected living area, the deck beyond the sliding glass door. The lawn wore a sparkly layer of early-December frost. "Is everyone else still asleep?"

Her father planted an elbow on the table and raised his fist to his mouth. Her question caused him stress.

"Well, Evan is outside," Svetlana said, with a strained smile. "She's been camping in the backyard for a while now. Sleeping in a tent with one of those wireless heaters." She paused as if to make sure Natasha knew what she meant by wireless heater. "She likes to, you know, sight the stars. As I'm sure you do."

They shared a knowing look and Natasha said, "Yes, I do enjoy a view of the night sky." Then she felt compelled to say, "Evan is your daughter."

"Yes. She's eighteen. You look to be about the same age?"

Natasha wouldn't answer that. In her case, age was relative and hard to explain. "Has she met Dad yet?"

"No, not yet," Evander said.

"And the others?" Natasha asked. "How many children do you have?"

Svetlana, in the middle of sipping her coffee, drew back as if distracted by a burned tongue. She replaced the cup upon the table and said, "Just Evan."

Something inside Natasha slumped. Her expectations? Her hope? Her overall trust in the universe? Svetlana had wanted many children. A big family. That was part of the legend. Living with Andrew *and* having lots of children.

But maybe having one child and the man she loved was enough.

"I can't wait to meet my grandfather," Natasha said to alleviate the awkward silence.

Evander twitched in his chair; Natasha thought he may have tweaked his back. But then he said, "He's not actually—"

Svetlana reached across the table and touched his hand. "It's okay." She turned to Natasha. "Andrew has passed. About thirteen years ago now." She lifted the top of the glass sugar bowl and replaced it, her hands jittery.

How can this be? This was the universe in which Svetlana and Andrew would be granted a good life. The one in which there were no Jovians! The couple and their children were to live happy lives, and no one would try to stop them.

The clock on the wall above the kitchen table ticked out the seconds. Suddenly the moment felt knotted. Stuck.

"I'm sorry," Natasha said and wished she had nothing to be sorry about. "I don't know what to say. I'm surprised."

"Yes. So was I, believe me," Svetlana said, gazing at the tabletop. "But I still feel he's near, still watching over us. Every day," she added, an obvious attempt to make the best of a bad situation.

Her grandfather's soul lived in a star, Natasha remembered, and she wondered if that's what Svetlana meant.

Evander took his mother's hand and squeezed it. "I'm sorry," he said.

That's when Natasha noticed how startling white her father's hand was. Like quartz, the wrinkles like striations running circles around each brittle knuckle. Powder blue veins tunneled curved lines from wrist to each finger. She dared leave the ancient terrain of his hand to observe his face. Ugh. Despite the medicines he'd taken, the time travel had pushed him well beyond octogenarian. Anyone would easily mistake him, a son, for Svetlana's father, or grandfather, more likely. How strange this must have been for Svetlana.

Except that she'd come from their world, so she knew. The possibility of strange multiplied wherever Jovians dwelled.

The question of how he and Natasha would get back home proved more worrisome. With her sensitive heart and his speeding age, would either of them make it back to their time and universe alive? Elsa remained on Io—there were no AI humans in this universe—so Natasha couldn't console herself with the prospect of Elsa being there to stabilize her father should he begin to fail en route.

As her thoughts fleetingly revisited Nadia and Dmitri waiting for their return, she drifted visually out the sliding glass door. Svetlana's backyard boasted many beds of dark-green bushes and miniature evergreen trees. While Natasha observed them, someone walked up the steps to the deck. A person wearing a puffy blanket from shoulder to foot. Messy bed-headed brown hair in a long-layered but overall short cut, hers was Evander's face, only with a female softness—and youth, obviously. As the girl neared, Natasha noticed her dark brown eyes. *Like Great-grandmother's,* she thought.

In this universe, Evan was Svetlana's child. Her human child. Would she and Evander share a personality? Would Natasha feel like she already knew her as well as she knew her father?

The sliding door pulled back, and Evan stepped in, then turned to push it closed. As she approached, she said, "Oh, hey," without focusing on any one of them.

"Hello," Natasha said, and Evan met her with a brief smile before she bowed her head slightly and stopped beside the kitchen counter, leaning her hip into its edge and then fidgeting underneath the blanket she was wrapped in. Not shy, necessarily, but not displaying a lot of self-confidence either.

"Evan, these are your relatives Evander and Natasha," Svetlana said.

"Good morning," Evander said, "so sorry to stop by unannounced—"

"It's not a problem." Her long bangs reached past her nose and screened her eyes. She shook her head to get them out of the way. Her brown hair was shorter in the back and much longer in front.

"It's lovely to meet you," Evander added.

"Yeah, you too," she said, as if this were a run-of-the-mill introduction and not a visit from otherworldly relatives —because as far as she knew, it was. "I didn't know we were having company today, or I would've got up earlier." She craned her neck in the direction of the clock above the kitchen table.

"It is only ten after seven," Svetlana said. "You're fine."

Evan's mouth dropped open. It was admittedly early for visitors. "Lemme just go brush my teeth," she said. "I'll be right back."

"Okay, honey," Svetlana said. She sipped her coffee. "Take your time."

Natasha observed the manner in which Evan shuffled away with the blanket draped across her shoulders. That was not something she'd ever seen her father do. Maybe they weren't so much alike after all. A door closed down the hall.

Evander leaned back in the chair, a thread connecting him and Svetlana eye to eye.

Natasha wondered what thoughts passed through that thread. Could her father be envious of Svetlana's daughter on some level? If he'd time traveled with Svetlana years ago, he could have lived in this house with her. He could have led a normal life. *Without Jovians.*

Had he wanted that?

A sustained silence went on for too long. Natasha raised her arms overhead and stretched. "What's the plan for today? Is there one?"

Svetlana said, "Your dad and I have to talk and—"

"I figured you'd already done that," Natasha interrupted. "How long are we staying?"

Her father didn't answer right away.

"Dad?" she said.

"I don't know yet," he said, with some restraint. "A few days, probably. Let's see how it goes." With a strange smile, he directed his words to Svetlana: "Natasha has a somewhat blunt way about her. You'll get used to it."

This made Natasha sit up. "Have I been rude?" she asked. Truth was, she hoped they *wouldn't* visit long enough for Svetlana to get used to her blunt ways. She needed to take her father home. And she didn't know how long she wanted to stay either, considering the pressure and pain in her chest that morning.

"Not at all," Svetlana said. "I thought you and Evan could go to the café and have some breakfast together. Would you like that?"

"You won't be coming with us?" Natasha said.

"In the Jupiter System we had nothing but liquid meals for weeks," Evander said, "so I'm sure Natasha would love that. Wouldn't you?" The intensity with which he spoke imparted a "Please say yes" message.

Svetlana put on a smile. "Your father and I have already eaten, but you girls should go. Order the chocolate chip pancakes or French toast. Both are delicious and very filling."

Svetlana could have mentioned the café's awesome cat kibbles, and Natasha would have been game. "Yes, I'd love to," she said.

At that, her grandmother stood, hurrying across the kitchen to a nook where she kept the kind of old-fashioned bag women of yesteryear toted with them everywhere they went. Would she call it a *purse* or *pocketbook*? Nadia used to carry a *bag*. Now that Natasha had reached the age of bag carrying, she doubted she ever would. A chip had been imbedded in her neck for most things, including funds and identity, rendering the purse, bag, or pocketbook defunct. Her unitard even sported space for tampons.

Svetlana returned with paper bills and handed them to Natasha. They were gritty to the touch, each one stamped with the number twenty. Natasha recognized it as money. Actual money you could hold in your hand. She wasn't used to that.

A tapping rhythm, like a short downpour of rain played within her chest, and she froze in place. What was it? She held her breath and waited for it to pass. When it did, she folded the money and slipped it into her thigh pocket. "Thank you," she said.

SVETLANA LENT her long sheepskin coat to Natasha, and Evan led the way to the nearby café. The town of Kirksberg, Pennsylvania—or, *Kecksburg*, Evan had corrected her—appeared pretty much the way it did in Natasha's universe, except for the slight change in name and a few other things, such as vehicles with engines that emitted toxic exhaust. The skies here lacked clarity. A gray layer of haze muddied the otherwise crisp winter blue. Was this what they called pollution? There were no Jovians here, and without Evander to clean the air, the planet most likely suffered the fever of global warming. She wondered if this version of Earth would eventually die, and decided it most likely would.

Nadia had often taken Natasha to eat at The Sheridan Café. As a child, Natasha enjoyed grilled vegetarian cheese and drank something called a black-and-white oat milkshake while her mother sipped a coffee equivalent and greeted neighborhood friends in an effort to live what she called a "normal life." Whatever she thought *normal* could be for a former First Lady who'd married the most famous and beloved of Jovians.

The waitress came up behind them and handed

Natasha a menu. "Hey, Evan, how's it going?" she said, making a snapping sound with something bright pink in her mouth.

Evan removed her big coat and settled into a booth with shiny green seating. Before they'd left the house, she'd brushed her hair with its long side-swept bangs, changed her shirt, and put on a baggie pair of black pants. The fact that her eyes were a dark shade of brown rather than blue-green like Evander's seemed wrong—but she still resembled him quite a bit.

"What was that in her mouth?" Natasha whispered once the waitress had gone.

"Oh, it's just chewing gum," Evan said with an amused smile. "You don't have gum where you come from?"

"I don't think we do. Or maybe my parents just didn't let me. I was five when I left home."

"Where are you from again?" Evan asked.

"Earth," Natasha said, her voice devoid of joking, though her lips curled with mischief. "But a different universe than this one."

"Okay." Evan's eyes lingered a moment before she went back to scanning the menu. The waitress returned and asked for drink orders.

"I'll have water, lots of ice," Natasha said, and Evan added, "Yeah, me, too, I guess."

"Two waters it is." The waitress spun away, stopping at the table beside theirs.

"So," Evan closed her menu and put it aside, "my mom says you and your dad are relatives, but she didn't say from which side."

"From *your* side, actually. And my side. Or, the Jovian side," Natasha said, knowing all of that would sound mysterious.

Evan chewed one of her fingernails. "I don't know what that means." Her knee jiggled under the table.

Evan differed from Evander in her lack of absolute calm. Maybe his charm and maturity, too, his way of making a person feel liked. Though, she also embodied a familiarity that could not be denied: her mannerisms, facial expressions, the way her eyes lingered after she spoke.

Overall, Evan was proving herself to be smartly cautious, and that was good.

"What's healthy here?" Natasha asked.

"They have really good mushroom burgers."

"Perfect."

"Are you vegetarian?" Evan asked.

"Of course," Natasha said. "I can't believe they serve old-fashioned beef burgers here. I have to stop myself from barging into the kitchen and lecturing the cooks on the error of their ways."

Evan laughed. "I know what you mean."

The waitress returned, and Evan told her what they wanted.

Instead of scribbling it down, the woman eyed the watch upon her wrist. "You sure? It's not even nine o'clock yet."

"We were up super-early," Evan said.

"Gotcha," she said, pointing with her pen before speeding away.

"Listen," Natasha said, getting down to business. "I'm going to tell you something that may surprise you."

Evan provided her full attention.

"My father, the man who's talking to your mother right now, is actually your brother."

"Oh, wow, he's *that* Evander? I wasn't sure."

She was not as shocked as she should be.

"Someone has already told you," Natasha said.

"Told me?"

"About the Jovians. About my father. Who was it, was it your mom? Or maybe you've had a visitor? Was it Uncle Jimmy?"

Evan took the straw out of her drink and fiddled with it. "All these years, I thought it was just a story. So, you really are from another universe?"

Natasha tried speaking directly into Evan's mind: *You bet I am,* she said.

Evan turned first a shade of white and then blushed red. A puff of a cough escaped her parted lips. "That was a little scary . . . but so cool!"

"I wasn't sure it would work," Natasha said. "Don't worry, I'm not reading your thoughts. I don't have that ability yet."

"Yet?" she said, her eyes dilating with awe.

The waitress stopped by and slid their plates onto the table. "Here you go, ladies. Enjoy."

Evan thanked her and grabbed a French fry, then dropped it and rubbed the oil from her fingers. "Don't eat them yet," she said, "you'll burn your mouth off."

Natasha didn't plan to. She needed her mouth for talking more than she needed it for eating. "So, the person who told you about the Jovians, was it an old guy, messy hair, sizable stomach?"

"I believe you're describing my grandfather, Grandpa James."

Natasha thought about that for a second. Uncle Jimmy was Andrew's birth father, so they could be talking about the same person. But Uncle Jimmy was also Jovian, so that *didn't* make sense for this world.

"You look unsure." Evan pressed on her mushroom burger's bun to make it more manageable, Natasha supposed, before lifting it to her mouth.

"I might know your grandpa. In my world, his name is Uncle Jimmy, and he kidnapped me three years ago—but don't worry, there were very important reasons he did it."

The way Evan laughed with abandon startled Natasha into silence. She wasn't used to such unencumbered displays of emotion.

"I'm not worried," Evan said through a mouthful of food. "He was my grandfather. I trusted him completely." Then, not quite so boldly, she added, "And I just met you, so . . ."

Natasha detected the possibility of a trust issue between them. "What did he tell you?"

"He basically said that Evander, and possibly some others, would one day visit, and I needed to listen to what they said. It would be important." She dipped a fry in ketchup and blew on it. "A very serious matter," she said.

"That's true. It is," Natasha said.

"Wait a second. I just realized something." Evan paused to wipe her mouth with a paper napkin. "If Evander is my brother, then you're my . . . niece. Is that right?"

That brought another eruption of laughter.

Natasha eased into the booth's backrest. "If you think that's weird, you're really going to like what comes next. I'm only eight years old. I've been alive the equivalent of eight and a half Earth years. According to my dad's bodyguard."

"Evander has a bodyguard?"

"Dad was the president where we come from, so we've had bodyguards for as long as I've been alive."

They stared at each other. Natasha could see that Evan had become stuck in her thoughts. Soon enough, however, she swiped her bangs to the side and said, "That's crazy. I always knew Mom wasn't telling me something."

"You have good instincts," Natasha told her.

"And you're eight years old. You don't talk like an eight-year-old, and you sure don't look like one."

"I like how nothing freaks you out. You're showing a lot of potential right now."

"I can't believe you just said that. That's something my grandfather always said to me."

Natasha liked the way the conversation was going, and the fact that Uncle Jimmy tried to prepare Evan for their arrival—even if it was Uncle Jimmy from a different universe.

"Potential for what, though?" Evan asked. "What's going on? Why did you and your father go through the trouble of visiting us?"

"He needs to talk to your mom. I think something happened before she came here. The thing is, I need to get him home to my mother and brother as soon as possible, so we can't stay long."

"You came all this way just so our parents can talk?"

"Seems ridiculous, I know. But my dad insisted it had to be done. He's not getting any younger, I'm sure you've noticed."

"I did," she said soberly. "Whatever he wants to talk about must be really important." Evan finished the last bit of her mushroom burger, then said, "You haven't touched your food."

As hungry as she was, Natasha pushed her plate out of the way and leaned in. "Listen, it's not just about my dad. I might have an important reason to be here too."

"Which is?" Evan picked up a few fries and dipped them into the tiny paper cup filled with ketchup.

"I'm pretty sure I'm supposed to tell you a story."

Evan smiled crookedly and exhaled a resigned breath. "The Jovians really like their stories."

Natasha put on her game face. "This one is about you."

"Really? Oh wow," Evan said, covering her mouth as she chewed. "Wait, I can't tell if you're joking."

"I've never been more serious in my eight-year-old life."

Chapter 13

Outskirts of Philadelphia, Pennsylvania

D mitri didn't like the cart they'd been using for a wheelchair, a big metal food-shopping basket so old that the store's logo, once etched into the plastic flap, had completely rubbed off. The metal rungs dug into his back and left sore indentations in his skin—and it felt undignified to be transported like one would transport bags of rice. Alexandria placed cardboard on the bottom and lay a dusty blanket she'd found in an abandoned building over it, but it wasn't exactly soft or comfortable. Plus, it smelled moldy.

Gripping the push bar with both hands, Alexandria leaned into the wagon, applying her weight in a downward motion so the two front wheels levered up a few inches from the ground, clearing the curb and riding up the short ramp. She struggled to force the small metal wheels over the threshold as they made their rattly entrance into the food kitchen's dining hall.

"Darn cart," Alexandria grumbled in Russian. "Never should have left home. Never will again if I ever find a way . . . " Her words collapsed into nothingness.

Once a day, when Alexandria's hunger bested her agoraphobia, they ventured out from the hideout they lived in.

Dmitri wished she'd let him eat more, but he couldn't tell her because while his mind worked as it should, the rest of his body remained asleep. Unresponsive and unfeeling, except for the occasional undulation of pins and needles that traveled his shoulder or leg, sometimes the small of his back. Every now and then he could open his eyes some of the way, but other times he couldn't open them at all. Only yesterday, he'd lifted his head in the morning just to have it faint right back. Alexandria had missed the whole thing.

He hadn't spoken a word since the day she'd carried him to the old abandoned shed ten days ago. He couldn't imagine that much time had passed, but each night after the sun went down, Alexandria scraped another notch into the wooden wall in their hideout, so he knew it to be true.

Ten days ago, he'd been literally bursting with energy.

After he exploded the door at the airport, and grabbed Alexandria's hand down the hall, several of Conseco's team had chased them to the elevator just as a man walked out. And that had been the only reason they escaped. The elevator doors promptly closed, and he and Alexandria rose to the first floor. After that, it had been easy to blend into the crowded corridor of arrivals. Instead of leaving the airport, as their pursuers surely expected them to, they ducked into one of the airport's bars. Bad weather in Chicago had caused a backlog of departures that left hundreds of people with hours to kill. Plenty of time for them to have a drink—or many.

Amid the party atmosphere, Alexandria and Dmitri (and his boiling energy) became lost in the milling crowd. Dmitri began to sweat, and he couldn't stop fidgeting, which was fine because the music pulsating through the bars' speakers inspired people who couldn't find an empty seat or barstool to dance in place while they drank and told stories. After a few minutes of blending in, Dmitri and Alexandria pulled up their hoods and joined the stream of arrivals who followed signs that led to ground transportation.

Hand in hand, with his zapping energy transferring between them—"I have so much energy when we hold hands!" Alexandria exclaimed—they slipped through rows of cars in the parking garage and followed signs to the highway. They jogged along the shoulder for a time, then slipped into whatever brush grew beyond it and pressed forward until they found themselves at the foot of a bridge. The traffic backed up for as far as Dmitri could see. But the bridge offered a narrow walking lane.

Dmitri said, "Let's go," and started toward it, but Alexandria pulled back, her hand slipping through his fingers.

"I'm not going up there." She gazed at the bridge and then quickly looked away, into the woods, her movements flustered, like a nervous bird.

"But we have to." He gestured strenuously for her to retake his hand. "They're going to find us if we don't hurry."

She turned and pointed into the woods. "Let's just go that way."

He frowned at her. "What's over there?"

"Nothing is over there, Dmitri," she cried. "I just can't do it. I can't cross this bridge. I hate bridges. Once we get up there, I'll freeze, and we'll be stuck. What if I accidentally jump over the side?" She covered her mouth and then rubbed her eyes before her alarmed expression crinkled into a cry.

"It's a short bridge," he said. "I can carry you. I promise you won't jump. I won't let you."

"I'm too big. If you carry me, my legs will drag behind you, and we'll draw too much attention: a skinny boy lugging a big old lady like me."

"I can do it," he said.

Traffic continued to move at a glacial pace beside them, the hum of engines trailing along the highway's endless curves and flow. He had no idea how short or long the bridge was. All he knew was they needed to cross it.

"I just blew up a wall, so I'm certain I can get you across this bridge one way or another," he said.

"Oh, I didn't know what happened," she said, gazing once again into the woods as if she might take off in that direction. "I heard a loud bang and then cement crumbling, and suddenly you were calling my name—"

"We have to hurry," he said, holding out his hand. "Come on."

Not far away, in the long line of stopped traffic, a car door slammed. A quick look told him it was a tall woman dressed in white. Javenport. Probably not the Javenport he'd met because she'd short-circuited in the blast. A different Javenport.

"My hand will give you the energy you need," he said, "and I will not let go."

She nodded, her mouth slack. "Okay, I guess." She moved toward him.

With fingers entwined and energy coursing between them, they started up the hill of the bridge and veered into the walking path.

"Pull your hood around your face," he shouted. "Don't let them see you!"

The wind reached for them, pushed them forward, seemed almost like it wanted to help—then it spun around and came at them. Javenport's presence somewhere amid the traffic inspired Dmitri to move fast even when his muscles began to ache.

Soon rocky ground replaced the rushing water beneath the bridge, and the forest emerged in the near distance. The ground came up close beneath them, and as soon as Dmitri saw a clear space without rocks, they left the walking path, hopped the cement divider, and dropped to the ground below. Then they ran.

They didn't rest until they reached a shadowy grove of pines. Out of breath and in pain, they let themselves fall upon the pine-straw-covered ground. Curled into fetal positions, neither of them spoke for several minutes.

Dmitri rolled onto his back. The rest had restored him, and he assumed Alexandria would feel the same way, though she remained panting on her side.

"We better keep moving," he said as he stood. He reached for Alexandria's hand to help hoist her when a sudden whirl of dizziness overtook him. Like a glass bottle that cracks, Dmitri's strength spilled out. He stood on his own two legs one second, then lost all feeling in them the next. His knees gave out, and he hit the ground.

"What? No, no, no," Alexandria shouted. "What are you doing?"

He couldn't even open his eyes.

Poor, nervous Alexandria frantically crawled to him and turned him over, then checked for breath coming from his nose. "Mitya, where have you gone?"

She brushed the pine straw from his face before shaking him and patting his cheek. Her jagged breaths cascaded over his face, and he imagined her sweaty complexion turning red. Though he couldn't move his body nor open his eyes, he remained fully conscious with no way to let her know.

"Okay, I can see what you want me to do, and this is not fair. You want me to carry you even though it is you who are supposed to carry *me*."

Alexandria scooped him up with both arms. His head fell back on one side, one limp arm dangled in the middle, and his feet bobbed freely on the other side. She carried him for he didn't know how long. Every once in a while, she plunked down on the ground to rest, grumbling about how unfair it was that he wouldn't wake up, and then she stood again and continued on for a time before dropping down once again. In this way, they eventually reached a neighborhood with close-together houses. Dmitri's lids bobbed open now and again, and he caught glimpses of unkempt yards with rusted metal fences. Old, beat-up cars, the kind that ran on gasoline instead of solar or electric. Homes left in the hands of decay and disorder.

Alexandria took him to an abandoned shed in between two houses. Where were they? He didn't know. They'd flown into the airport in Philadelphia, so he supposed they'd entered the outskirts of the city.

That night was cold, and Alexandria dressed Dmitri in every piece of clothing he'd brought with him—two sweaters, two pairs of pants, two socks. She had only what she'd worn to his house and her raincoat, which she wrapped around herself like a blanket.

Cars chugged by with their radios thumping. The slough of feet over a gravelly street startled them both from peace, the laughter of groups of people they didn't know trailing behind. He and Alexandria remained in the shadows of their little broken-down shed. The worst part was that he couldn't tell her to stop crying or that they would be all right or even that he would recover, because he couldn't move, couldn't speak. But he knew in his heart they would be okay, that soon enough he would regain his strength.

The question was, how long could they hide before Canseco and Javenport, or someone else, found them?

In the meantime, Alexandria took Dmitri to this free cafeteria once a day, where she carefully propped him up and spooned broth and water into his mouth and whispered for him to "Get better, please get better, Mitya." Her constant tears left red rings around her swollen eyes. How could she have so many tears? He was feeling some small bits of strength, but she didn't know. The pins and needles came to him each morning and sometimes in the afternoon. Soon he'd be able to move. His strength would return, he knew it would.

Alexandria rolled Dmitri in the old shopping cart to an empty table and pulled out a chair for herself.

And suddenly he opened his eyes.

Alexandria squealed when she noticed. At the same time, a man in a blue apron approached them. "I've seen you around here a few times now," he said. "You okay?"

Alexandria startled, then shook her head so that her long, dirty hair covered most of her face.

The man had a deep, kind voice and way about him. "Where you from?" he asked.

"No English," she muttered and drew the wagon with Dmitri closer to her.

The man gestured to Dmitri with the rag in his hand. "Does he need medical attention?" He pulled up a chair from the table beside theirs, and Alex's complexion turned a shade of gray.

"It's okay," he said, placing the cloth on the table. "You're not in any trouble."

"No English," she said again, her voice quivering.

"I don't mean to upset you." He stood slowly, rubbing

the cloth across the surface of the table, the muscles in his bicep bulging with dark, indecipherable tattoos. "If you want to go to the shelter, there's a brochure over there, on the way out. It's a safe space for unhoused people. They might even have a wheelchair they can give you."

Alexandria said nothing. She just sniffed up her tears and put on a blank face until the man walked away.

After that, she stood in the food line and came back and fed Dmitri clear broth. "Finally you open your eyes," she said, smiling down on him. "Soon you will move for me, right? Please, please, Mitya, say you will."

Dmitri breathed in deeply and tried very hard to make his vocal cords work, but nothing came. Alexandria put an apple in the kangaroo pocket of her sweatshirt, and then took him, in the cart, to the bathroom, where she locked the door behind them. There, Dmitri withstood the discomfort of having someone in the stall with him, helping him to go. Not that this was new to him, nor was it something Alexandria hadn't done before. He'd lived with it forever, and it didn't normally bother him—it was just a fact of life—though as he got older and his body started to change, he felt a sense of indignity at times. It had to happen, so it was not something he allowed his thoughts to linger on.

He wanted to go to the shelter but knew Alexandria worried someone would look for them there. Instead, they'd stay in the shed in between two abandoned houses. Cool, dark, and confined, the shed had everything Alex's agoraphobia demanded.

As they followed the bumpy sidewalk to their home, he thought about how even someone who was not afraid to leave the house would be fearful in their circumstance. People were after them, and because Dmitri's power had drained away and took his everyday strength with it, it was up to Alexandria to keep them safe, not to mention, to make all the decisions.

He wanted to remind her about the money he'd taken from his mother, but until the rest of his body started working again, he couldn't so much as signal or write her a message. Alexandria wouldn't want to leave their abandoned shed anyway. They'd been safe there so far, and that would be reason enough to stay. The people looking for them would be checking hotels.

In the meantime, he'd withstand the hunger, the awkwardness of the metal wagon, and the dirt of the abandoned shed—and concentrate on regaining his faculties.

In the morning, he woke with a terrible crick in his neck. Arching his back, he stretched his arms—realizing all at once that he could move. He sat up and made a strained sound as his neck and shoulders veered off to the side for no reason. He welcomed the familiar, jerky motion.

Alexandria jolted from a light sleep. "Dmitri? You're moving!"

"It is-ah coming back," he said, smiling in his normal way.

"Oh thank goodness, finally!" she whispered in Russian.

"Now we can go to Great-grandmother's," he said.

"What? No. I want to go home," she cried.

He knew she was going to say that.

"I don't trust your Great-gran. I don't trust anyone."

"'Cept for me," he said.

She lowered her chin and slumped tiredly.

"Don't be afraid, Alex. They will help us."

"The Jovians will help *you*," she said, her hands shaking

and tears returning. "I'm just some Russian they don't know."

"I need more food. Hungry!" he said as forcefully as he could.

"No. I don't like to go out. I don't want to feed you like this anymore."

"I am healing. Feed-ah me!"

She sniffled and looked away. "I don't know how much more of this I can take."

"Stop crying," he said. "You wrinkle like an old lady when you cry."

She turned and gazed at him, a soft hurt in her eyes. But then a smile crept over her face.

"I will take you out for food, and then we will go to the liquor store, and you will buy me vodka," she declared, punctuating the thought by swiping away the tears that had collected in the swells under her eyes.

"You know I have money in my bag."

"Of course."

"You could have taken it."

"I'm not a thief."

"Yes, I know-ah," he said, his brow teetering as he did his version of an eye roll. "Thank you, Alex, for taking care of me." He made the most gracious face he could, but who knows what she saw.

She bit a piece of skin from her dry lips. "Just get back to normal, please. I want to go home."

Chapter 14

Kirksberg, Pennsylvania

"Hey guys, the fog is making surprisingly quick progress today," Fran said. "Looks like it's been heading inland all night. I've sent you all a report."

Nearby Coalition members turned their attention to the wristcomms and various screens and devices about the room.

Connie glanced up from where she lounged on a couch someone had squeezed in between two computer stations, but she didn't move. Lisa spoke with Anders in the entry to the library and gave Fran the one-second finger.

"Have you seen this, Connie?" he said, pointing to the paper screen he was reading. "Come over here for a minute."

They'd taken some time off to regroup after Drew died —just a few days—but it hadn't helped much. Connie remained listless and uncaring, like an injured animal. Dressed in the same black army boots and black tee and shorts every day (a punk rock look, though Fran doubted she knew much about punk rockers), she was the epitome of a loved one in mourning. He'd always suspected Drew and Connie were more than co-leaders in the cause, even if neither of them publicly acknowledged their relationship. Fran recognized love when he saw it, just like he recognized mourning.

He also worried Connie's behavior pointed to something more than grief. She displayed the slumpy low energy of one who didn't care what happened to the world at large, though something about her vibe simmered aggressively below the surface. He'd watched her gaze at the ceiling for hours, her expression displaying an intensity common to those who hatch plans of ill demise. And sometimes she literally disappeared for hours at a time. Fran didn't know if that was because he couldn't see her wandering among them inside the bunker, or because she'd left the premises.

Could she be planning to avenge Drew's death in some way? And if so, which of the Jovians would she target?

Whenever she made her presence known, Fran struck up a conversation with her, hoping to entice her to resume her position as Coalition leader. He asked what steps she wanted to see them take moving forward. He wanted her to know she remained a crucial part of the organization and needed to resume her responsibilities.

He even tried to ask her how she was doing, as a friend would, but she had yet to respond to questions of the personal kind.

The atmosphere in the bunker had changed quite a bit without Drew's oversized ego filling it up. The clones and hybrids continued to work as if he were still with them, guiding them, inspiring them. All of them dedicated to a new world where clones enjoyed freedom of choice, the same way Drew had been.

Monitoring the situation with the Moon Children was number one on that list.

Connie rose from the couch with the enthusiasm of a sloth, dragging the heels of her boots across the floor. She collided with the chair beside Fran and gazed at the screen with tired eyes. The map Fran had pulled up showed a thick fog over some parts of the Great Lakes and the surrounding land, and there were even some cloud patches following the country's tributaries, like veins carrying a disease to distant parts of the body.

"Some of that could be regular fog, no?" Connie asked.

"Yeah, I'm sure some of it is. It's hard to say."

"If all of it is the Moon Children, they're doing a darn good job of spreading for a race that doesn't travel well," Connie said.

"It's troubling because there's absolutely nothing we can do to stop them when they're in vapor form."

"Caroline can probably stop them."

Could it be that simple?

"What do you mean?" Fran lifted his coffee and took a sip.

"I mean, if Edmund knows how to deal with them, then she must know too."

"I just assumed Caroline wasn't the best negotiator in the family, that Edmund could persuade their leader, and Caroline wouldn't be able to."

Connie placed the screen on top of the bar. "You're right about that. She wouldn't. She has the emotional intelligence of a one-year-old and zero likeability."

He laughed with unexpected vigor. This was more words than Connie had spoken in days. Still, she didn't join him in his laughter. Not even a grin.

"But she knows what needs to be done, is my point,"

Connie said. "She has information we could most likely use to contain them, or maybe even banish them."

"Uh-huh," Fran said, wondering if there was more to what Connie was saying. In the days after Drew died, she'd flat out blamed the Jovians for his sudden death. It didn't make sense to Fran because Drew had died of a heart attack the same way Andrew had. By way of DNA, it really was "written in the stars," and Fran didn't understand why she couldn't see that. Fran assumed that choosing to feel vengeful appealed to Connie more than choosing to feel her loss.

"So, what are you saying?" he asked. "You want to speak to Caroline?"

Connie leaned back in the chair in a carefree manner as if casually considering it, but he could tell her thinking went far beyond casual. She was only acting the part, and as Drew had pointed out, Jovians were not the best actors. In reality, Fran suspected, she'd been thinking about this for days, and she wanted him to get on board with whatever plan she'd hatched. He sensed a simmering-teakettle kind of energy just below her easygoing exterior.

"Talking to Caroline, I think, could be very helpful," she said. "Possibly extremely helpful."

"Yeah, but something tells me she won't take a call from us."

She breathed out a laugh that had nothing to do with good humor. "No, she won't."

"Are you thinking of showing yourself at one of her meetings?"

"No," she said, holding his gaze. "I'm thinking of going into the tubes and bringing her back here."

"Here? To the bunker? On her own volition?"

"Probably not."

Now he laughed the way people do in response to a

ridiculous idea. Because this was damned ridiculous. And reckless, too.

"I'm serious," Connie said. "I think we should escort her here and—"

"Make her want to take her true form?" he said loudly.

"She can't take her true form if she's in the bunker. There's not enough room."

They both tipped their heads back and observed the rounded ceiling one-and-a-half stories above. Crazy to think it wouldn't be high enough to house her alien body.

"That's true," Fran said. "But even if you could get her here, what about her Leonards? You know they'll figure out where she is. Once you bring her here, you'll have revealed our location and endangered all the clones who live here."

"I have a plan for the Leonards," she said with Drew's level of confidence. "Trust me."

"I'll trust you when I hear the plan and like it."

Lisa joined them. "What's up, guys? This conversation seems to have taken a loud and animated turn. Did something happen?"

"Connie thinks it would be a good idea to drag Caroline over here and have a chat about the Moon Children."

Lisa looked to Connie, no judgment on her face. "You think she'll work with us?"

Fran grumbled. "Not voluntarily."

"She might," Connie said.

"Be honest," he said. "You just told me you basically want to kidnap her."

"But maybe we won't have to." Connie's wide-eyed response reeked of false innocence. "Maybe she has a reason to want to work with us."

Mysterious ideas like this one made Fran want to spit. "Explain," he said.

"Well, right now many of her clones and hybrids trust us and want what we want for the future: freedom for clones and hybrids. They're behind us, not her. We're leading them—or Drew was leading them, mainly, but their loyalty endures for the moment," she said, her voice softening at the mention of Drew. "The oneness is broken, so Caroline doesn't have the dictatorship she once had. Without taking her natural form, all she has under her command are her security squad, her Leonards, and whatever devout clones are left, which is not many."

"The equivalent of an army, as small as it is," Fran muttered.

"Her power is seriously lacking," Connie said. "But President Abela doesn't know that. She still thinks Caroline reigns over all clones and hybrids. The one thing Caroline does have is the ability to take her true form and retake control that way. But she hasn't done that since the Battle of Philadelphia three years ago."

That captured Fran's attention.

"You would think she would have taken her true form by now just to re-assert her authority, to remind the clones who's boss," Connie continued. "And I've been watching her closely every week, staring at her because she doesn't know I'm there. Ever since David died, she's different. I can't put my finger on it, but I sense something's up. Like, she looks seriously worn out."

Lisa raised her brow. "Someone's been doing her homework."

Fran wondered if Connie wasn't just projecting. "Tell me what could be up, for instance. Give me some possibilities." He might have been as impressed as Lisa was, but he didn't want to let on quite yet.

"Well, her grandson left the planet to consult with Edmund, her obviously disgruntled former partner, and then David died as we all know. Then, during the Mars launch, she barely escaped the Moon Children, and soon after Miranda and Leo, who weren't as lucky, became ill and quickly left for Mars."

"Who does that leave Caroline with?" Lisa said.

"No one," Connie said. "She's alone. For the first time, she doesn't have anyone to support her."

"She has her Leonards," Fran said.

"Yeah," Connie said, "and you know what they're like."

He grunted in agreement. "Not exactly a joy to be around. Definitely too caveman-ish for Caroline's tastes."

"Exactly," Connie said.

"But something tells me she wouldn't care if she ended up completely alone," Fran said.

"I think it's taking a toll," Connie said. "I've seen changes in her. She seems sad at times. And it's not like Caroline to display emotion."

Fran remembered how Caroline hadn't mourned Andrew at all. "And this plan of yours has nothing to do with wanting revenge for Drew's death?" he asked.

"Fran, stop," Lisa said. "How could you say such a thing?"

"Why do you blame the Jovians?" he asked, staring Connie down.

Her thin, angular face sharpened as a dark defiance crept into her eyes. She pressed her lips together in a straight line, probably to keep contained the harsh language she wanted to spew. Perhaps he'd hit the nail on the head.

"They knew Drew had a heart problem," she said, her words thick with venom. "Their own son had died, and Drew had the very same DNA. They could have sent him to Mintaka for a transplant. Years ago, Drew made the request. He was Caroline's highest in charge, her favorite, and she still denied him. No explanation. She simply said no."

"I'm so sorry, Connie," Lisa said, putting her hand on her shoulder. "That's horrible."

"So, this *is* about revenge, then," Fran said.

"This is about saving the planet from the Moon Children," Connie insisted, and she banged the counter with her fist. The activity within the bunker went silent around them. "After that, it's about a better life for the clones. That's what Drew wanted, and that's what I want. I'll never stop fighting for our freedom."

Fran had been correct: simmering teakettle.

All the Coalition members within earshot raised their fists in the air and shouted, "Here-here."

"I understand," Fran said. "Let's get a plan together. This could take a while."

Connie's mouth fell open. She looked starstruck.

Lisa touched her arm and said, "Are you okay?"

"I just didn't think you two would agree with me," she said. "Especially, him." She jutted her chin in Fran's direction.

"Well, I do," Fran said. "Dire times require dire plans. And you know the Jovians better than anybody. Plus, I trust you. Don't you know that by now?"

The defeated vibe that had weighed Connie down for days seemed to have toppled from her shoulders, and for the first time in weeks, she stood straight, her head held high.

"I've always trusted you," Lisa told her.

"And her gut is never wrong," Fran thumbed toward his wife. "So let's get to work."

Chapter 15

Kecksberg, Pennsylvania

A Universe Without Jovians

When Natasha and Evan returned from their trip to the café, they went to the front door of the house but found it locked. They knocked but no one came. "They're probably sitting in the backyard," Evan said, so they walked down the driveway beside the hedges that lined the side of the house. Soon they arrived at an old-fashioned wood gate.

The gate opened to a stepping-stone walkway that led to a three-step staircase up to the deck. The murmur of conversation wafted toward them, and Natasha touched Evan's shoulder. "Don't go up yet," she whispered. "I want to hear this."

The girls crouched beside the stairs, where they could view the back of Svetlana and Evander's heads through the deck's spindles without being noticed. The mother and son sat side by side in a pair of chaise lounge chairs, a blanket over Evander's legs.

"So, you're happy?" Evander said. "Or you were? Living here? Being married to him again."

"You sound exactly like Andrew," Svetlana said. "He asked the same questions. And I told him, 'Yes, I am happy. I love my life.' Then he died, and believe me, I wish he hadn't. But people die, whether it is in this world or the Jovian one. I wasn't prepared because I thought we were safe here. I assumed his heart condition would not carry over. But no one in life is safe no matter what universe you live in," she said. "We had five wonderful years together. He was able to be a father to Evan. That's something the other universe did not grant us."

"I'm happy for him in that way, and for you," Evander said.

Svetlana turned toward him with slow deliberation. "I didn't expect to have a girl," she said, glancing at him guiltily. "I assumed I would have another boy, a different . . . you."

"I'm sure it was a shock," he said, "but it doesn't upset me, if you're worried about that. I told you some things would be different."

"Yes," she said, "you tried to prepare me. You told me I was going to a world without Jovians, and you said it would most likely be different in other ways as well. I guess what I'm trying to say is that I've missed you. I've missed you so much." Her voice strained. "You have no idea. I'd see other young men with their families, and each time it broke my heart."

"I'm sorry." He reached out to hold her hand. "I'm sorrier than you know."

Natasha wondered if she should suggest she and Evan leave. Would hearing these things hurt Evan's feelings?

"There's something I have to tell you," Evander continued. "Something that has weighed on me for years."

"I'm sure that whatever it is, is not as bad as you think," Svetlana said.

"Back when you still lived on the Jovian Earth, after the family took me to Jupiter and you searched for me," he said in a slow and careful manner, "Caroline convinced me that it would be best if you left Earth. At the time, I agreed. You weren't happy, and I knew that. I told her I could make it happen, that I could get you on the spaceship that would take you away. But I should have thought it through more carefully. I shouldn't have pushed you."

"You didn't do it for Caroline," Svetlana said with an intensity that could have been mistaken for anger. "I *know* you did it for me, that your intentions were good. Because you felt it was the best thing. And you wanted me to have what I longed for. It was a selfless act."

"I did want that for you," he said, easing back. "It wasn't until later that I grew to regret it. I shouldn't have pushed you so hard."

A cold wind rushed across the yard and flustered the dead leaves high in the branches of the yard's tall oak. Natasha wondered if that would be the end of the conversation.

Evander's voice wavered when he next spoke. "You could have stayed in that world with me. Sometimes I think you should have."

"Evander, no," Svetlana said. "You had important work to do. I *wanted* to be with Andrew without his family bearing down on us. Please believe me. There is no reason for you to feel guilt."

"The fact is, I sold you on the idea." He rubbed his forehead. "That's my strength, convincing people to do things, giving them the courage. But, as it turns out, Caroline may not have had our best interests in mind."

She shook her head with vehemence and adjusted her position on the chair so she could face him. "I don't care what Caroline wanted. I'm not angry with you, if that's what you think. You went on to be the president who healed the planet. It was for the best that I left. I might have killed Caroline otherwise, and then you would not have been elected because your mother would have been a murderer."

He laughed, but Natasha recognized that laugh. It required effort.

"I also promised to protect the humans," he said. "And right now, every one of them is in danger."

"That can't be your fault. You are only one man."

"Whether it's my fault or it isn't, I can't protect them," he said with the undiluted honesty Natasha admired. "Edmund has sent the Moon Children to Earth." He paused and looked to the sky. "The results will be devastating."

"I don't know what that is, but I am sorry to hear it," Svetlana said.

"They're a species from the Jupiter System, and they're deadly. They'll kill the clones and ravage the land. There will be no stopping them."

Svetlana laughed angrily. "That's what I don't understand about Jovians. They say they want to help, but then they do something like this. It doesn't make sense."

"He sent them to stop Caroline. She's become possessive of Earth. As if it's hers to do whatever she likes. She's made an army of clones, some of them violent. And she showed the entire world her true form."

"What form is that?"

"Her Jovian form. She's one of the largest that ever lived. And when she did it, when she stood six stories high for all the world to see, she frightened the entire planet into bowing to her rule."

Svetlana went silent and pale. "Is there no American president? No Earth leaders of the human kind?"

"Oh, there are, but the American president quite readily does Caroline's bidding."

With an aura of concern, Svetlana lay back once again, stretching her legs and gazing pensively at the sky. "I suppose every universe has its tragedies. Caroline never knew how to play nice with others."

"I wish I could put it aside, not worry about it, but I can't. What happens there affects what happens here. If there's a tragedy there, there will be a tragedy of some sort here as well."

Evan grabbed Natasha's arm and whispered, "Is that true?"

"It is," Natasha said.

Svetlana made a disgusted sound, a cross between a moan and a groan. "Of course there will be a tragedy. It's never simple with the Jovians. Even when I get away from them, I am not free of them."

"I'm so sorry, Mom," Evander continued. "I'm sorry I failed you. I promised I'd take care of the humans—"

"You could *never* fail me," she said. "Never. You have a pure heart. I've always known that. Whatever is happening on Earth is not your doing. And I *chose* to come here. You gave me a second chance at a happy life. How many people are granted such a wonderful thing?"

He said nothing in response, and Natasha knew why: it would take more than one conversation to rid him of years of guilt, to topple his self-appointed responsibility to take care of everyone and everything, especially his family.

"No more about this," Svetlana said. "I want to hear about you. Tell me about your health. You look quite tired

—probably from bearing the weight of the world upon your shoulders. Do you need a doctor while you are here?"

"I don't think so," he said.

"How long will you stay?"

"I don't think I'll be leaving." He turned to face her.

"So, you'll stay," she said, with cautious optimism. "I didn't realize that was an option."

Natasha watched her father's sad smile appear, and she knew all at once what he meant.

"Unfortunately, I won't be staying either," he answered softly.

Svetlana squeezed her eyes shut. "Don't say that."

Natasha bowed her head and stared at the ground. It was just as she suspected. Well, she wouldn't let him do it. They had to go home. She wasn't going to leave him here.

Evan put her hand on Natasha's shoulder and whispered, "Are you okay?"

"I'm fine," she said, giving the answer she wished were true.

Evander took Svetlana's hand and leaned toward her. "I need a promise from you."

"Anything," she told him. "You know that."

"Bring Natasha home. Bring her back to Nadia and Dmitri."

She pulled back her hand, but he continued to hold it.

"You want me to time travel?" she said, glaring at him. "Oh, I don't know, Evander—"

"I'll show you how. It's not difficult," he said.

She stared at the hand that gripped hers until he finally let go and sank back into the chair.

"I'll do anything for you," she said, "but don't make me go back into that world. If Caroline knows I'm there, she might not let me leave. I'm afraid I'll be stuck. And then what will Evan do?"

"All you have to do is take Natasha home," he said, pleading. "You don't have to leave the ship. You can make the return trip immediately."

"But what if something were to go wrong?"

"I'm sorry to ask you to do this. I wouldn't, except that she's so young, a lot younger than she looks."

Svetlana nodded with a pained look. "Just like you, I suppose. A baby and a grownup at the same time."

"Yes."

"But what about Evan?" Svetlana said. "She's young too. What if I don't make it back? She has no father. Her grandparents have passed. She'll be alone. I can't. I just can't."

Evan met Natasha's eyes. "Should we be listening to this?"

"No, but I have to," Natasha whispered. "You can leave if you want."

"But you *will* make it back," Evander said loudly. "I wouldn't ask you if I didn't believe that. I even asked Uncle Jimmy, and he said he saw signs of—"

"*Don't!*" Svetlana stopped him. "I don't want to hear Uncle Jimmy's 'it's written in the stars' opinions."

"I'm sorry," he said, "I wouldn't ask if—"

"Natasha can stay here," she said firmly. "She can live with us. It's safer here. Bad things are happening on your Earth, so this will be better for her."

"She can't," he said in a quieter tone. "She can't stay here, and she can't stay on the other Earth for very long, either. It's her heart—"

He turned his head and immediately stopped talking. He'd seen them, crouched beside the deck's short staircase. Natasha ran up the steps, with Evan behind her whispering, "Wait. Are you sick?"

Natasha shouted "We're back," crossing the deck with an abundance of enthusiasm.

Enthusiasm had never been her thing.

"Hi, girls. How was your breakfast?" Evander's air of normalcy was anything but.

Up close she could feel his exhaustion, see his white, crinkling old age, and sense his heavyheartedness.

Beside him, Svetlana clasped her hands, the fingers gripping each other as if desperate to withstand the moment.

THAT NIGHT, once they'd entered the guest room they shared, Evander handed Natasha three polished black stones that vibrated in her hands. She sensed their power and wondered if she were to drop them, would they explode?

"Are these traveling stones?" she said. "Where did you get them?"

"They are, and I found them in my pants pocket this morning. That's how it sometimes works in the multiverse. What you need comes to you as you need it."

"Okay, but why give them to me?"

"I want you to hold them."

She didn't like that idea. "Why can't *you* hold them?"

He stepped away, toward his bed, and busied himself with the blanket there: pulling it taut, smoothing away wrinkles.

"Dad," she said, sitting on her own bed and carefully placing the stones on her night table, "you're going to make it back. You promised Mom you would. And what about Dmitri? He needs his father."

"I didn't say I wasn't going back."

"Yes, you did. I heard you tell Svetlana. And I also

heard her say she won't take me home. So you don't really have a choice."

He sat on the bed and hunched over his knees, then rubbed the crown of his head. What little hair he had left formed white tufts gentle as sea spray.

"You'll just have to take your medicine," she continued. "You'll be fine, I know you will."

He sat up straight. An odd, empty expression rested on his face. "There's no medicine left to take."

"How can that be?" she asked. "They didn't give you enough for a return trip?"

"They did. But I sensed it wouldn't work, so I doubled the dosage—"

"Did they say you could do that?"

He sighed and looked away, ashamed perhaps of his own misguided actions.

"Check your pockets," she said, hopefully. "If what you need comes to you—"

"I didn't mean *everything* you need."

Why is he making this difficult? She removed one of her uncomfortable vintage shoes and on a sudden volatile whim, flung it across the room. She hadn't even known she was going to do it until it released from her hand and thumped the wall above her father's bed. Worse, it hadn't nullified the gnarl of frustration within her.

"Natasha," he said, calm as ever. "What are you doing?"

She hunched over sheepishly and attempted to erase the scowl from her face. "I'm sorry," she said, spitting the words.

They both sat, each on his or her own bed, in silence.

"You came here to die," she said, unable to look at him. "And now you're asking me to let it happen. You're going to give up, and I'm supposed to let you." She paused in wait of a response that did not come. "That's not fair. If that's what you planned to do all along, you should have told me."

He opened his mouth to speak but no words came. Which meant she was right. This had been his plan.

He removed one sneaker, then the other, and placed them on the floor at the foot of his bed.

"You don't know how sorry I am," he said. "But how would telling you have helped? I needed to come here. This was my last wish. You've given me a great gift, don't you see?"

"It's not fair," she said. Heat welled in her eyes, and she wanted to surrender, to give in to it, but she couldn't. She couldn't let him go. "Maybe if you had told me, I could have prepared myself, or I could have made you take me home like you were supposed to instead of coming here. I wouldn't have agreed to this had I known. Maybe then you could have seen your wife and son one more time. You could have told them goodbye."

At that, her head started to spin the way it did whenever she reached a place beyond overwhelmed. Thoughts funneled around and around in a spiral that blurred into a stream of nothing she could grab on to or decipher or rationalize.

"You are extremely levelheaded," he told her, and the sight of his sad, drooping eyes acted like an anchor that stopped her, steadied her. They were still blue-green, still bright and filled with all the good in the world. "That's why I felt we could talk about this and you would understand. There's no way to prepare for a loved one's death," he said gently. "Even when their passing is slow, or when they know the end is near, the pain comes just the same."

"I'm not a rock," she said, hating the pout in her voice. "I *have* feelings."

"We can talk like this because you are consistently sensible, always practical," he told her. "You are the foundation upon which I stand."

She wanted to remain angry, but his flattery massaged her negative disposition. "I always thought Elsa played that role," she said. "I'm just your . . . eight-year-old adult." She smiled, allowing him the break in tension.

His cheeks turned a pale shade of pink, hinting at embarrassment. "I'm sorry you've grown up so fast. That is obviously my fault, my genes." He held out his hands and observed them with a scowl. "You've inherited the best and the worst of me."

"I agree with that," she said. "And I couldn't be happier about it."

"You'll be okay. No matter what. You can handle anything, Natasha. You really can."

That he thought so made her proud.

"By the way," he added as if this were an ordinary conversation, "your brother tried to reach me today."

More secrets. Why hadn't he told her sooner? "Well, that's good news, I guess," she said.

"Did you know Dmitri was an early bloomer in the communications department?"

"Early? I assumed he was late."

"He's telepathic. Possibly telekinetic as well."

Now *that* was interesting. "Really?"

"And yet, oddly," Evander said, rubbing the scruff of his chin, "when he reached out, I couldn't decipher what he was trying to say. And I know he couldn't hear me."

"Which is another reason you need to live long enough to get home," she said, with a flick of her brow.

The angst that had clouded the room a few moments before crept back in.

"Please, Dad, I know you can make it home if you try. Please, do it for me."

He nodded and stared numbly into the floor. "I wish I could."

"But you heard Svetlana. She won't bring me back. How will I get home?"

"I think she will. Be kind to her."

"If she doesn't take me, I'll just go myself," Natasha said, knowing he wouldn't like that idea.

"Please don't say that. You can't go alone."

"Why not? I can handle anything. You just said so."

"Svetlana can keep you from panicking if something were to happen with the ship . . . or if you were knocked out of your sleep cycle."

"You're afraid I'll panic if I wake mid-journey? I have *never* panicked in my entire life."

"Your 'entire life' has been just eight years in which you have time traveled exactly once," he said, his determination rising with the volume of his voice.

She bowed her head in surrender. He was dying; she shouldn't argue with him. Besides, she had little evidence to stand on. He was right.

"I know you have ice water in your veins," he said gently. "I've seen you handle your share of difficult situations, but there's more to the trip than I've told you. It can be dangerous. Promise me you won't go alone." With his shoulders slumped and head bent, it appeared that exhaustion had taken him into a deep hunch, though he still managed to sound stern.

"I promise," she said. "But I have to get back to Mom and Dmitri. Can't you see that I want to get home as much as you wanted to come here? Not to mention, they'll need me when they hear what's happened to you."

He stood and pulled back the topmost blanket, then

crawled under it, not bothering to change into sleepwear. He closed his eyes and rested upon the pillow before rubbing his forehead again.

Natasha wondered if he had a headache.

"I'll talk to Svetlana in the morning," he said.

She regretted her firm stance. "I'm sorry I'm being difficult."

"You're not difficult at all." His voice was tired and soft, like a breeze that rustles the curtains. He cleared his throat and followed with a wheeze. "You're just as you should be, and I love you."

"I'm going to die young, too," she said, thinking he might feel better to hear it.

"You're *not* going to die young," he said, his irritation strengthening his voice.

"It's okay. My life will have meaning. Just as yours has."

"Natasha, please."

"Sometimes my new heart feels like it's not beating consistently. Like da-dum, da-dum, da-da-da-dum da-dum. And this morning I had a pain right here." She pointed to the center of her chest, though she realized his eyes were still closed.

Why was she so compelled to worry him? Was it just so he would keep talking to her?

"You don't believe you're healthy," he said through a sigh, "but your new heart is perfect. The doctors from Mintaka are ages ahead of the human doctors—"

"And yet, they still can't help you," she said, staring him down.

He clenched his jaw, but his eyes remained closed. "I love you, sweetheart, but I must get some rest. Can we talk tomorrow?"

From the sound of his fading voice, it was obvious he

teetered on a cliff that would drop him into the valley of sleep.

"I'm going to shower." She grabbed her night clothing from where it sat on the dresser. "I love you too."

His head sank deeper into the pillow. "Enjoy the water," he whispered.

She went to him and kissed his cheek the way he used to kiss her goodnight when she was a little girl. "I will."

Chapter 16

Kirksberg, Pennsylvania

Days after the FBI failed to enter Starbright, Caroline occupied her "throne" at the head of the conference table. As second-in-command, Head Leonard took the chair across from her with Andy, who managed the lab, and three other Leonards lined up shoulder to broad shoulder in the middle. Their billy clubs occasionally knocked into the table, and Caroline regretted sanctioning them every time she heard the tinny clunk. It had been Miranda's idea for the Leonards to carry weapons of various sorts. "Tools of self-defense," Miranda had called them. And now Caroline wondered why she had agreed. She'd be sure to make changes before Miranda returned from Mars. For now, the beings at this table represented Caroline's team, weapons and all. It was quite simply the best she could do without Jovian support.

A fog had settled over Kirksberg early that morning—natural fog according to local weathermen and Starbright forecasters—and rain fell in a steady drizzle. She was surprised when Head Leonard had requested an emergency meeting.

"The Moon Children," he told her, "are readying for attack."

"That is not what our meteorologists are saying," Caroline said. "What we're seeing this morning is natural fog. Besides, there's no body of water large enough to accommodate them near Kirksberg."

Leonard grunted. "I can smell them a mile away, and whether you believe they are capable of traveling long distances or not, I smell them now."

She was in the middle of replying when her head became as dense as a lead ball, one she could no longer hold upright. Her chin collided with her chest and her forehead bounced into the tabletop in front of her. Darkness flooded her mind, and she could not move in response to any of Head Leonard's commands to "wake up."

Someone jiggled her arm. She wanted to tell them to take their hands off her but couldn't find the words. She couldn't lift her head or open her eyes.

"What's happening to her?" Leonard said.

A vitals checker pressed into her wrist. "Pulse is normal, she's breathing," Andy said. "Blood pressure is high. Very high."

Their conversation muffled and faded as if someone had placed cotton in her ears. Through the darkness came a distant voice that said, "Grandmother."

Evander. He sounded frail, far away.

"Where are you?" she answered in her mind.

"Grandmother, you must stand down."

"There's no oneness. How have you reached me?"

"I have perished."

The words whisked the breath from her body.

"No!" she said. "I don't believe you."

"She's shaking," Head Leonard shouted.

"Her pulse just climbed to 172," Andy said through

bustling sounds of quick movements. "Put her on the table. It must be her heart."

"You love Earth as much as I," Evander said, his voice light and kind, "but you must stop."

She wanted to reach out and bring him closer, to invite him to sit and talk with her. She was desperate to see him again, to tell him she was the keeper. That all along she'd been the keeper.

"Edmund is coming," he said. "The Moon Children are coming."

"The Moon Children are here," she said.

"Stand down, Grandmother. I beg you. Don't let this happen."

"You don't understand," she said. "I can't stand down. The keeper does not stand down."

Evander didn't reply. The sound of wind pressed through Caroline's mind, leaving it empty and dark.

"Evander? Wait, don't go. Come home. I want to see you."

The last traces of his presence receded, and a horrible void spread through her chest.

The sounds of the ordinary world returned. Caroline opened her eyes and tried but failed to sit up, laid out as she was across the conference table.

"She's awake," Andy said, putting the paddles down upon a medical cart at his side.

She gathered her strength before trying to sit up again, this time with Andy's support. "Slowly. No hurry," he said.

The room spun around her. Her legs hung over the table's side, and wearily she straightened her back.

Andy continued to grasp her upper arm, holding her steady. Head Leonard attempted to do the same, but she stopped him when her raised hand collided with the metal side of his face, emitting a sharp *clink*. "I'm fine." She shrugged Andy off, and he stepped back and busied himself with the medical cart. Soon, though, he returned to place his fingers on her wrist.

"No more," she said, pulling her hand away. "Back up, all of you."

She didn't want any of them to see her in this state.

Evander is dead.

"Go," she told them, struggling to hold onto her last shred of calm before the storm of emotion spilled from her.

"Let's just get you in a chair first." Andy grasped her arm and attempted to guide her, but she drew back and shouted, "No!"

He spoke gently: "Ma'am, you may have had a—"

"Get out." Her head vibrated with the impending loss of control. "All of you, get out of here now!"

Andy stepped backward toward the exit. Head Leonard gestured for the other Leonards to leave. They moved swiftly, weaponry clinking at their sides.

A fire burned in Caroline's chest. The pressure of the heat swelled painfully up her throat, stretching and seething.

Andy lingered by the door, eyeing her with concern. "She shouldn't be alone," he told Leonard.

"Leave! Both of you," she yelled.

Leonard shoved Andy through the door and followed directly.

Caroline fell into the closest chair. *Evander is dead.* She covered her mouth with the intention of keeping the thunder at bay. She'd seen humans cry before and dreaded the tears rising in great swells from her body, the nose running, her face crinkling like a piece of paper bound for the garbage pail. *Evander is dead.* The sadness came with unbearable heat that spread across her face and distorted her mouth. *Evander is dead.* Her chin quivered and collapsed, taking her mouth into a horrible frown. The tears emerged like acid rain across her face.

She'd rather someone cut off her arm than experience the subtleties of human mourning. The pain of losing a limb, she could handle. Like a limb, Evander had been a part of her, she realized now. And that was not the way of a Jovian. This sadness and loss was not Jovian. She never wanted feelings, and now she couldn't stop them from coming. Could not ignore or deny them.

Constance did this to me.

Like an ocean in turmoil, Caroline's emotions churned everything that once was settled.

Feelings made one weak. How would she hide them from the Leonards? From the other Jovians? If she couldn't control herself, she would be doomed. *Earth* would be doomed.

She'd never wanted to take her original form more than she wanted to in this moment.

"Constance!" she cried. "Where have you gone? Come back and restore my power."

The conference room remained silent, though Caroline detected activity outside the door.

She thought of Evander again and sank into her sadness. "I'm sorry. I'm so sorry, Evander." She closed her sore eyes and drew a breath through her swollen nose. Her emotions seemed to have come to their end, or perhaps only the tears had ended. Would the pain settle now? Was it over? She wiped her eyes and considered how to explain her behavior to Head Leonard and the others.

Before she could decide, Leonard burst into the room. "Ma'am, you have to see this."

A reprimand formed in her mind as he gripped her upper arm and pulled her from the chair. She would have stumbled, but his strong hold lifted her clear off the ground. He guided her to the nearest window and pointed downward. "They've arrived," he said.

Emergency alarms began to blare beyond the conference room walls. Caroline followed Head Leonard's darting finger to the ground below. Two Andrew clones had collapsed by the back entrance and lay swollen and coughing on the platform by the door. The poison had arrived.

Leonard said, "The woods across the way," and her gaze lifted to the trees just beyond the row of parking spaces. It was as if someone had rolled a silver blanket across the surrounding forest and beyond, its thick, wispy fingers reaching for them.

Caroline checked the clock by the door. It read 8:45 a.m. Employees were just arriving for the workday.

Images of Miranda at the Mars launch flashed in her mind, how her face cracked and bled. How sick she and Leo became.

"Get the two Andrews inside, and then seal the doors," she said, her pulse flying in her veins as she realized she, too, was in danger this time. With the door opening and closing, with the many employees rushing into the building, the fog would be free to enter as well.

Leonard met her gaze, staring at her with an intense curiosity. She tried but couldn't vanquish her response to her own horrific thoughts.

"I've already sealed the doors," he said with utter calm. "No one can get in or out."

She bowed her head and rubbed her nose, which had started to run again.

He tilted his head, his eyes boring into her as if he were observing the results of a surprising scientific experiment. "It isn't like you to fear," he said. He reached out with his large, gloved hand and flicked away a tear that remained upon her cheek.

For perhaps the first time in her life, Caroline didn't know what to do.

She wanted to lead without emotion, *and* she wanted to cry.

She wanted to slap Head Leonard back into line, *and* she wanted to crawl under the desk and hide.

She pulled in a breath and stood straight, fixing her blouse, finger-combing her hair. "What can we do about this? Our employees are dying out there."

"I'll take care of it."

That answer didn't satisfy. "If we don't let them in, they'll die," she said, volume rising. "We can't have a large number of deaths occur at the doorstep of Starbright International."

Through the window, she watched clones of Miranda and Evander shout and pound the back entrance while the Andrews became incapacitated. Finally the door flew open and the thin Leonard who'd volunteered to return Miranda and Leo to the Velostar showed up on the staircase platform.

"He's opened the door," she said urgently. "The fog will get in!"

Thin Leonard began to drag the injured inside. Others pushed through them and rushed in as well, the fog and its misty arms following after. Caroline smelled the stench of ammonia to such a degree that her eyes watered.

"You need to get in the tubes, Ma'am," Head Leonard said.

"Go ahead," she said, her head dizzy with the poison. "I'll stay here."

"The tubes, Caroline. Now."

She took a step and wavered dizzily. "I . . . can't—"

He grasped around her waist with his big, rough hands and lifted her over his shoulder as he would a bag of cement. He began to walk like that, Caroline's upper body oscillating as he carried her out of the conference room and into the balcony corridor.

She wanted to insist he release her, but the ammonia had drained her of energy, leaving her lightheaded and feeble. She gave in, powerless, as he moved down the hall. Alarms rose and fell with startling volume, and red lights spun from the tall ceiling. "Retreat to the basement immediately. All personnel retreat to the basement immediately," the automated system, a replica of Miranda's voice, smoothly commanded.

And then they passed an unmoving body in front of the laboratory entrance. A man wearing a white lab coat. He lay face down on the floor as if hit by the blast of a grenade.

"Andy," Caroline said and beat on Leonard's back. "Andy needs help!"

Leonard ignored her. He took the spiral staircase to the first floor, Caroline's face bouncing off the taut muscles of his wide back.

"You'll have to return for Andy," she said, tasting the horrible ammonia as she coughed. "It's getting stronger."

She felt the deep vibrations in his chest as he spoke. "Hold your breath," he said.

They reached the red room, which sprawled with injured Andrew clones, and worse, some Evanders, and the few Leonards, including the thin one, who tended to them.

Head Leonard entered the room and gave the order to "Get to the basement." Those providing aid grabbed the injured by the hands and arms, and dragged them away. They left the dead behind. Leonard locked the back entrance once again before setting Caroline on the ground.

She tried not to see too much, tried not to linger on the bloated bodies and the blood puddled on the floor around them, nor the living just outside the back entrance door, enfolded in fog and thumping their panicked fists, elbows, and shoulders against the blood-smeared windows. Leonard opened the door and pushed the nearest individuals off the platform, shouting, "Get back!"

Then he slammed the door and locked it again.

"No one will see you now." He nodded in the direction of the hidden tube entrance. "Get in there."

"Open that door as soon as I'm gone," she said. "And don't forget about Andy."

She didn't like the way Leonard laughed when he said, "Yes, Ma'am, I will."

CAROLINE RETREATED TO THE SMOOTH, cool interior of the planetarium while she waited for the fog to pass and the dust to settle. Feeling like she'd been run through the mill, as humans sometimes said, she took to one of the lounge seats at the center of the room and pressed a button on its armrest. As she reclined, stretching out her legs and laying back her head, the bright ceiling lights faded and the deep purple night sky with its glittering Milky Way covered the ceiling and curved walls of the egg-shaped room. Beethoven's *Moonlight Sonata* came through the speakers.

Surrounded by stars, Caroline observed her slowing heartbeat, and noted how the tension in her body abated. She exhaled a long, relieved breath, grateful for this moment alone. Grateful for the galaxy above her head and its vast stretches of space. It was wonderful to leave Earth behind for a few moments, even if only virtually.

She tried not to think about what had happened outside Starbright's walls, tried not to imagine how many clones died awful deaths and what questionable things Head Leonard might have done to protect the building— to protect *her*.

The fog would have passed by now, and her team of technical experts and media enforcement would be on the job making sure no one—human, clone, hybrid—spoke to outside sources. No one would share videos, photos, audio, or anything else. This attack would not be documented the way the media had broadcast the one that had occurred after the launch in Florida. Queen Jovian could not be involved in—nor blamed for—another poison gas cloud. She could not give any legitimate FBI directors reason to want to take her into custody or shut down Starbright, and she could not allow the Moon Children to sow more fear than the National Guard already struggled to suppress.

Her team would contain it, make it go away.

But how would she make the Moon Children go away?

Mars appeared on the horizon, its red glow, soft and pale at first, growing brighter and more aggressive as the music continued to set a melancholy tone. It was no coincidence the Moon Children had showed up at Starbright's door. *Her* door, more specifically. It was a message from Edmund, Caroline was sure. One he needn't have sent. He wanted her to witness firsthand what they could do to her world, her clones, her beloved bright blue planet. He wanted her to know that the Moon Children knew exactly where she lived and that they would stop at nothing to remove her from power.

But he also knew that she would not let him do that. That she would do whatever needed to be done to remain at the helm and to fulfill her role as the keeper.

If his intention was to kill every living thing on Earth, she would make sure she was the very last living thing left alive.

She would go to whatever lengths it took, without question.

As Mars passed into the distance on the ceiling above, a comet sped across the sky, and the door to the planetarium opened.

"You wanted to see me?" Head Leonard's words came in along with a flash of light from the corridor. He stepped forward, returning the room to darkness.

Caroline didn't turn on the lights for him, and he remained where he was, unable to see.

"Come in," she said as she sat up.

She enjoyed watching him squint and hesitate.

His left cheek, the human half of his head, wore smears of blood.

His steps upon the tile floor tapped out an unsure rhythm that pleased her. She sneered when he walked into one of the seats and stopped abruptly.

"That's far enough," she said. Then she stood and slowly approached him until they were face to face, the light from the sky coloring the pale side of his face a cool shade of violet. "I am going out," she said.

He glanced at her and nodded subtly. "I'll ready the Velostar."

"No. I'm going alone. I'll need an auto-car. An ordinary one."

His brow rose. "That is not recommended."

"It won't take long, and I don't want to draw attention. You and the others will stay here."

"Where are you going?"

"That is none of your business," she said. "I am your superior, Leonard, and I suggest you remember that."

"Of course, Ma'am," he said, snapping to attention. "Is that all you require?"

"How is the head of the laboratory?" she asked. "How is Andy?"

"He's taking treatment."

"He'll live?"

"Yes, Ma'am," he said gruffly. "He will live. If he doesn't, I'm sure we can make you a new one."

She became snagged on Leonard's insolent eyes for an elongated moment, weighing the pros and cons of slapping the human side of his face. It was a desire that she allowed to pass. "Andy saved your life, if I recall correctly. He was the only one who didn't give up on you."

"Maybe he should have let me go," Leonard said, surprising her.

She didn't know how to respond, so she said nothing.

"What happened to you today?" he asked. "During the conference. Andy said it might have been your heart."

Her words emerged with jagged edges: "My heart is fine," she said.

Then she remembered how Evander had whispered to her, *I have perished,* and her throat clenched.

"It was the ammonia, a reaction to the fumes," she added.

"Of course."

"You can leave now," she told him.

He moved without hesitation, as if only waiting for her permission.

As soon as the door closed and the darkness resumed, Caroline lowered into the nearest chair.

The entire security squad surely had discussed her questionable mental and physical state. If only she could take her natural form, her power would not be debated. Without it, she needed a different show of strength. She needed her clones to stand behind her, to remember who was in charge and how much power she wielded.

She closed her eyes and thought of Evander: how cruel she'd been when she last saw him. How she practically banished him from Earth, from his home. Her emotion swelled painfully once again, threatening to reveal itself, to leave her with nothing but weakness. She was so far from the being she once had been.

Was there no way to rid herself of these terrible feelings?

She lay back in the chair and gazed upward once again. In the distance loomed Jupiter, big and bold and beautiful, with its tempestuous cloud rings and brilliant, steadfast eye. Its swarm of moons made circular orbits like bees around their hive. She swore she could feel the enormity of Jupiter's gravitational pull, the swell of its influence. The mere sight of its gargantuan size gave her comfort. The warmth of its deep, piercing rust and orange and red struck her as painfully beautiful. It stung somehow, as if burning her eyes.

"Dmitri," she said, just then remembering how badly she needed him. "Where are you?"

Chapter 17

Kirksberg, Pennsylvania

"Okay, so we're really doing this?" Fran said, checking the various items of combat strapped to his body. He wasn't thrilled about storming the castle that was Starbright International, especially not this late in the day and not after the Coalition members he'd sent to do recon reported the appearance of the Moon Children.

As he, Lisa, and Connie came together in the pubspace to make final preparations, he second-guessed himself: How the hell had Connie convinced him that taking Queen Jovian from her home was a good idea? He wondered if Connie didn't possess some of the powers of persuasion that had benefitted Evander so much when he was president.

"The timing is perfect," Connie said. "Many members of the security squad suffered injuries this morning. Several clones and even a few ordinary humans allegedly died too. Not only are they weaker than ever, they're preoccupied with the disaster that just occurred."

"And the media hasn't caught wind of the incident," Fran said. "We're sure about that, right?"

"Yes, we're sure," she said, gesturing to the clones seated at nearby tables scrolling paper screens and vigorously typing in front of the computers. "We've scoured every network out there—old, new, legit, illegit, dark, light—since this morning. And you know as well as I that what happens at Starbright stays at Starbright," she said, a bit too cheerfully for Fran's taste.

"Don't worry, Fran," she said sedately. "Starbright has shut down for the moment, their security is licking its wounds, and Caroline has most definitely withdrawn to the tubes."

She placed a heavy hand upon his shoulder and met his concern head on. "Attack when they're weakest, as Drew used to say."

Fran rubbed the scruff of his chin. "Yeah. I generally agree with that, but are we sure the Moon Children aren't still out there, hanging around? I don't want to go on a mission to abduct the queen and end up walking into a poison cloud."

Connie gave him a dead-eyed Jovian stare. "You know they're not."

"We've covered all the bases, Fran," Lisa said. "We're ready. The members of the Coalition are re—"

A sudden knock on the bunker's metal door made all three of them cower where they stood. Fran glanced around, noting how the surrounding clones seemed just as surprised.

"Did anyone go out today for any reason?" he asked in a fierce whisper.

Lisa checked her wristcomm. "Not according to the sign-out."

"The camera is showing a single person." Connie tossed a paper screen onto the table in front of her.

"Prepare yourselves," Fran called to the others.

The clones scattered, taking cover behind tables, half walls, and columns.

Connie was on the move. "Whoever it is, is wearing sunglasses and a hood. Looks like a small adult. I'll go up and check the spyhole." Before she finished the sentence, she'd gone into camouflage mode, blurring into the background and becoming all but invisible.

Fran wanted more time to contemplate the best way to handle this unexpected intrusion, but he let her go, considering her invisibility and how he would have chosen her for the task anyway.

Now she whispered from the platform at the top of the stairs: "You won't believe this."

"Try us," Fran said.

"It's Caroline."

A murmur passed through the pubspace. The clones crouched as if ready for anything—though they most certainly were not ready for this.

"You have to be joking," Fran said. "How is this possible?"

Then again, he knew how. They were dealing with Jovian royalty, plain and simple. Of course Caroline was aware that the Coalition had hunkered down in their bunker. She probably even knew what they planned to do that morning. He rubbed the top of his head. So much for plans. "We should have known," he muttered. "What are we, stupid?"

"She looks smaller than usual," Connie said. "I'm opening the door."

"What? No!" Fran remained in one place though he sustained the sense of stumbling and falling on his face.

The bunker's hefty door pulled back with a familiar metal groan, and Connie became visible once again as she said, "What the hell are you doing here?" in a surly tone that made Fran cringe.

He and Lisa bolted up the stairs. Fran reached for his weapon out of habit but decided it best to leave it holstered. What good would a gun do against a giant alien?

There, just outside of the open door, an older woman wearing a windbreaker and jeans stood. Connie was right: Caroline looked small. And older somehow, but not in the usual way. Not in a wrinkled-face kind of way. She had removed her sunglasses, and he recognized her alarming brown eyes with the unearthly gold flecks. And the prettiness. She'd always been pretty. Although, her pretty seemed to have been dipped in something dull. Weariness, maybe? Something major must have happened to put her in this condition. Her slender bones looked so delicate. Her overall guise, so . . . ordinary. Very much unlike herself. He wondered if the Moon Children's poison was to blame. Starbright had been attacked. Maybe she'd been affected.

Or maybe playing weak was her strategy.

"Fran, it's good to see you," she said, her kindness disabling him further.

He remembered all at once that Caroline wasn't just the six-story alien that had shocked the world three years ago. She was Andrew's mother—the mother of his best friend and college roommate—and he'd known her for years. She was the same woman who had fawned over Max when he was a baby and hired Fran to head up the security squad when he was out of a job. And yet, for the past three years he'd thought of her as nothing more than "the scary alien," just as the rest of the world did.

He'd almost forgotten she was other things as well.

"Hi, Caroline," he said.

"And Lisa." She turned in Lisa's direction, offering a subtle smile. "It's been such a long time."

"It has . . . and it's so . . . good to see you," Lisa's words twisted with uncertainty.

After that, Fran didn't know how to proceed. They'd been preparing to breach Starbright's walls and take this woman—a dangerous hostile—back to the bunker against her will. And now here she was, all sweet and innocent, at their door?

"Would you like to come in?" Lisa asked.

"One second." Fran stepped forward and gently nudged Caroline aside so he could scan the surroundings. Where's your bodyguard detail? They're not coming in."

"I came alone," she said, her voice soft, slightly hoarse. "I didn't tell them where I was going."

"Why would you do that?" Connie said, her face hard with seriousness and arms crossed over her chest like they often were.

"Because I want you to trust me."

That was stranger than strange. "You don't go anywhere alone," Fran said. "Do you forget I used to work security for you?"

Her gentler tone of voice seemed to indicate some form of regret when she said, "Things have changed, Fran."

He saw no evidence of Leonard or the squad as far as he could see.

"Please, come in," Connie said, with a snaky, mean-spirited edge that Fran recognized but Caroline may not have. "Come in and tell us how your world has changed. I'll tell you how it has changed for us as well. For one, Drew is dead. You remember Drew?"

Fran pulled a frustrated breath. "Caroline didn't kill Drew, Connie. And let's not go there right now."

"What better time than now?" Connie pursed her lips as she brought the two sides of her militaristic jacket together. "She's out of the tubes, for once. On her own. And even if she didn't kill Drew, it *was* her fault."

"I had nothing to do with Drew's death," Caroline said, standing straighter, more like herself.

"Well, you didn't let him get the heart transplant he needed. So you kind of did."

"The only heart transplant Jovians can receive occurs on Mintaka and will not survive Earth's gravitational force and magnetic spectrum," Caroline said. "There was no point in Drew undergoing the transplant. He knew that as well as I."

"Okay, okay," Fran said, trying to reel them in before the argument snowballed and Caroline's size expanded tenfold. "Caroline is here, and I assume she wants to talk. The least we can do is let her."

"Yes, that's why I'm here," she said. "We are up against a formidable enemy."

"The Moon Children," Fran said. "We heard the scene at Starbright today was pretty gruesome."

"It was." Caroline bowed her head, then slowly lifted it to him. When she met his gaze, he felt none of the electrified shiver that once raised his hair and Svetlana's. Had Caroline changed so much that she no longer raised his hair? Had she lost her . . . whatever supernatural energy it was that once caused his follicles to stand at attention in sheer terror?

"Dead people seems to be your thing lately," Connie murmured.

Fran ignored her. "Okay, let's do this," he said, waving Caroline in. "Careful as you make your way down the stairs."

The irony that he was inviting her into a property she

owned did not escape him. And why was he being so cordial, anyway? Caroline was the enemy. She couldn't be trusted. Connie was right: the injured-animal guise could be a fake. And yet Fran's gut told him it wasn't.

From the gentle way Lisa reached out to Caroline and helped her down the steps, it appeared that Lisa's very reliable gut told her the same thing. "Can I get you something to drink? Some tea maybe?"

Connie groaned. "She's not your grandmother, Lisa, and she's not your guest. Remember that." She pushed past all of them and thumped her way down in her bulky black boots.

According to protocol, most of the clones cleared out of the pubspace and only senior officers remained: a dozen clones and hybrids, all prepared for confrontation.

Fran, Lisa, Connie, and Caroline, who appeared particularly small boned and unassuming, settled around one of the circular tables. She clasped her hands and rested them in her lap.

Who is this woman? Fran wondered.

She wasn't exactly Caroline, and she wasn't exactly someone else. One thing was sure, however: mourning and sadness oozed from her pores.

"I am here because I want to help," she said.

"Doubtful," Connie muttered under her breath.

"Let her speak," Fran said. If Caroline wanted to feign weakness, that worked for him. He preferred her small and humble over enormous and powerful any day.

"In the past few weeks, much of an entire generation of Andrew clones has perished. Some of them, like Drew, for instance, passed due to heart failure. But the majority have succumbed to the fog cloud that is the Moon Children."

"Tell us something we don't know," Connie said.

"The Moon Children have spread from Glacier Bay to Canada and the Great Lakes, traveling along the rivers throughout the land. We expect them to cross oceans and begin to show up in Europe, Russia, every country in which water is plentiful. Small-scale attacks like the one that happened at Starbright this morning will become more and more frequent."

"That's what we don't get," Lisa said, "how fast they're multiplying."

"They don't multiply," Caroline said. "The hive mind is many and one at the same time. If there is one Moon Child on Earth, there are countless Moon Children on Earth."

Lisa nodded, but Fran could tell she didn't get it. He didn't either, but he didn't care. Outside of how to rid the planet of them, he didn't want or need to know specifics.

"They're here because of you," Connie said in a malicious tone. "Because Edmund wanted to stop whatever terrible plan you have for Earth."

"It doesn't matter why they are here," Caroline said. "It matters only that they *are* here. The Moon Children are an unstoppable force. Poison when they want to be. Desperate for a better life. We will not survive them unless we band together. Humans, clones, Jovians, all."

"We're not banding together with you," Connie said.

"Is that what you want?" Fran asked Caroline. "You want us to work together?"

"What she wants is obvious," Connie said with a scowl. "She wants to control us. She wants to *own* us. That's why she's here, pretending to be some kind of caring matriarch. Like she ever gave a crap about anyone."

"But I do," Caroline said, leaning forward with urgency. "I have always cared. I will do whatever is necessary to save this planet. That is why I am here."

"Okay, okay, we can all agree that we want Earth to survive," Fran said. "Right, Connie?"

She didn't answer, angry thoughts clouding her demeanor. She slunk back, the teakettle within her simmering.

"Wait a minute," Lisa said. "I don't see what the problem is. If you want to rally the clone population, why don't you just do it? What do you need us for?"

The room's focus shifted, landing palpably on Caroline, who stared straight ahead, a Jovian blankness in her eyes.

"I can't," she said softly.

"You can't," Fran paused, "do what exactly?"

"I can't command the clones anymore. I have . . . lost that ability."

"Because David died, and the oneness is gone," Fran said. "But what about your natural form—"

Connie perked like a dog that has been tossed a ball, her head tilting in astonishment. "She means she can't do it," she said slowly. And then her words gained momentum when she added: "She can't take her natural form. I knew something big was going on. That's what you mean, isn't it?"

She sounded far too delighted than was comfortable for Fran.

Caroline bowed her head. A moment of silence unified those present as they waited for her response.

"That makes so much sense," Connie said, all smiles and energy. "How did it happen—and when? Was it Constance? Did she strip you of your natural form? It had to be Constance!"

Without waiting for an answer, Connie stood and shouted to the clones beyond the conversational circle.

"The clones are free. Do you hear me? We're free!" She waved a defiant fist in the air.

Unable to sit back and watch this act of disrespect, Fran grabbed Connie by the wrist and gently pressed down. "Please stop. Get a hold of yourself."

Connie reclaimed her arm and let out a subtle sort of growl.

"What good is it to be free when the Moon Children are out there, killing every clone they pass?" he said. "I understand wanting to be free. I'm totally with you there. But now is the time to come together, to save humanity in all its different forms."

Connie slumped back into her chair, insolence wrinkling her brow.

"Please excuse Connie," Fran told Caroline. "She's still in mourning."

Caroline gave no response. She clasped her hands together and waited.

"What do you propose we do?" Fran asked her.

She straightened up a bit as she took in a breath and seemed to rally her dignity. Then she began to speak: "Once the Moon Children have spread across the planet, there will be no turning back. It won't just be clones who die. The air will become thick with ammonia. Entire forests will fail. Crops. Plants of all kinds. *Life* of all kinds. The ground and the air will become toxic. Those who survive will be taken back to the age of hunters and gatherers. Survivors will be forced to find a cave—or bunker— to live in."

"They'll have to live underground," Lisa said.

"Most likely, yes," Caroline said soberly.

"Before it gets to that point, can't you negotiate with them?" Fran said. "The Moon Children have a monarch, so why don't you talk to her? Make her understand she's killing the planet. You said she wants a better life for herself and her people, tell her we share the same concept."

"I don't know where she is," Caroline said soberly. "And I have no means of finding her."

Connie laughed loudly. "What Caroline means to say is that without David and the oneness, she's useless."

Caroline did a good job of ignoring Connie. Her eyes met Fran's briefly when she said, "My great-grandson will be here soon."

"Dmitri, you mean," he said.

From what Fran remembered, the kid showed signs of impressive power when he was a disabled eight-year-old playing with a set of keys on a blanket on the floor. He'd read Fran's mind and responded to him that way too.

"What she's not telling you is that Dmitri will be the recipient of David's power," Connie said. "He'll bring the oneness back. If it doesn't kill him first."

They all looked to Caroline, who armed herself with one of her Jovian stares.

"He lives in Russia with his mother," Fran said. "I helped them get settled there."

"He *was* in Russia." Caroline boldly raised her chin, though a lifelessness remained in her eyes. "I don't know exactly where he is, but I expect him soon."

"Then I guess I better help you find him," Connie said in a threatening manner. "I bet I can find him before you do."

Caroline didn't flinch.

Fran caught Connie's eye and sent her an unspoken reprimand he hoped she'd receive. If he'd known she was going to be so disagreeable, he never would have okayed her plan to seek Caroline out. Thank God this meeting was going as well as it was. Thank God they hadn't tried to abduct her.

"What about Evander?" Fran asked hopefully. "He can negotiate with anyone, human or alien. He should have been back by now. Has anyone heard from him?"

"Yes," Caroline said, turning toward Fran with robotic stiffness. "I have heard from him."

"And?" He couldn't help but become excited. Maybe Evander was headed home, and that meant Max was too.

Caroline became exceedingly still. When she finally blinked, Fran swore her eyes glistened. "He's dead."

"What, when?" Lisa said before covering her mouth.

"I found out yesterday," Caroline said.

"Who told you?" Fran asked.

Caroline's demeanor grew long, and she breathed with deliberate slowness, trying to temper the pain, Fran assumed.

Finally, she said, "He did."

No one spoke for a full thirty seconds, maybe longer. Fran knew that when it came to death, Jovians had unusual ways. It was possible Evander had come to Caroline after he died. Fran wondered how and when he'd passed. Was Max all right, and Natasha? Had their spaceship blown up? Collided with a meteor? He braced himself for the answer.

"Don't believe it," Connie said. "She's trying to win us over with her heartfelt sadness. Then we'll help her, and she'll rally her troops and get back in their heads, so she can take over the world again." She turned to Caroline. "I know you better than Fran and Lisa do. You're lying."

"I have never lied in my lifetime," Caroline said, her voice rising scarily in volume. "Not to you, not to anyone. Evander is dead." A tear escaped from her eye.

An actual fucking tear. Fran nearly slipped off his chair.

Lisa and he exchanged glances.

"What about the others, those who traveled with him?" Fran asked.

"Max," Caroline said. "As far as I know, Max and Natasha are fine."

"Okay." Fran bowed his head and cleared his suddenly parched throat, feeling like he'd dodged a bullet. He thought of Nadia and didn't look forward to telling her that her husband was dead. "Putting all of that aside for the moment, I'm going to ask you again, what do you want from us?"

She brought her hands together, settling them into her lap once again. "I want your support as leaders of the Coalition. I would like you to get the word out to the clones and hybrids before each attack comes, so they can seek safe shelter. I could make a public announcement, but they don't trust me anymore. They won't listen to me, and I understand that. But they *will* listen to you."

"So, you want to help the clones, is what you are saying?" Lisa asked carefully.

"Yes, I want to help them."

"Bullshit," Connie said. "She can't be trusted. That's why Constance took her power away."

"I will share everything I know about the Moon Children if you help me to protect the clones."

"Will knowing everything you know be enough to stop them?" Fran asked.

"No, it won't," Connie said. "Wiping Caroline and the Leonards off the planet would be a better plan than working with her. At least then we'd have a guarantee that she'll never regain power."

When Caroline turned to Connie, she seemed to grow bigger, straighter, stronger. Something dark and shadowy dropped over the room. Even Connie slunk back, and for a second, Fran worried that Caroline had lied about not being able to take her true form. But her body did not transform or grow. Instead, she said, "That would be a grave error," with such conviction that the skin across Fran's back broke into shivers. "If I die, so will this planet."

"Do you know that for sure?" Fran asked. "Or is this another one of those Jovian prophecies?"

"I don't know whether it's a prophecy or not," Caroline said, easing back into the chair as if it were a throne, as if she still ruled the world and no one could take that away from her. "All I know is that without me, Earth will die and with me, it will survive. It's the reason I live on this planet, the reason I exist, the very reason I was born to this world."

The statement hit Fran hard. He blinked for a moment, allowing its enormity to become absorbed. Then he scanned the room around him. Everyone in the pubspace had shut their mouths, and with a serious dose of preoccupation overtaking their faces, no doubt became lost in their greatest fears.

"Okay," Fran said, withstanding a strange mix of trepidation and hope. "With you, it is."

The room released a breath. Connie even seemed humbled as she rubbed her forehead and bit her bottom lip.

"So, what are our next steps?" he asked.

"Watch the waterways and study the satellite images," Caroline said. "Monitor them for steam rising, for fog in the area. Then warn the residents in those places. We'll need to mass-produce NOxygen clips that the population can carry wherever they go, as well as Oxygen tanks, for those who become sick."

"Yeah, okay." Fran nodded. "I assume Starbright can help with that."

"Yes," Caroline said.

"Good, good." He pointed his index finger in the air. "And one more thing. If we're going to work together, if we have any chance at all of trusting each other, I think you have to stay here, with us, for a little while. Would that be all right? So we can discuss all of this further. And, of course, as a show of good faith. You can have your pick of rooms—"

"Yes, I will stay," she said.

He hadn't expected her to agree, let alone so readily.

Connie shot up from her chair, outraged. "What about the Leonards? They'll come looking for her."

"Not if I forbid them," Caroline said. "They'll do whatever I tell them to do."

"Are you sure about that?" Fran asked in a harsh tone before he realized how disrespectful he sounded in light of who he was speaking to.

Caroline flashed him a look he absorbed in the pit of his stomach. She was sure. The gravity in her brown, gold-flecked eyes did not waver.

"Good, good," he said, bowing his head in apology. And yet, he needed his message to be clear. "Tell them the second we see one of them within a mile of this bunker, the deal is off."

Chapter 18

Outskirts of Philadelphia, Pennsylvania

For four days after Dmitri was able to speak again, he continued to feel pins and needles all over his body—even his head—and the whole of him ping-ponged between moments of movement and long stretches of not being able to move. On the fifth day, he woke in the abandoned shed, just a few feet from Alexandria, as usual, and knew right away that something had changed. His legs and arms had resumed their familiar, unpredictable ways, and he couldn't have been more grateful.

He'd been in the middle of a dream when he woke, one he couldn't label good or bad. Both Father and Great-grandmother occupied space in his mind, which comforted and disturbed him, because they did not arrive in that space together—he sensed much distance between them. Father called to him from a place beyond the black sky, but the words didn't reach Dmitri fully formed. Each time he heard Father's voice, lightning flashed and the thunder that came with it snuffed out the message and boomed throughout his body.

Great-grandmother's presence arrived with that storm. He sensed her reaching for him, maybe even desperate for him. Her voice came through much clearer than Father's when she said, "Dmitri, where are you?"

Alexandria helped him into his wheelchair, an old thing with cracks in its brown, soft-plastic seat that was so much more dignified and comfortable than the metal cart he hoped never to ride in again.

"Are you certain you are ready to leave?" Alexandria asked.

She acted quite caring and motherly, but underneath, he knew, she hoped he would say no. If Alexandria had her way, they would stay in the abandoned shed until they remained the only two beings on Earth.

His answer filled the pit of his never-quite-full stomach, and he gazed at her with great determination and seriousness. "Yes-ah," he said. His limbs were alive with movement. It was impressive, how much work his body did on a daily basis. He wondered if this renewed strength came from Father. Or maybe Great-grandmother. Or, he realized, it could be that he'd healed on his own.

He was so grateful to be back to his old self.

Alexandria finger-combed her long hair, frustrated with the knots. "I wish we could take a shower, at least, before going to Starbright. I'm embarrassed about how we look. They'll think I don't take good care of you."

He pointed to the shelter's brochure. "We could go—"

"It's not safe," she grumbled.

"They gave us a chair."

"I don't trust them. I guess we just have to show up dirty."

Dmitri figured that in her mind, nowhere could possibly prove safe enough from Conseco and Javenport, and whatever other forces that sought them. "Let's go," he said.

The quicker he could get her to leave the safety of the shed, the better.

Alexandria pushed him a block or two and stopped in front of a liquor store because she needed vodka for courage. He liked this store. Its ramp at the entrance provided a smooth uphill climb. The vodka helped Alexandria the way the ramps helped him. She needed it to keep her journey smooth.

The storekeeper, a bored-looking man wearing a T-shirt that said "Destruction," sat on a stool and watched a paper screen tacked to the wall. As they walked in, he lowered the volume and an advertisement for soda came on. Alexandria left Dmitri in front of the checkout and slipped down the first aisle. A few seconds passed, and she returned with a small, clear bottle and a grin that he found worrisome. *Vodka makes her a bit too happy*, he thought.

Meanwhile the paper screen played a dramatic ensemble of musical notes—DAHN-DAHN DAHN!—and a photo of Great-grandmother appeared. Across the top, a headline read, "Queen Jovian, Dead or Alive?"

The reporter, a woman in a bright yellow suit, said, "It appears Caroline Jovian of Starbright International fame has not been seen since a poison fog rolled through Mars Launch 3.0, which she attended in Florida earlier this month. Rumors of her possible death have circulated across multiple media outlets and one unnamed agency has unofficially verified her demise."

She is not dead, Dmitri thought. *I heard her voice only hours ago*. Unless . . . what if it had been an ordinary dream?

No, he never had ordinary dreams.

"Hurry Alex," he said, eager now to reach Starbright.

"Okay, okay." She stopped admiring the bottles of alcohol and placed the one she would buy on the counter.

"Shame, isn't it?" the storekeeper said. "We finally find someone who can lead this country the right way, and now she's dead."

Alexandria hunched forward so her hair fell around her face. "President Abela has died?"

He shook his head as he took her money. "No, not the president. The president doesn't do squat. I'm talking about the queen. Word is Queen Jovian is dead."

Alexandria's eyes opened wide. She turned to Dmitri, who shook his head as best he could.

Alexandria eyed the screen tacked crookedly to the wall. "Looks to me like they're saying she is missing."

"Yeah, that's what they're saying . . . but you know how these things work. She was too powerful. I'm sure someone put a hit on her."

Alexandria focused so intently on him that for a second Dmitri worried she might punch his face. "How would they even get to her? She's only been in public once since the day she scared the crap out of the whole world."

He handed her some change. "Yeah. She's probably dead."

Alexandria grumbled as she resumed her position behind Dmitri's chair. "You have no evidence and yet you are certain—" She leaned toward Dmitri and whispered into his ear: "Don't worry, he has no evidence." Then she paused, pulled the bottle out of its paper bag and twisted off the vodka's cap. She helped herself to a drink right there in the middle of the store.

"You can't do that in here," the man said.

"Oh, I can't? I'm so sorry." She tipped the bottle back again, taking another long swallow. "It's just that I am very thirsty in the morning."

"I told you, you can't do that!" he said. "Go on, get out of here."

"Yes, yes. Thank you so much for your hospitality." She laughed as she screwed the cap back onto the bottle and shoved it into her hoodie's pouch. Then she carefully maneuvered Dmitri out the door and down the ramp.

"What was that-ah?" Dmitri said, trembling with a giggle.

"Can you believe that guy? The news station he watches is nothing but a scam!" she said. "I highly doubt Caroline is dead. Don't you worry, Mitya, you're going to see your great-grandma again."

"Yes," he said. "Please do not get drunk."

"I won't. But you know it helps me. Plus, I'm celebrating. I feel like something long and horrible is ending. We are finally getting out of this place." She laughed dramatically, a little like a madwoman, before adding, "And we're going to one that's much scarier."

Then she began to run, bumping over the sidewalk's uneven concrete squares and shouting *woo-ha* in a loose, tipsy way like someone who hadn't a care in the world.

ALEXANDRIA WASN'T ACTING as carefree hours later when the orange Auto-rider they'd flagged down headed toward the expansive Starbright International building. They'd passed right through the unmanned security squad gate, glided down the hill, and observed the dried-up and dying landscape. Trees, grass, and once-blooming beds of flowers appeared to have succumbed to a torrential downpour of acid rain that left behind crispy bushes, stiff dark-brown stalks missing their flower heads, and the slender trunks of young trees felled across the lot's empty parking spots.

There were no cars here.

"What day-ah is it?" Dmitri asked.

Alexandria frowned and shook her head.

"Today is Monday, December 11, and the time is 9:22 a.m.," the car's simulated driver reported in its deep, robotic voice.

The vehicle pulled up to the front entrance. More brown-leaved bushes decorated the mulch beds. Dmitri cringed at the dark splotches marring the sidewalk and pavers leading up to it. It looked like blood. Worse yet, dark red-brown handprints and smears soiled the otherwise majestic front doors. The glass entrance suffered massive, cracked panels as if someone had tried to beat their way into the building.

"What happened out here?" Alexandria asked. "It's like a battlefield."

Dmitri didn't know what to tell her. Something terrible most certainly had occurred.

Alexandria patted her sweatshirt's midsection and pulled out her bottle of alcohol. "I told you I didn't want to come here. I'm scared. I want to go back to Russia!"

"This Auto-rider does not drive to that location," the car's automated voice replied. "We have arrived at your destination." The trunk of the car popped open behind them. "The fee for this trip has been paid. Auto-driver thanks you and wishes you a good day."

Alexandria shook her head and whispered, "I'm not getting out."

"Please gather your things and exit the car," the speaker said in a blunt tone.

Both passenger doors popped open.

Alexandria closed her eyes and drank from the bottle of vodka.

"Be careful exiting," the car said.

"We must go-ah," Dmitri said. "We must see if—"

"If Great-gran is here. Yes, I know," she said loudly. "Something tells me she's not home right now."

"When we get back to Russia, you must stop drinking so much," he said.

"Of course," she said. "When I get back to my safe, boring life in Metka, I won't need it anymore."

She replaced the bottle into her sweatshirt pocket before exiting the car. She stepped toward the trunk and, with a struggling groan, pulled out the folded-up wheelchair, banging it against the car's back bumper. The clicks and clacks that followed restored the chair to its usable form. Soon enough, she'd rolled it to Dmitri's side of the car.

A sudden sensation buzzed its way up the trunk of his neck.

"Smells disgusting out here," she said, pulling the neck of her sweatshirt in front of her face and covering her nose with it. "Like burned bodies and ammonia."

"I am sorry, Alex," he said fluidly, without effort. "But it will be okay. I know it will."

"Of course it will," she said with no indication that she believed it would.

She unclipped his seatbelt and hugged him around his waist. The ease with which she assisted him out of the car and set him in the chair made him think she was so much stronger than she believed she was. Look at her, thousands of miles from home. His cousin who rarely left the house! As soon as they were clear of the back seat, the Auto-driver closed its doors in unison and sped away.

"Hey," Alexandria said, the alcohol softening her eyes, "I just realized, you're speaking the way you do when you can walk on your own." Then she laughed. "And I'm slurring."

She was right. His limbs had stopped fidgeting. His feet

remained flat upon the footrests. He tried to move them, to put them on the ground, but they wouldn't budge. The energy was building again, but he couldn't walk yet.

"Let's wait a few minutes," he said.

She gazed skeptically at the building. "Let's not. It's too creepy to hang around here. Feels like someone's watching us through one of those windows. Has the old lady said anything to you today?"

"Yes, in my dream this morning."

"You didn't tell me."

"She still needs me," he said.

He didn't know what to do. It was doubtful he'd be able to convince Alexandria to approach the front door considering its horrible cracked glass and smears that hinted at past violence. Then he remembered. "There's an entrance in back. We should go there. I think it might be better."

He only hoped the back didn't look as bad as the front.

Alexandria stared with parted lips at the building as they entered the sidewalk that wound around its side. "Do you really think Caroline is here?"

His father once told him members of the security squad, like the government's secret security, worked around the clock.

"Someone has to be," he said.

When they came around the corner, she hesitated mid-step. "What is that domed roof?"

"That's the planetarium," Dmitri said, and a sudden burst of joy coursed through his veins. "I will show it to you when we get inside. There are planets and constellations in there, and it's very beautiful. Father taught me how to work it before he left to find Natasha."

"And what's that other thing, farther up? I can hardly see it, but it might be stone?"

"That's the observatory. I will show you everything," he said eagerly.

As they approached the staircase that led to the back entrance, Alexandria stalled. A tattered jacket hung from the handrail, fluttering like a wind-ripped flag near the top of the steps. "Is that what the security squad wears?" Alexandria asked.

Dmitri could see that it was but said nothing.

"Maybe they're all dead," she whispered. "Oh my God, Mitya, maybe the newscast was right. Maybe your great-grandmother—"

"No," he said, scanning his mind for any sign of her. "I would know."

"How?"

"I just would. I'm sure I would. Please, Alex."

He needed her not only to climb the stairs but also to help him get up there. If she couldn't do it, he'd need her to go into the building alone, and he knew she wouldn't agree to do that.

She stared straight ahead, at the cement staircase. "That's about twenty steps."

"Carry me up?"

"I don't know if I want to see what's there."

"Nothing is there. But if I'm wrong, we can turn around and go back down. Don't worry, Alexandria. We will be all right. I know we will."

He spoke with conviction because the closer they came to getting inside the building, the more confidence stirred within him, and the more energy too. The pins and needles that sparked and flared within him grew assertive, and he worried the discomfort that had come with it the last time would reappear. He could raise his arms a couple of inches and tap his toes against the wheelchair's footrest.

Something told him he was where he was meant to be.

In this place. At this time. Great-grandmother needed his help, and he had come for her.

He scooted to the edge of the chair and placed a hand on each armrest. He dropped one foot, then the other onto the ground. Pressing with his arms, he attempted to straighten his legs . . . but then dropped back into the seat.

Alexandria squatted in front of him and said, "Do you think you can get on my back?"

"I will try." He leaned forward and threw his arms over her shoulders, clasping his left hand around the right's wrist like a necklace. Then he pulled until he slid off the seat and encircled his legs around her middle.

Slowly, she lifted to standing, gripping his elbows. "Are you good?" she said.

"Yes," he answered with loud enthusiasm. "You can do this."

"I hope so."

She began to climb one careful step at a time.

Halfway up, she muttered, "I bet the door will be locked."

Dmitri closed his eyes and pictured the two of them entering the building. "Somehow we will get inside. I am sure of it."

She sighed and took another step. "After all this, you better be right."

When they reached the ripped and soiled jacket fluttering in the wind, Dmitri saw what he'd hoped not to see. Worse than the front entrance, the platform at the top of the steps exhibited dark and extensive blood stains. A formerly clear-plastic oxygen mask rested on its side, red and mottled, its tube jaggedly torn from a tank. Someone's once-white handkerchief lay crumpled and crusty, stiffened as if due to rigor mortis. A twisted bandage lay flat and trampled at the platform's center.

How many died here, and how? Why?

"I knew it," Alexandria cried. "Why are we doing this!"

"You can't stop now. We're almost there. Just a little further. Please, Alex."

"I can't."

"Close your eyes. There are only three more steps."

"The smell," she said. "If I close my eyes I won't be able to see where I'm going."

"Close them, and I will count the steps for you."

"Okay, okay. They're closed," she said.

"One."

Slowly, she raised one leg, then the other.

"Two," he said.

She coughed but then followed with another step.

"Just one more, Alex. This is the last."

She did it.

"Now, very slowly," he said, "walk forward two steps and stop." He wanted her right up against the front door. The less she could see of the disaster, the better.

She'd reached the door and stood still. "Now what?"

"I'm going to try to stand. Do not open your eyes."

"Believe me, I won't," she said.

As she let go of his elbows and he released his legs from around her middle, his arms slowly slid to her waist and his feet reached the platform. He continued to hug her while he tested his legs. The muscles twitched and one of his knees gave out. He straightened it, regained balance. So far, so good.

Blood spatters marred the door and the security panel that hung beside it. A rainbow arc of brown-red crossed from one side of the screen to the other. Dmitri leaned toward the panel and considered how it might work. One button said "Swipe" and another said, "Eyes."

"I think I can—" The screen flashed, and the door lock

clicked. Either someone had been watching them or the building had recognized him and unbolted itself.

He released Alexandria and pushed the door the rest of the way open. "We're in," he said, moving forward on unsteady legs. "We've made it!"

Then he turned back and grabbed Alexandria's hand. "Open your eyes," he said, and he pulled her inside.

Chapter 19

The Jupiter System

Relieved to take off from Europa without killing any of the small silver people, Max programmed the trip to Io, only two hours away. When he reached the moon's docking station and maneuvered inside as he should—without need for an unexpected crusted-ice landing—he thanked the stars that Europa was an undeveloped habitat with undeveloped residents. He would have been far more embarrassed to have accidentally landed on Io when he'd been trying to get to Europa. As it was, he didn't care what the silver people thought of him considering none of them knew how to fly or even how to build a spaceship . . . or any other mode of transportation, as far as he could tell from what he'd observed.

Once inside Io's terminal, a Jovian (basketball-player tall, slender, and as shiny as a brand-new sports car) waved the *Sparrow* into an available hoverslot, of which there were many. Max supposed what travelers had been saying must be true: the trend on Earth was to journey to Mars. Traveling to the Jupiter System was old news.

He raised his arms in a stretch, wondering when he had last slept, and looked forward to a room with a bed.

As he disembarked, a woman in white walked out of the main building. Elsa! How cool was that? Wherever Elsa was, he would find Evander. Which meant whisking Evander away was going to be easier than he'd thought. Still, he was surprised Elsa came to meet him at the docking station. Must be an important reason for that. A message or a meeting he needed to go to, maybe?

With a spring in his step, he climbed down the ladder and hurried toward her. "Elsa! It's been too long. It's so good to see you again."

Elsa bowed her head in a coy manner. The action struck him as emotional. She was an AI, so this was strange. An air of caution came over him.

"What is it?" he asked.

"I have important news to deliver." Her crystalline blue eyes showed signs of hesitancy. Fear, maybe.

"Okay, well, don't hold me in suspense. What is it?"

"Evander has passed," she said, and she bowed her head.

He stared, waited for the words to make sense, then repeated them to himself. She could not have said what he thought he heard her say.

"That can't be right," he said.

"I'm afraid it is. Evander time traveled to see his mother. The movement through time exacerbated his cellular propulsion."

"Exacerbated what? I don't under—"

"His body aged at even greater speed than before. And, as it turned out, he reached the end of his life."

"Why would he do that? He knew even regular travel wasn't good for him. Why would he time travel?"

"He wanted to see Svetlana."

Max blinked at unprecedented speed. He breathed in deeply, again and again, until it was like he had slipped underwater.

"You have taken too much oxygen." Elsa placed her hand on his shoulder. "Breathe out through your mouth."

"Yes, okay," he said, as if breathing incorrectly was no big deal to him.

"Evander is with the stars now," she said.

He didn't know what that meant. Surely it meant something to Jovians, but it didn't mean anything to him. "He's in a better place," Elsa said, and she tried to appear okay, but her eyes hinted at held-back misery.

"Okay," Max said, nodding on the outside while he longed to collapse internally. "I forgot something on the ship. I'll meet you in one of the entry rooms, or something."

Desperate to get away, he gestured to the *Sparrow*, the vessel Evander had given him. The one thing in his life that inspired memories of Evander more than any other object. Any second now he would lose control, crumble into the child he used to be, and bawl like a baby.

He turned and started up the ladder, slowly at first because the wretchedness growing within him weighed him down, and then faster as desperation to release his misery fueled him to seek a safe place.

Once through the airlock, he let go. The tears barged upward as the memories unearthed: the day in the tubes at Starbright when Evander suggested Max come with him to Io, then teaching him to fly, then introducing him to Natasha and Uncle Jimmy, and promising they'd return to Earth together. Max had assumed the future held a long stream of adventures he and Evander would share.

He had learned so much from Evander, not only about flying but about life, about being a good person. He'd been taught by the best. The smartest and most even-keeled. He considered Evander family.

But now he wondered if Evander had known he would time travel once he reached Io. Had he asked Max to leave so Max wouldn't try to change his mind?

"I should have made you go home," Max muttered, his voice gravelly with tears. "We were supposed to go home!"

He dropped to the floor, and his poor heart took a sorrowful beating while he accepted the punishment. Lying on his side on the floor, he wondered what Evander would think of his collapse into hysterics. Was it a dignified response or a childish display? He decided it was neither. Evander would tell him to have his cry but then to summon the courage to carry on, to face reality. What else could a person do?

Max stopped crying and wiped his nose, then heard what sounded like the pad of bare feet coming from one of the berths. He sniffed as he sat up and wiped his nose again. There, in front of him, stood a bright, silvery sight that obscured his vision.

"Oh, no, no, no. When did you get here?" he shouted.

It was one of the creatures from Europa, up close and out of its element, which somehow made it easier to see. Child-like and slender. In the darkness, he'd thought they were short and squat, but this individual's dimensions were similar to a small human's. Its head seemed more oval than he'd imagined, too, more elongated. Not so round compared to the group he'd met a few hours ago.

"I didn't say anyone could come with me," Max said, more to himself than to the being. "Crap, now you're stuck here, all by yourself, do you realize that?"

Could this day get any worse?

The creature communicated using hand signals.

"Syndi," he alerted the ship's AI, "I need you to interpret."

Syndi said, "Individual uses the language of hands to say, 'Do not be afraid.'"

For some reason, Max took it as an insult. "Why the heck would I be afraid?"

"She says her name is Elara," Syndi added.

"That's a very nice name, but what is she doing here?"

"Elara says she is here to travel with you. She says, 'Do not be afraid.'"

"I'm not afraid," he said and followed with a forced laugh. "I'm worried for her. She's here when she should be on Europa with the others."

"Visitor says, 'No, Elara should not be with the others. She says, 'My people have sent me to return with the seeds.'"

"You don't have to do that. I promised I would come back with them, and I will." He stepped into the command center and dropped into his captain's chair, then flicked a few buttons.

"Visitor says, 'Elara will fly with you.'"

"Syndi, tell her I promise to bring the seeds back. It will take some time, of course but—"

"Excuse me for interrupting," Syndi said, "but she says, 'Elara will bring them back.'"

At this point, the silvery being stood right behind Max's chair so that when he turned around, they were nose to nose. He saw two eyes and a smiling face: the apples of her cheeks, the point of her chin. It was like staring into a block of ice.

"You want to come with me?" he said. "All the way to Earth?"

"She says, 'Elara must.'"

"I guess I could. Maybe? I mean, I had another

mission but . . . I failed. I should have brought him back right away, when I was supposed to. But he wouldn't let me. What was I going to do, insist that he get on the ship?" Max grabbed his head, wanting to stop the disappointment that brewed below the surface, the pain of losing his friend and mentor. Evander must have known he wouldn't make it home. Elsa said he'd wanted to see Svetlana again. He needed to tell her something.

Whatever it was must have been really important.

"Now he's dead," he said softly to himself. "I don't know what to do. I need to talk to Ida. What's gonna happen to Earth now? My parents live there, and Evander won't be able to fix all the shit that's going down. Caroline will—" As he spiraled, he noticed the glow from Elara reaching for him, touching him with what he swore was a softness that soothed him.

She made two fists with her three-fingered hands and pushed them together.

Syndi said, "Elara says, 'Trust.'"

"Trust what?" Max wiped his nose on his sleeve. "Trust her?"

"No," Syndi said. "Elara says, 'Trust in the stars, in the black of the sky, in the . . .'"

Elara raised her arms wide and tipped back her head. As she gazed upward, the heavenly glow that surrounded her body grew brighter.

Max wanted to understand. "Does she mean the universe?"

Syndi didn't answer.

"Do you mean the universe?" he asked.

Instead of using her hands to speak, Elara uttered, "Uni-verse.'"

Chapter 20

Kecksburg, Pennsylvania

A Universe Without Jovians

With a heaviness that had not been there the night before, Natasha threw back the sheet, kicked her legs over the side of the mattress, and slowly stood. Her father's empty bed held her rapt. He was gone. She'd thought maybe he would be there. But he was really gone.

The striped cotton shirt he'd worn the prior night lay crumpled on the floor. She went to pick it up, squeezed it between her hands, and brought it to her face, breathing the scent of him.

"I wish you didn't have to go," she whispered. She trembled as the sadness welled up from her chest and became lodged in her throat. Tears gathered in her eyes. For a moment, the pain and loss grew, threatening to take her to the floor.

Instead of crumbling, though, she willed herself to stand. She let herself feel it, let the fact that her father wasn't coming back sink in and take hold. He was gone.

He had said goodbye. It was her job to go on, to move forward in his place.

She had to get home.

She centered herself before exiting the room and heading down the hall. As she considered what she would say, she stepped up to the kitchen's entrance and peered inside.

Svetlana, in her fuzzy black robe, leaned over the table and placed a platter of pancakes at its center.

"Evander is gone," Natasha said with the same softness she remembered her mother using for sensitive situations.

"What? Where did he go?" Svetlana lifted a pitcher of juice from the counter and filled one of the glasses on the table. "He didn't say anything to me about going out this morning."

Natasha held out the shirt with both hands. "It was last night."

Svetlana put the pitcher down. "But he'll be back, right?" She placed her hands on her hips, confusion flashing like heat lightning across her face.

Natasha bowed her head. "He went to sleep. He's gone. I'm very sorry." *Isn't that what adults say when someone dies?* Again, she offered the shirt Evander had worn the prior day.

"Went to sleep? Or went out?" Svetlana took the shirt but didn't wait for an answer. She left the kitchen, her robe wagging side to side as she moved down the hall in the direction of the guest room. Natasha followed behind.

As they passed the door to Evan's room, it opened and Evan, in pajamas, came out rubbing her eyes. "What's up?" she said.

Natasha pointed down the hall and continued to follow Svetlana.

"Evander?" Svetlana tapped on the guest-room door.

"I'm sure he just went for a walk or . . . maybe to buy a newspaper?" The door, ajar, slowly spread open. Svetlana peeked in before entering. She hadn't taken more than two steps before she stopped to stare at his empty bed. The topmost blanket was rumpled but hardly appeared slept in.

"You'll have to take me home." Natasha spoke to Svetlana's back. Evan was behind her now, standing in the doorway. "He fell asleep before me. I showered and then went to sleep as well."

Svetlana remained unmoving, still staring at the empty bed.

"He came to me in my sleep," Natasha persisted, not knowing what else to do. "He told me he was sorry and that he had to go. Then he walked off, into some dark place I couldn't see."

Svetlana turned toward her, a scowl on her face. "That's called a dream." Then she lifted Evander's shoes from the floor, the sneakers that had appeared on his feet when they'd arrived in this world. A watch he'd worn lay on top of his strewn pants. "Why are his things on the floor?" she asked.

"It wasn't a dream." Natasha took pains to speak gently. "He's gone. It was his time. I'm sorry." Once again, she bowed her head.

"You don't look that sorry to me," Svetlana said bluntly.

Natasha pursed her lips. "Yes, I am, and I'm very sad. It's just that . . . I can control my emotions better than most humans. My mother always said it was due to my Jovian genes."

Something happened to Svetlana's face then. Some kind of revelation clicked behind her eyes, as if she were seeing Natasha in her true form for the first time—as if just then she remembered that Natasha was one of "them."

"I'm mostly human," Natasha said quickly, feeling Svetlana's disdain.

"Uh-huh," Svetlana said. "Either way, I cannot take you to your home. You will have to stay here. At least until I figure out what has happened to Evander. I can't imagine why he wouldn't tell me he was leaving. Or where he went."

"I'm not sure he knew when it would happen," Natasha said. "He said he was going to speak to you in the morning. But he's not here anymore. Not in this universe, I mean."

Svetlana seemed to break a little then. She bent over and covered her mouth with her hand. Just as quickly, though, she stood straight. "I'm going to look for him."

"Mom, stop," Evan said. "We have to tell you something."

Svetlana's face became rigid with restrained fury. "We, who? You and—"

"Natasha," Evan said in a quiet voice that made her seem afraid.

"The two of you have something to tell me?" Svetlana said loudly. "*Evan* has nothing to do with any of this," she barked in Natasha's direction.

"Please just listen to me," Evan started to explain but Natasha rode over her words.

"There's a Jovian prophecy," she said. "It's called 'The Lost Sister.'"

"Now is not the time for this." Svetlana glared in their direction.

"The prophecy is about me," Evan said.

"I doubt that, honey."

"If you'll please listen." Natasha spoke loudly as she began to recite in a bold voice:

The leadership's mother,
   sent across time,
   had with her a child,
   who crossed the sublime.
   She laid to rest the resistance,
   sidestepped the queen's insistence,
   and rendered a solution
   for all mankind.

Amid the awkward silence that followed, Evan produced an audible gulp.

Svetlana raised her brow. "That's it? That's not written very well."

"I'm sure I'm leaving a word or two out. I was groggy when I first heard it."

"I'm the child," Evan said. "You're the mother sent across time."

Svetlana frowned. "Girls, please. That could be any of thousands of people. Or even just a fairy tale. Sounds like a poem Uncle Jimmy made up."

Evan's lips parted as if about to reply, but then she bit the inside of her cheek.

Svetlana jumped on it. "This is something you learned from Uncle Jimmy—I mean, Grandpa James?"

Evan nodded. "When I was little he used to sing something like it all the time. I thought it was just another children's song. But now Natasha has told me this similar story, almost the same words. Grandpa wouldn't have shared it if it didn't mean something."

Svetlana threw back her head and groaned at the ceiling. "He cannot be trusted."

"That's not what my father told me," Natasha said in vigorous defense. "He said Uncle Jimmy was the *only* one of the Jovians who tried to help you."

"Yes, that is true. He did," Svetlana said, giving in with a reluctant sigh, "and I do love him, but that does not change the fact that he sometimes . . . gives bad advice."

Svetlana's feelings for Uncle Jimmy seemed conflicted, to say the least. "It doesn't matter," Natasha said, "because Uncle Jimmy *didn't* tell me. A Jovian on Mintaka did, someone I'd never met before."

"Either way, it's just a story." Svetlana said without hesitation. "Stories and dreams are not reasons to take a time trip, or to wage a war, or to do whatever you intend to do once you reach whatever world you're heading for. And it doesn't mean it's about you, Evan. You're a regular human. You are not part of the Jovian universe. They can't know you."

"Right," Evan said. "Because, as the prophecy tells us, I'm lost . . . in so many ways, apparently."

"That's not what I said."

"You didn't have to, Mom. I am what I am. Just a dumb, directionless teenager who lives with her single mother and grew up very lucky in a nice, suburban home, with a back deck and a caring father who loved her. A father whose DNA gave her the desire to observe the stars because she always felt like there was something out there for her. Something far, far away beckoning."

"We've talked about this," Svetlana said. "I absolutely agree that you have inherited your interest in outer space from your father. And I told you, if you want to space travel, you can become an astronaut the way the rest of the human beings on this planet do."

"Right. Except the Earth I need to travel to is in another universe—not a place our astronauts have ever been. This is my chance to do something. To be who I'm supposed to be."

"You *are* who you're supposed to be," Svetlana said straightening her spine. "That story could be about anyone."

"So the prophecy is just a coincidence? Even though Grandpa told me about it?"

"I don't know, Evan. Maybe."

"They need me," Evan insisted. "You just don't like Jovians."

At that, Svetlana's shoulders crept up to her ears and her fingers curled like claws, vibrating with frustration. "You don't know what it's like to live in a world with them," she said. "They think everything revolves around what they want, the plans they have for Earth, for the solar system or . . . galaxy. You have no idea what they'll ask of you. They don't care about humans. They don't even care about other Jovians. When your father died in their world —" She stopped short, looking to Natasha. "I've never spoken to Evan of the Jovians. I never had a reason to."

"Well, now you do," Evan said. "Tell me. I need to know."

"Fine," she said with fire. "When your father died the first time, in the Jovian world, his mother didn't even cry. She didn't so much as wear black to his funeral. His father gave a soulless speech. Their lack of emotion was so obvious, I actually believed they might have killed him."

"I'm sorry you had to go through that alone, Mom, I really am."

Svetlana simmered in her anger and memories of bad feelings. "I promise, if you go back there, they will ask you —without giving a second thought to your health or life or safety—to give yourself up to their cause."

Evan nodded. "That might be true. But my brother,

who I didn't even know until a couple of days ago, did care about them and their world. He cared very much. Enough to take this time trip knowing he probably wouldn't make it back home to his own wife and son. And I think I owe it to him to at least try."

Svetlana stepped backward, then eased onto Evander's bed as if she'd run out of the strength to stand. "You've always been so noble," she said. "And impressionable. I just want you to have a good life. That's why I left that world. To rid my family of Jovians and all the chaos that comes with them. You're safe here. Their world isn't for you. Let them work out their own problems. We don't owe them anything."

Evan looked up and half smiled. "Sometimes safety is overrated," she said.

"Says someone who has yet to face real danger," Svetlana muttered.

"You're right," Natasha told Svetlana. "You and Evan don't owe the Jovians anything, but if something devastating happens in my world, something equally devastating will happen in this one. My father told you that."

"He did," Svetlana said with ease.

"And do you trust *him?*"

The look in Svetlana's eyes said, *How dare you?*

"Last night my dad said that you will take me home. He trusted you to make that decision."

"I already told him I couldn't. I told him why. You are welcome to live here with us, for as long as you like."

"I'll die if I stay here. He told you that as well."

"I know. I know. I'm sorry. I just . . . Give me some time to figure all of this out. I need to talk to your father. I need to think."

"My father is gone," Natasha said. "He's not coming back."

"You keep saying that, but people who die don't just disappear. Where is his body?" She rose from the bed and opened the closet, then dropped to her knees and checked under the bed frame.

"His body isn't here because he doesn't belong to this universe," Natasha said. Then, remembering how her father had told her to "be kind," she said, "I'm so sorry. I know he was your son and that you loved him. I know that years ago you came here even though that meant losing him, and that was very painful for you. I understand how upsetting it is that you'll never see him again."

Svetlana whispered, "Never see him again." She sank to the mattress and lifted Evander's shirt to her face. "He was just here."

Evan came to her side and hugged her. Svetlana reciprocated for a moment as she stared blindly across the room. Her long hair fell into her face like curtains closing as she slumped. A moment passed, and she let her daughter go, then sat up. Wiped her eyes. "I need to be alone for a while. There's breakfast in the kitchen, if you want, and—" She rose from the bed with some difficulty, as if unused to balancing the new sorrow she carried on her back.

"Don't worry about us," Evan said. "We'll be fine. Go rest. Let us know if you need anything."

She continued out of the room, hunched over, her heavy spirit dragging behind like the train of a dress. Natasha lowered her chin out of respect as Svetlana passed clutching Evander's T-shirt in her fist.

A moment went by before Evan turned and raised her shoulders as if to say, "What now?"

Chapter 21

Kirksberg, Pennsylvania

Like Starbright's back entrance, the opening to the tubes seemed to anticipate and encourage Dmitri's arrival. All he did was step in its direction —with wary legs at first and then with greater confidence and ability—and the wall began to open to a fluorescent-glowing tube.

"Are you doing this, or is the building doing this?" Alexandria asked.

"Starbright is a special place," he said. "It must assume Caroline wants me here. Or maybe Great-grandmother knows I'm here. Maybe she's doing it. Come on."

He moved to take Alexandria's hand, but she refused. A look of terror brought out the whites of her eyes. "Do you think Caroline is in the building right now?"

Dmitri stood completely still as he searched for Great-grandmother in his mind. The oneness he once observed daily still eluded him. "I don't know. All I know is that she wants me here."

"Well, I hope she doesn't mind that I've come along with you. I don't think I can take much more excitement."

"She will love you for getting me here," he said gently. "She will celebrate you."

Alexandria cowered at the thought. "I really don't want that kind of attention," she said sheepishly.

"And this will be fun." A flash of excitement lit Dmitri up the same way David's electricity energized his body. "I've never been in the tubes either."

"But your father told you about them?"

"He said they are a safe zone for the Jovians."

"You're sure they don't lead to some dungeon where they'll hang us upside down?"

He laughed and this time when he reached out to her, she took his hand. He led the way in with Alexandria following close behind. Together they passed sealed door-ways and ascended modest inclines. With every step, the feeling that he was supposed to be there became more evident. He even sensed that maybe, in another life, he had done this before. That maybe this was his destiny. And something else he had never considered before: the need to come to Great-grandmother's aid was also the need to come to this place.

"Where are we going?" Alexandria asked.

"Into the tubes," he said with a smile.

"Yes, but where do the tubes go?"

"Everywhere," he said, beaming with excitement. "To the observatory and the greenhouse and the executive wing."

"Greenhouse?" she said.

"I'll show you."

They walked for a few minutes, hand in hand. Soon they came to a door with a wooden sign attached, some-thing written in another language.

Alexandria sounded out the words: "*In via lactea*? What does that mean?"

Dmitri didn't know offhand, but an overwhelming desire to touch the sign made him reach for it. Its surface felt as powdery soft as beach sand.

The door opened.

A beautiful scent like the crisp air of autumn reached for them. Also, water. And rocks. The night sky. Flower gardens.

He and Alexandria stepped inside, allowing the door to close behind them. They stood in silent awe of the cool stone space with light cascading through the hole up top. In the very center of the room, it created a spotlight of the sort one would see on a stage.

"Is this place . . . magical?" Alexandria asked.

"It's wonderful," Dmitri said in an airy whisper. He felt so happy here. He wanted to dance. An internal rhythm began to move his feet. Tap, tap, tap-tap-tap. He swung his arms, bent at the elbows, back and forth, the momentum taking over. He pulled off his backpack and tossed it aside; it slid across the floor, creating a gentle echo when it hit the shadowed wall. Then he began to dance like the Koryak, the indigenous tribe of Russian people. He thumped the floor, turned in a circle, moved his arms back and forth, and waved them overhead. their bells chiming in his mind.

When he entered the stream of light, the rays touched his head, ran their fingers through his hair, connected him to something that warmed his insides: not only his body but the thing that made him *him*. His soul? He continued to move unhindered, like a breeze that never quite reaches the ground. The rhythm of the earth lifted his spirits and directed the motion of his flesh and bones.

Alexandria watched from the side of the room as he spun and thumped under the light that poured forth from the ceiling. She smiled as she said, "Are we sure this is a good time for celebration?"

He danced over to her, grabbed both of her arms, and made her move along with him. She couldn't help but laugh. "Maybe my vodka bottle is empty because you have been drinking it too?"

"I am dancing because we're here. We're safe. We are alive!" he shouted.

"You're a pretty good dancer, I have to say."

She laughed, and that made him even happier.

"We made it!" Dmitri shouted.

He moved back into the stream of light, relishing the warmth on his crown, then tipping back his head, feeling it on his face, breathing in deeply, savoring the pure, Earthy scent.

While Alexandria continued to dance outside of the spotlight, Dmitri bobbed at its center, facing it full-on as he let it fill him. He sensed its energy becoming absorbed, and an electric vibration began to course through his veins to the thrum of his heart. It tingled and zapped like charged blood flowing through his limbs, tickling the tips of his fingers and toes the same way it had the night David died and the green cloud surrounded him.

He closed his eyes and wondered what would come next. Would the energy stay like this, or would it grow too big the way it had at the airport?

When he opened his eyes again, he saw a pair of black soldier boots beside the shadowed wall, sitting there by themselves. Who had left their boots in this room?

And then the boots stepped toward him.

How strange.

Alexandria continued turning in circles a few steps away. "Woo-hoo, I feel it," she said. "I feel like I'm bathing in starlight, like I'm finally getting clean!"

That's when the person in the boots showed herself. A blurry, hard-to-see woman slowly became visible. She had an angular face and brown shoulder-length hair, braids to each side. She was a small woman, shorter than Mother. And familiar to him, though he couldn't think of her name. Her clothing seemed wrong. Much like a soldier's uniform, only the pants weren't pants. They were shorts.

His thoughts moved at light speed, as he simmered with the newfound energy.

"So, you made it," the woman said and clapped her hands a few times. "All the way from Russia."

Instead of responding with words, instinct told him to walk out of the light, into the shadows behind him.

"Dmitri, who is this?" Alexandria said. "Where are you going?"

Beside the wall, a stool waited for him. The one David meditated upon? "Take it," a man's voice in his head told him. "Take my chair and rise."

David had spoken to him before. David, who wanted to transfer his energy.

An electric shimmer rode Dmitri's spine, and he lifted the stool. He carried it to the center of the room, where the light streamed the brightest. Its gentle, smoldering rays swirled around him like a force that would keep him safe. He put the stool down as he'd been told.

"Oh no, you don't," the woman said. She hurried toward him but couldn't seem to pass into the lighted area, couldn't enter the bright circle. Dmitri observed her but didn't speak.

"If you think I'm going to let this happen, you're wrong," she said.

"Who is this person?" Alexandria asked.

"Leave the room, Alexandria," Dmitri said. "It's all right."

He stood in front of the stool, safely within the cone of light.

Instead of leaving, Alexandria came away from the wall and lunged. She pushed against the young woman's shoulders and threw her back. "Get out of here," she growled. The woman stumbled away but didn't fall. She floundered for a second before regaining her footing and coming right back at Alexandria. Alexandria held her ground, catching the woman's swinging punches, one arm and then the other. She gripped both arms and pressed forward, trying to move her toward the exit door—but the woman disappeared.

Aghast, Alexandria lost her hold and suffered a blow to her chin. She recoiled for a moment, rubbing the sore spot before turning back to Dmitri.

"She's gone!" she cried. "Where did she go?"

"Take cover by the door," he said and pointed at the wall. Something was happening inside him. The electricity pulsed faster, stronger, surging through his veins. He worried what might occur should he move too quickly.

Hunched with fear, Alexandria ran to the wall and cowered beside it.

"I'm Connie, a Jovian. I only want to help you." The woman's voice came from a place close to him, perhaps just through the light right in front of him, though Dmitri couldn't see her. "Caroline doesn't care whether you live or die. She killed David. She'll do the same to you. Trust me, you don't want to take his place."

Dmitri stared at the stool before him. It blurred as if vibrating, as did his body, the two of them on the same plane, meant to come together.

"If you do this, you will die," Connie said. "Do you understand?"

"Take your place, Dmitri," David's voice told him in his mind. "Rise to meet your potential. Accept your destiny."

Dmitri tipped back his head, and the light cascading from above surrounded him like water. Energy seeped into his pores, zapped through his limbs, pulled them taut and then let them go as if he were riding a rolling wave of energy. It was power like he'd never felt before.

This was his destiny.

He climbed upon the stool and sat with his back straight. Soon his body rose like smoke rising from a flame. The energy held him suspended, and his back arched. His arms and head fell to one side, his legs and feet to the other. His body formed the shape of crescent moon curved over the stool.

The light glowed around him, a neon shade of green.

He sensed the woman, Connie, wanting to help him, her heart pounding loud enough for him to hear. "Leave," he told her.

"I can't," she said. "Please, Dmitri, listen to me. It's for your own—"

"Leave!" he shouted, and sparks rained from the ceiling.

Footsteps tapped across the floor and then the door to the tube opened and closed with a thud.

"You must go too, Alexandria," Dmitri said, his voice buzzing and strange.

"I'm not going anywhere without you! What are you going to do?"

"Go!" he shouted, not knowing what was about to happen, only that David's power was supreme and fierce.

Alexandria began to sob. "I can't. I don't want to. Do whatever you have to do, Mitya. Whatever happens to you will happen to me too."

The sound of her cries made the boy inside of him cry as well. He imagined holding her hand the way he did whenever things got rough. Alexandria had always been there for him. Was there for him still. She was being strong for him, so he would do the same for her.

"I am holding your hand," he said.

Then he raised his head and straightened his back so that his legs pointed downward. His body became the shaft of an arrow, like one of the keys in his cluster. The light from the oculus multiplied and then flashed. A *boom* shook the room as if some natural barrier had been broken, and a bolt of green and white and electric and life entered Dmitri like searing hot metal that scalded his insides. Just when he thought he couldn't withstand anymore, it rocketed out of his mouth, a projectile of energy aimed through the hole in the ceiling. He heard an explosion as it collided with the atmosphere and then rippled over the curves of the earth, moving at the speed of light.

In his mind, he saw the results of what had happened. The thick cloud coverage that crisscrossed over the country's numerous waterways ruffled as if pulled up by its corners and shaken out like fresh laundry. The hazy, gray blanket broke and dissipated, and the winds that followed whisked away any leftover wisps.

He'd given himself up to the sky. He knew that now. He'd become one with the earth and the sun, with the dark matter and black holes and star nurseries—with the universe and all its thriving, relentless energies. The chatter of Jovians entered his mind like roiling rapids, a natural force of sound and thought pouring like a surging waterfall into his being. He let it in, allowed it to flow. It knotted and twisted and moved indiscriminately at first and then stretched and pulled and straightened and calmed, eventually becoming a stream riding a gentle slope through a glorious wood of oaks and pines, daisies, rocks, roots, and soil. He heard Natasha's voice for the first time in years. She said, "His body isn't here because it belongs to another universe." Dmitri thought he knew what that meant, but before he could settle on the meaning, the gaggle of voices in his mind drew him away. He recognized the sounds of Dana and John talking about the whale population. He heard Uncle Jimmy laughing and Constance speaking kind words. Farther away, his Great-grandfather, Edmund, gave orders to "Change course." He heard Caroline say, "They'll do whatever I tell them to do." Miranda and Leo were laughing as Miranda said, "Imagine her shock when she sees what we've done." He heard all these words as great numbers of other, roving thoughts slipped past him so fast they hardly registered at all.

With each second, those sounds and sentiments and voices consolidated word by word and sentence by sentence until they formed a gentle hum that hung like an atmosphere inside his mind. He found he could hear everything and nothing at all.

His body once again lowered onto the stool in the center of the observatory. He sat perched like an ordinary person. Much like David used to sit, with his legs crossed, hands resting upon his knees. The light from above continued to funnel into him, effortless and strong. His consciousness continued to expand. He was no longer a mere child of eleven but an otherworldly being connected to everything in existence.

When he spoke, his voice buzzed like electricity in his ears "Alexandria?" he said.

"Yes, Dmitri, I am here."

"Are you all right?"

"I am. Are you?"

He was still himself, still the boy who once shot paper balls across the room, who needed a wheelchair and spoke in a distinctive manner, but he was also something new. Something that had once lay quiet inside of him had been brought to the forefront, zapped with David's electricity, shocked to life. He was Jovian. He'd always been Jovian.

"Come out from the shadow," he said.

A moment later, slow and cautious steps approached. Alexandria appeared with her head bowed, eyes hesitantly raised, legs shaking.

"Do not be afraid. You are strong. You have always been strong," he said as he extended one arm. "I would like my keys. Can you retrieve them for me?"

Alexandria rushed back into the shadow. The sound of zippers opened and closed. Dmitri anticipated the trill of metal as she pulled the keys from the bag's front pocket. She returned quickly, her awe sharpening her soft features, the frightened hesitancy in her step, gone. She held the keys out to him. Her eyes gleamed every shade of blue in the spectrum.

"I am different too," she said.

"Yes. We are both different."

"And, are we also the same?" Her chin quivered.

"Yes, we are also the same."

He held the keys in his palm, the cluster of shining metals clinking. Raising them in his hand, he observed them all at once and saw in his mind's eye a kaleidoscope of images accompanied by Jovian voices. Great-grandmother sat in a circle with Fran and his wife, Lisa; Aunt Constance and Uncle Jimmy spoke with the oldest woman he'd ever seen—Ida, he believed, was her name; Edmund traversed miles in a spaceship with small silvery beings, the Moon Children, he recognized at once; Miranda and Leo —what were they up to? *No*, he thought. *They must be stopped.*

He grasped the keys tightly and closed his eyes. "Great-grandmother, come home," he said. "I have arrived."

Epilogue

Kecksburg, Pennsylvania
A Universe Without Jovians

The heat pinged and chimed as it passed through the baseboards, making soothing house sounds Svetlana knew well. Was it the dry, heated air that made her head ache and nose whistle when she breathed? Or was she sick? She didn't remember having a cold. She opened her eyes, her lids raw and puffy. There, above her head, Evander's shirt draped the headboard.

Evander is dead, she remembered, and her stomach became sick. She rolled sideways into a fetal curl. The clock read 7:04 p.m.

What day is it?

She remembered talking with Natasha and Evan. How they'd wanted to time travel and she didn't. How Evander, the prior day, begged her to take Natasha home.

Where are the girls?

She dragged herself from the bed, dressed in one of

her old sweaters and black leggings. Some urgency within told her to stop fussing and move. She stomped into her lace-less sneakers and entered the hall, combing fingers through unruly hair, wondering why there were no people sounds. No music to draw her in its direction. No chatter or giggles blooming from the guest room or living area. The only noise, the lonely tick, tick, tick of the hot water passing through the baseboard pipes.

"Evan?" she called.

The house answered with silence as suspicious as the so-called prophecy Natasha had shared. Svetlana entered the kitchen and shouted, "Evan, where are you?"

Her purse lay open on the kitchen table. She searched for car keys, which she found, wallet, which she found, phone, which she also found. Her phone's screen provided no news. No calls. No texts. The clean counter was devoid of a note saying they'd gone to the movies or the diner or library.

Damn it.

The metal sink shined. The breakfast and lunch plates made neat rows in the dish rack. The griddle had been put away, the pots and pans. So they had cleaned up—and then what?

They couldn't have gone, couldn't have time traveled without her. Could they? Would they? Did they even know how?

She rushed into the foyer. Switched on the light. Opened the closet there and grabbed her winter coat, shoving one arm through, then the other.

She flew out of the house, the wind slapping her with austere hands as she succumbed to a swell of heart-pounding déjà vu. The night the Jovians came to Russia to take ten-year-old Evander. That same sick feeling of knowing something awful had occurred rolled in like a storm cloud. She wrestled with the notion that it was happening again.

But there were no Jovians in this world.

Or there weren't supposed to be.

Natasha is Jovian.

Under a crisp night sky alive with sparkling stars, Svetlana ran down the same sidewalk where she'd taught her young daughter how to ride a bike, how to run a lemonade stand, how to play hopscotch. No way was she going to let the Jovians take her. They may have stolen Evander, but she would not let them have Evan.

When she came to the end of the road, she stopped. Would the girls have gone left, toward Main Street, or right toward the farmland and forests? Where did a person go to time travel? Where would they board a ship? More likely in the middle of a field than the town itself. She turned right and started at a jog once again.

Had Evan really left her, or was this whole thing ridiculous? Maybe they'd gone to the movies after all. It was possible Evan hadn't called or texted because she worried the phone would wake Svetlana from her sorrowful sleep. Her daughter wouldn't board a spaceship just because some distant relative told her a story about a lost sister, would she? As preposterous as it seemed, the nagging tug of knowing pulled like a tow rope, and the only way she could deal with it was to consider possibilities while the sidewalk passed below her running feet.

Just keep moving.

When Svetlana had emerged from her room that afternoon, the girls had made lunch for her and treated her gently. "Do you want more soup," they asked. "Can we slice you another piece of bread?" There was no talk of leaving. No talk of Jovians or other universes whatsoever.

Everything was on hold. At least as far as Svetlana was concerned.

Afterward, Svetlana, exhausted, had returned to the warm, dimly lit confines of her bedroom and sunk into thoughts of Evander. The occasional twitter of laughter and clink of kitchen pots reminded her the girls had volunteered to clean up. She'd wondered if later, in the evening, they would head out to the deck, maybe sight some stars?

With that thought, she stopped running and grabbed her forehead as it occurred to her where they might go to time travel. The deck in the backyard. Andrew's "sacred circle," the one he'd built into the boards. If anything in this universe contained a shred of Jovian power, that circle might.

She ran back home, fueled by the innate knowledge that she was right. She sped down the driveway, passed through the gate that opened to the backyard, and raced up the steps to the deck.

There they were. Two teens standing inside the circle Andrew had built. Natasha held Evan's wrists, and both girls bowed their head with closed-eyed concentration.

"Stop!" Svetlana shouted. "What are you doing?"

They gazed in her direction. Two sets of guilty eyes lit like coins in the backyard spotlights.

Svetlana marched up to them. "Evan? Are you . . . " She paused to swallow the backlash of what looked a lot like betrayal. "Are you leaving me?"

"It's not like that," Evan said, her expression pale and sincere. "I'll be back soon."

Natasha kept hold of Evan's wrists.

Three stones sat at the circle's center. There was something about them. They seemed alive and buzzing, as if tiny motors vibrated inside.

"Do you even know what you're doing?" she asked.

"It would be a lot easier if we had three people," Natasha said matter-of-factly.

Svetlana made sure to remain clear of the circle, to avoid touching the planks laid into wood boards. "You're not taking Evan. I told you, you can stay with us."

"It's not working," Natasha said with eerie calmness. "We need you. If you will just come with—"

"Evan, get in the house." Svetlana's desire to protect would not be hindered.

"You don't understand, Mom. I *have* to go."

"Both of you," Svetlana said, stepping a bit closer, though careful to remain outside the circle. "Come in the house. Let's talk this out. Maybe there's a way we can get Natasha home without going ourselves."

"There isn't," Evan said. "And I *want* to go."

"Okay, okay." She raked her hair back with frustration. "Come inside and tell me why you have to go. *Convince* me."

"It's simple." Evan was shouting now. "Natasha needs to get back home. I'm not going to let her die here. Evander died, and she will too, if we don't help her get back."

Svetlana pressed her lips together and squeezed her eyes closed. There had to be another way. "One day when you have children you will understand why I'm not going to let you do that. You are not leaving this planet. And Natasha can get medical care here. I'm sure there are plenty of doctors who can—"

"There's not one doctor on Earth who can help her," Evan said. "You know that. Evander asked you to help her. Do it for him."

Svetlana rubbed her forehead, her hands shaking, nerves frazzled, the moment slipping from her sweaty palms. She was losing this argument, just like she'd lost so many arguments with Evan in the past. The daughter who had an answer for everything. There had to be something she could say to change Evan's mind.

"And Natasha's not just some Jovian," Evan said, her voice laced with disgust. "She's your *grandchild*."

A hot, sick feeling coursed through Svetlana's body: something like embarrassment partnered with dread. She had never thought of Natasha that way. Or maybe she had, but she'd pushed it out of her mind because it changed everything. Was she willing to let her grandchild die? Evander's only daughter.

No. They would figure something out.

She bowed her head, and the stones in the center of the circle drew her eye. The way they gleamed brightly even amid the darkness. They seemed . . . alive. And now that she'd looked at them, there was something else: they tempted her to touch them. She had to hold herself back, though she wanted very much to pick them up, to study them.

"What is going on with those?" she said, and before she knew it, she'd reached for one.

Natasha shouted, "Don't!"

But it was too late. Svetlana already had. The stone was cold. Cold enough to freeze her skin. It felt as if she'd been bitten, or stung, and she dropped it.

She thought that would be it, maybe she'd suffer a freezer type of burn, but it didn't stop there. The cold from the stone spread from her palm through her arm as if riding the tunnels of her veins. It sped through the stem of her neck, spun a circle through her brain, then oozed into the rest of her body leaving behind a pure, crisp cold like none she'd ever felt before.

After that, she found herself in a place of brilliant light and movement. Light so bright it blinded her. No longer did she stand upon her deck in the backyard. She'd joined hands with the girls and felt their presence, though she could not see them, could not see anything beyond the light that surrounded her. Together with the girls, she'd become something as weightless as wind, moving at indescribable speed. All of it too fast and overwhelming for logical thought.

It was like becoming the wind itself. Bursting into air molecules and rushing through caverns and valleys and sand beaches. Spreading out and exploring the whole world for one blink of a second before being called back and spilling into the form she'd known when she was whole.

That's when she'd stopped.

In the stillness, she once again experienced the weight of her body. Consciousness flowed into her mind like water arriving with her last memory. The backyard, the circle, the stones. Evan and Natasha. Where was she? Were the girls still with her? A click and then a pop broke the silence.

Air escaping. Pressure relieved. Tubes withdrawing from her nose and forearm. She sensed light on her closed lids the moment before she opened her eyes.

The walls of a pod surrounded her. The cover hummed as it retreated. She remembered the enclosure from the last time she'd traveled this way. The start of her journey. Maybe they hadn't left yet? But, no, this felt like the end of the journey, not the beginning.

She sat upright and then wished she hadn't. A roiling discomfort grumbled against her stomach walls, then flattened. Three pods lined up in the center of what appeared to be a small half-circle of a spaceship.

Another click and then a pop.

The cover of the pod to her right opened a couple of inches. She heard Evan cough.

"Mom?" she said, her voice gruff, on the verge of panic.

Svetlana tried to speak but only made harsh, gravelly sounds. Like the pointed bones of fish, her words stuck in her throat. She knocked on the side of the pod, then finally coughed the words "I'm here."

"What happened? Did we make it? Is Natasha okay? When did I change into a black unitard?"

"I am not able to move very well yet," Svetlana strained. Though she'd sat up with little problem, her arms and legs now refused her commands.

"Why haven't my tubes retracted?" Evan asked.

"I don't know. The last time I did this, I arrived smack in the middle of my bedroom—giving birth to you. There were no tubes for me to worry about."

"Oh, wow," Evan muttered. "Sorry about that."

Svetlana chuckled and then recoiled at the ensuing pain in her throat. With great effort, she flung one leg over the side of the pod and maneuvered the rest of the way out. Her spine creaked like something corroded, but she managed to stand. Three small steps brought her close enough to peer through the small circular window at the head of the still-closed pod.

Natasha was there. Sleeping. Or was she dead? She had aged. She looked more like a twenty-five-year-old than a teen. Like a blonde Sleeping Beauty. Except the hue of her lips appeared grayish.

"Natasha?" Svetlana tapped the pod's window. "Wake up, Natasha."

"What's wrong?" Evan said.

"I don't know if she's breathing. She looks beautiful but —" Svetlana continued to tap.

"Help her," Evan said. "Open the pod. Give her CPR, or something."

Svetlana searched for a way to open the pod, the engineering of which was smooth and all but seamless. "There's no way to—"

A click and then a pop.

The cover eased across, and Svetlana placed her hand on Natasha's cheek, patting it gently. "Natasha. We're here. You're . . . home. I think. Wake up."

"Natasha, cut the crap," Evan said. "Wake up. We need you."

"Give her a second," Svetlana said. "I'm sure she'll be—"

"The time travel might have killed her," Evan said, angrily. "You need to give her CPR. The tube in my arm is still hooked up. I can't get out."

Svetlana adjusted her position, preparing to press down on the young woman's chest. Isn't that what you did for CPR? Press just below the—Natasha opened her eyes wide, and Svetlana startled back.

"I'm here," Natasha said, blinking rapidly. "Where are we? Have we landed?"

"Thank goodness." Svetlana placed her hand on her own chest and eased back with relief. "One moment we were standing in the backyard, and now we're on some kind of Jovian ship. I think. I really don't know."

"We're not moving," Natasha said, sitting up. "We must have reached our destination."

Something mechanical hummed. "Oh, there they go," Evan said. "The last of my tubes. Finally."

Now that all three of them had been freed of their pods, Svetlana remembered to be worried. "Where do you think we are?"

The ship, no bigger than an average-size bedroom, made a hydraulic drawl and jolted as if something had clicked into place. Metal window shades peeled back, ushering in a strange blue light. Natasha pressed a couple of buttons in what resembled a pilot's cockpit and looked out the window. "This is Starbright. The docking station."

"Do you mean the basement?" Svetlana experienced a surge of panic. "Evan and I need to go back right away. We brought you here like you asked. Evander said I would be able to go home immediately. Quickly, before someone notices we're here. Program the ship to take us home."

Natasha patted the pockets in her unitard, as if hoping to find something in them. She went to the control station and read the screen, then started typing keys at superspeed.

In the silence, Svetlana fought back a bad feeling.

"It's not letting me prep for departure," Natasha said.

"Why not? Is it broken?"

"No, it's not broken. It's just not letting me—"

"Use the stones," Svetlana said. "Where are they?"

"We don't have them anymore."

"And you don't know how to send us back?"

"I do know," Natasha said with confidence. "It's just not letting me do it. Don't worry. I'll work around it."

"Hurry before someone comes. We can't be here." Svetlana stared warily out the window. "We can't be in this world."

"But Mom," Evan said, "I want to stay."

"That was not the agreement," she said, sounding more flustered than she wanted to. "We did what we said we'd do. Now you're coming with me."

"I told you I have something to do here. This world needs me. There was no agreement to leave as soon as we arrived."

"I can't listen to this right now, Evan. You don't belong in this world. Please, just . . . don't talk." She turned to Natasha. "Maybe if I get back in my pod it will start the process. That's how it worked the first time. I climbed in and everything else happened automatically."

Natasha didn't reply, busy as she was bringing up screens and typing in commands. A look of fierce determination had settled upon her face.

"Evan, get back in your pod," Svetlana said, climbing into her own. "If we're in our pods, it might work. Lie back and don't say anything more," she begged.

Evan didn't move.

"Please, Evan," Svetlana said, on the brink of losing control. "Just this once, do as I tell you!"

She put all her determination into the force of her eyes and glared at her daughter. With slow reluctance, Evan climbed into her pod, then huffed angrily as she sat in its center.

Svetlana lay back, role modeling the behavior she expected her daughter to follow. She held her breath and prayed for Evan to do what she needed her to do while she waited for the covers of the pods to close them in.

She stared at the ship's gray-silver ceiling.

Nothing happened.

"Natasha? What's going on? Will it work?"

"Not yet," Natasha said. "I've done everything right, so I don't know—"

"Keep trying. Just keep trying." Svetlana closed her eyes, her frustration boiling. Before she knew it, she was kicking the side of the pod. *I. Have. To. Get. Back. Home.* One kick per word. When that didn't alleviate her anger, she punched it: *I. Want. To. Go. Home!* She opened her eyes and gazed straight up. *Oh my God, Andrew. I'm here again. I'm stuck. Help me get out of here!* She threw punch after punch, kick after kick, and then let out a scream.

Evan shouted at her to calm down. "It's going to be all right."

"There is no way I'm staying here," Svetlana moaned. Then she threw two more punches, her knuckles beginning to swell.

A high-pitched squeal sliced through the room—or maybe just through Svetlana's mind. She stopped punishing the pod and lay there, chest heaving. A moment of intense silence came over her. She held her breath, eyes wide in wait of what would come.

Andrew, is that you? she said internally, remembering all at once that he used to speak to her in this world.

A sound rolled into her mind like an enormous wave crashing. It was followed by the soulful tune of a whale song playing in the distance. Sad and soothing. Attempting to comfort her. She felt, oddly, as if it could see her, as if it *knew* her. Was it Andrew, or something else? Something ancient and knowing that refused to be ignored. It was hopeful. And . . . inevitable. She eased into that word, *inevitable*, and relaxed into her pod.

Yes, it felt inevitable.

And now she knew that she wasn't getting out of there. Somehow she'd always known this was how her life would go, and there wasn't a thing she could do about it.

"Shit," she whispered with surrender. She grabbed her forehead and breathed in deeply, fighting back the urge to cry. Her next breath exhaled amid a quiet groan, reluctant and yet accepting.

"Mom? Are you okay?" Evan's concern was like a hand reaching for her, pulling her up from the depths, bringing her back to life.

Svetlana sniffed. "Um." She needed to be fine. For Evan. "Yes," she managed. "I . . . am fine."

"I'm really sorry," Evan said. "I'm sorry we made you come with us. If you can't go back today, I'm sure we'll be able to send you home soon."

"No, no. It's okay. I just had . . . a small meltdown. I'm better now."

"I can't get the ship's systems to reboot," Natasha said. "I'm sorry, Grandmother."

Svetlana's heart fluttered. *Grandmother*.

"It's okay, Natasha," Svetlana said. "It's not your fault. Thank you for trying. We better get up and see what's going on. See where we are exactly."

"Are you sure?" Evan asked.

"It looks like there are no other options right now." She tried to smile as she stood and stepped out of the pod.

Evan rushed over and threw her arms around her. Svetlana put her hand on Evan's back and eased into the comfort of being there for her child.

"Thank you, Mom. Thank you." Evan sounded a lot like the little girl she used to be, and Svetlana softened with the gesture.

She really wants me to stay. All along that's what she wanted.

"I'm here," Svetlana said, and she rubbed Evan's head. "Don't worry, I'm here."

Natasha, taking slow, cautious steps, approached them. "I'm here too," she said, and Svetlana took her under her wing as well. They stayed like that, a circle of three, each one of them frightened but much stronger together. "We'll get through this," Svetlana promised them.

The door of the ship rose suddenly with hissing strength, startling them. A massive man wearing a black security uniform appeared. His head was half human, half black metal like a robot's, and Svetlana held the girls tighter than before.

"It's one of Great-grandmother's Leonards," Natasha whispered.

Whoever he was didn't waste a second before stepping

onto the ship and grabbing the two girls by their elbows, snatching Evan and Natasha from Svetlana's hold.

"What are you doing?" Svetlana shouted. "Let them go!"

Two copies of this enormous, muscled man came from behind the one with the strange head and reached for her. "Don't touch me!" she said.

With a harsh grip, they led her through the blue-lighted space that resembled a subway platform, dark and windowless, while the girls moved in the opposite direction. "Where is he taking them?" Svetlana asked the men who squeezed her arms. "That's my daughter!"

Her captors said nothing as they pushed her roughly forward. Their various weapons clanked with every forceful step. Was this the new way Jovians treated people? Would she and the girls be punished for who they were? Would being Andrew's wife and Evander's mother be a help at this point, or a hindrance?

Soon enough, they came to the entrance of what appeared to be a tube. They stepped inside. It was round and bright white with smooth, arching walls and doorways to rooms or possibly other pathways. Svetlana worried that if given a chance to escape, she'd never find her way through this maze. How would she find Evan?

They came to a closed door. One of the brutes pressed his hand to the screen on the wall beside it. The door slid open, and a room appeared. An actual bedroom, with a bed and blankets and curtains over windows with virtual landscapes, much like the one she'd known in her home in Kecksburg. She stared in amazement for a moment before they shoved her inside.

"Wait," she said as she spun around. "Why are you doing this? Is this Starbright? Is Caroline here? Do you know who I am?"

One of the men smiled at her deviously and said, "Caroline doesn't live here anymore," just as the door slid closed in front of him.

She ran at it and banged with her fists, shouting, "Let me out of here!" over and over again, though she knew it was no use.

They were already gone.

She was locked in.

And this was the next chapter in her destiny.

A Note from the Author

Thank you so much for joining the Jovian Universe's cast of characters on this journey. I hope you've enjoyed experiencing their ups and downs and getting to know them inside and out.

As I write this, I am busy creating Book 5, the final installment in the series. I've lived with these characters for so long, I don't know what I'll do when it's finished. Don't be surprised if I decide to write some supporting pieces down the road.

If you've enjoyed this book, please leave a review (or just a rating) wherever you like to write book reviews. Reviews have the power to rocket a novel into the stratosphere. I appreciate and send good vibes in response to every kind review I receive. Thank you in advance for taking the time to type a few sentences worthy of your thoughts!

If you'd like to reach out to me, subscribe to my newsletter, or read my blog, you can do so at AuthorKimCatanzarite.com. I love to hear from readers and always reply to messages.

Acknowledgments

If it's one thing authors need, it's support from the loved ones in their lives and in the reading and writing community at large. I consider myself very lucky in that vein.

Thanks to everyone who helped raise this novel up and bring it to publication. Specifically, Ron Skelton, Patricia Olson, Lynn Gale, and Aggie Jae for beta reading; Breanna Teramoto for her amazing developmental expertise; and the proofreading pool comprised of Nicholas, Bobbye, Julie, Ron, Katy, and Malia.

An abundance of thanks to Philippa Willitts for her sensitivity editing, feedback, and overall invaluable input.

Where would a book be without its early readers? Thank you Zoe, Debra, Sudasha, Annette, Lisa, Barbara, Joe, John, Mark, Ashlee, Ron F., Rosemary, and everyone who read it after I wrote this list!

To my Bookstagram friends: you inspire me and make me laugh. Special thanks to Alana Faye Wilson's Sci-fi Engagement Group.

Here's a shout-out to all my Writer's Digest University students who have taken an interest in my novels and blog.

I also want to mention my husband, Joe, who forever keeps my spirits up, and my new adult, Jupiter, who's always willing to brainstorm the mysteries of the universe.

Finally, thanks to my parents, Joan and Ben, and my sister, Jennifer, for celebrating with me every step of the way.

About the Author

Kim Catanzarite writes character-driven science fiction and dark fantasy novels. Her books are a mix of heartfelt family and friendship drama, fast-paced adventure, engaging plot twists, and unique imagination. She is the author of the Jovian Universe series and the Angel of Death series. Kim lives in New Jersey with her husband and daughter.

www.ingramcontent.com/pod-product-compliance
Lightning Source LLC
Chambersburg PA
CBHW022022310726
48972CB00006B/1762